OUR STREET

Our Street

Compton Mackenzie

NEW ENGLISH LIBRARY
TIMES MIRROR

To
RALPH PINKER
In affection and
gratitude

First published in 1932
First published by Robert Hale in 1971
© 1931, 1932 by Doubleday, Doran & Co. Inc.

*

FIRST NEL PAPERBACK EDITION FEBRUARY 1973

*

NEL Books are published by
New English Library Limited from Barnard's Inn, Holborn, London, E.C.1.
Made and printed in Great Britain by Hunt Barnard Printing Ltd., Aylesbury, Bucks.

45001351 0

CONTENTS

OUR STREET

I HAVE little doubt that it was originally called our street in order to disguise with a kind of family joke the fact that in our hearts we felt a little ashamed of its being the only street among all the genteel roads and avenues and terraces that were proclaiming the difference between our suburb and the larger suburb of Fulham beyond, from which, by putting West in front of Kensington, we fancied we had as successfully dissociated ourselves as North Kensington had prudently detached itself from Notting Hill or South Kensington extricated itself from Brompton. The democratic present should be informed that the name of the Old Court Suburb had a reassuring ring about it, clink of old silver, in the days when Queen Victoria reigned. Streets abounded in Fulham, and to find a street in West Kensington seemed like a grubby finger pointed to remind us that we were only an imitation of the authentic Kensington. To be sure, our street had a most aristocratic prefix; but few of those who lived in Beauclerk Street ever used that prefix. We left it to be mispronounced by the tradesmen, and we found it only one of the countless deplorable habits of the Spinks at Number 13 that they would never conform in this matter.

'After all,' as I once heard Miss Lockett who lived at Number 3 say to Mrs Clyburn who lived at Number 15, 'what is good enough for Lady Marjorie Doyle and General Brackenbury and dear Doctor Arden should surely be good enough for those scaramouches.'

Golliwogs had not been invented in those days; but if they had been Miss Lockett must have called the Spinks golliwogs. Years later, when I first saw a group of golliwogs in a toy shop, my mind went back at once to the Spinks and to that house in our street which always gave the effect of having been denuded of carpets, curtains, and cushions by the noisy crowd of children with mops of dark curly hair who lived in it.

Mr Spink was the editor of a weekly paper called *Bohemia*,

and if anybody ever expressed outwardly his occupation Mr Spink did. He was a tall, swarthy, rawboned man who always wore a long frock coat and a wide-brimmed dark sombrero hat.

'A regular organ grinder,' I heard the General say once. In those days the most modest type of soft hat outraged the feelings of people far less conventional than General Brackenbury.

Mr Spink's hair was nearly as untidy as that of his children and it hung in a mat over his grubby 'choker' collar like Virginia creeper over a wall in winter. He wore a large Ascot tie of black satin in which was stuck a cameo in sardonyx of Medusa's head. When I first saw this cameo I thought it was a portrait of Mrs Spink, whose own hair bore a resemblance to the snaky locks of the Gorgon. Mrs Spink must have had gypsy or Creole blood. She used to wander fecklessly about that barn of a house, always dressed in loose silk wrappers of flame and orange and scarlet; and with her bright dark eyes and perpetual chattering and habit of cocking her head on one side she seemed like some tropical bird whose plumage had been dimmed and ruffled by a captivity and whose cage was not kept as clean as it should be. There must have been quite eight or nine children, from Annie who was nearly seventeen down to Rudolph who was about two; but they all looked so much alike, boys and girls, and they all behaved in so much the same harum-scarum way that it is difficult many years later to distinguish them individually in the memory.

In those days a family like the Spinks was still regarded as a menace to the gentility of the Neighbourhood. I have given Neighbourhood a capital letter because it meant a great deal more to us than could be expressed without some such emphasis. It would be easy to sneer at our snobbery in managing to believe that the outskirts of Fulham were an extension of Old Kensington. I dare not fancy what Mr Thackeray might have written about us, had we come into existence while he was still alive. Yet, looking back now on that Neighbourhood, I believe that the desire to safeguard our gentility was due less to pretentiousness than to a die-hard effort not to admit the power of wealth over inherited traditions of behaviour. Nobody in our street was rich; but our being unable to afford to live in a neighbourhood of long-enjoyed social repute was no

8

reason why we should allow ourselves to be irrevocably banished from the world to which we belonged. We were like those first colonists of New England who built over again across the Atlantic the familiar towns and villages of home, and if only somebody had had the wit to think of it we should have been called New Kensington instead of West Kensington.

Mr Lockett was the accepted mouthpiece of our aspirations for the future of the Neighbourhood. He had actually been a resident of Old Kensington, and he had only moved this much farther west because he was convinced that the value of house property in West Kensington would rise. With Mr Lockett it had been no question of a retreat. He had deliberately migrated from Young Street (where Thackeray himself once lived in that old bow-windowed house) under a conviction that he was making a wise investment in buying 3 Beauclerk Street, West Kensington. He was for ever advising everybody to buy his house. You might often see him at the corner of our street in earnest conversation with General Brackenbury. The General, slim and upright in his grey frock coat, would be standing with his arms behind him and tapping his back with the ivory knob of his malacca cane; Mr Lockett would be shaking his forefinger just below the General's chin to point the force of his argument. And depend upon it if you passed within earshot you would hear that Mr Lockett was saying something like this:

'You'll be sorry one day, General, that you didn't take my advice and buy Number 19. Property here is going up. When I saw our street first, there wasn't a single house taken. Boards up at every gate, TO BE LET OR SOLD. In fact they hadn't finished painting the outside of your house. They'd only reached as far as Number 13, where those wretched Spinks are living now.'

At this the General would bring one of his arms quickly round to the front and give a contemptuous twist to the ends of his white moustache, suggesting by his action that he was tossing the whole family of Spinks out of West Kensington and into Fulham or Hammersmith.

'I wrote off to my old friend Doctor Arden who was retiring from the army and looking out for a practice,' Mr Lockett would continue. 'I told him to buy Number 1 which had two

9

extra rooms and a side entrance, being the corner house. I saw at once it was the very place for a surgery. "This is a rising neighbourhood," I warned him. "Buy now before house property goes up. I'm going to buy the house next door to you." Yes, yes, that's what I told Arden, and I cannot understand a man like you, General, who knows the world in and out preferring to take a house on lease.'

We had all of us heard over and over again the story of Mr Lockett's discovery of Beauclerk Street; but we were so fond of Mr Lockett himself that we none of us minded listening to it once more. Although Mr Lockett had lived in Young Street and had even been personally presented to Mr Thackeray when he was a young man, he was himself a fervid Dickensian.

'Thackeray is too cynical for me,' he used to proclaim. 'He hasn't the humanity of Dickens. Head is not enough. We must have heart as well.'

Whether it was that Mr Lockett by reading so much Dickens had turned into a Dickensian character himself or whether he enjoyed Dickens because he was born a Dickensian character, it would have been hard to decide. Some think that people who love certain animals grow like them, others that people love certain animals on account of a natural affinity. My own belief is in the second theory. I knew a boy in our neighbourhood who was always in the company of a bull terrier, and he could scarcely have grown so like a bull terrier himself in so comparatively short a time. He even had pink rims to his eyes. I believe that Mr Lockett must have been a Dickensian baby in his cradle. He was a short man with a florid face and protruding eyes, and he wore curly mutton-chop whiskers of what must originally have been an exceptionally vivid carroty hue, though by the time I first remember him a considerable number of grey hairs had toned down the colour. Top hats and frock coats were worn every day of the week by most of the male residents in our street, and Mr Lockett's top hat had a curly brim like John Bull's, beneath which there was such a rich crop of wiry reddish curls that when he took his hat off and discovered a completely bald crown it gave one a shock, because it was so difficult to understand what could have caused such a luxuriant growth to vanish so abruptly.

Mr Lockett was the organist of a large and what we used to call a fashionable church in South Kensington. He was also a noted singing master of the period. It was always said too that he could have been a teacher of the piano second to none if he would.

'But there's a point,' Mr Lockett used to declare in that resonant metallic voice of his, 'at which a man may become a miserable slave, and that point is reached with the first lesson he gives on the piano.'

Sometimes Mr Lockett would invite me to walk to church with him and sit up in the organ loft during the service. When I look back on those walks it always seems to be a windy morning, and the skirts of Mr Lockett's frock coat are always being blown out across the pavement on either side of him as we hurry along; and as Mr Lockett rams his silk hat more firmly down on his carroty curls and bows his head the better to make his way against the wind he is always asking me the most searching questions to test my knowledge of Dickens. Once, I remember, just as he had asked me where Mr Pickwick's hat had blown off and what had been the direct result of its being blown off, Mr Lockett's own hat blew off and went bounding away down the empty Sabbath street, for in those days on a Sunday morning London was more quiet than the heart of the country is nowadays. People were continually bemoaning the dreariness of a London Sunday, and I daresay it was a very dreary affair. Yet now to recall those isolated footfalls and down the high empty high-road perhaps the passing jingle of a glossy Sabbath-breaking dogcart bound for Richmond makes them seem in retrospect as staid and pious as the silent streets of Winchester in Keat's *Eve of St Mark*, and in recalling them the mind ponders wistfully a peace for ever lost, a spaciousness for ever shrunk.

Mr Lockett's hat went bowling along that morning as if it were tired of going to church and wanted to follow that fast dogcart to Richmond; but even while he was running after it he kept on probing me about Mr Pickwick's hat until presently his own blew into the front garden of an old-fashioned cottage long ago pulled down to make way for flats. The hat bowled along up the path until it was stopped by the threshold of the door, over which a funny old woman in a cape hung with bugles of jet and a bonnet to match was just emerging with her prayer book.

'Well,' said the old lady severely, 'first it's cats and then it's

11

hats in my poor garden.'

The scene was like an illustration in one of those morocco-bound volumes of Dickens from which Mr Lockett used to read us. He picked up his hat and banged it down on his head so hard that his carroty curls puffed out more defiantly than ever beneath the curly brim. Then he raised the hat to the old lady, bowed very low, banged it on again, and hurried on his way to church, still pressing me to give him every detail of the course Mr Pickwick's hat took on the common at Rochester. How deeply Mr Lockett loved Dickens! Even in the little room up in the organ loft where he put on his cassock and surplice there was a copy of *Great Expectations*, which was Mr Lockett's favourite volume for the penny readings he would give in aid of the various clubs and charities connected with the church of which he was organist. Although St Jude's was a good step from our street, Mr Lockett seldom gave one of his readings without some of his neighbours being present. He took these readings most seriously and he always wore evening dress at them, with a large red silk handkerchief tucked between his frilled shirt and his waistcoat. Sometimes the pathos of the great novelist's scenes would be too much for Mr Lockett, and the tears would trickle down his cheeks to settle like dewdrops among his whiskers. Yet, however much he was overcome by emotion, he never disturbed that red silk handkerchief which had been so carefully arranged by Mrs Lockett to cover just the right amount of shirt front. Instead, he would fumble with one hand in the tails of his coat until he found a big bandanna handkerchief with which he would mop up the tears provoked by the death of Paul Dombey or Little Nell. And we in the audience wept with him just as we would laugh with him when he leant back in his chair and declaimed the hopes of Mr Micawber or barked out the absurdities of Major Bagshott. And when he was reading about one of Dickens's dear and ridiculous old maids Mr Lockett would look so exactly like his own sister, Miss Lockett, that we would not dare to cast an eye in her direction for fear lest the little old lady herself should be embarrassed by our seeming to recognise what an excellent imitation Mr Lockett was giving of herself. Perhaps Miss Lockett was not really so old; but in those days, I fancy, maiden ladies grew older more quickly, or perhaps it was that some of us were so very young ourselves then. Miss

12

Lockett had the same kind of protruding eyes as her brother, and with them went such a shakiness in every limb that some-times it seemed as if they must one day pop right out of her head altogether. She was a little woman always dressed in black and always hung round with a gold chain of heavy square links, al-most as heavy a chain as an alderman's. She always wore, too, a large intaglio of Niobe as a brooch, and on one of her quiver-ing shrivelled fingers a mourning ring in which was set a minia-ture coil of lustrous auburn hair belonging, she told me once, to her grandmother. Miss Lockett's own hair was scanty and the colour of it a sandy grey; but she was never to be seen without a lace cap tied with velvet ribbons of some rich colour, and these took away all the sombreness of the black dresses she invariably wore. Miss Lockett had a drawerful of these ribbons which she once showed me, and I who was very small at the time gazed at it as if it were a coffer of gems. She would often be buying herself a new ribbon, and when we saw her descend-ing the front door steps of Number 3 and go walking down our street under a parasol of mauve and green shot silk we would say, 'There goes Miss Lockett to buy a new ribbon.' Often, when I was gone on a shopping message for one of my aunts, I would pass Rawdon's, the draper's shop, and catch sight of Miss Lockett seated beside a counter heaped high with cardboard drums that were wound round with ribbons of every colour and shade, and should I wait to stare into the window of Mrs Barlow's toyshop next door Miss Lockett would be sure to come out of Rawdon's rather dim interior from time to time in order to see how the ribbon of which she was contemplating the purchase of a yard looked in the full sunshine of the Terrace.

The Terrace! It must have had some prefix; but we never called it anything else, and to this day I do not know what its full name was.

THE TERRACE

THE TERRACE was a line of shops between Castlemaine Road and Beresford Road which provided the people in our street with most of the necessities and many of the luxuries of their existence. To be sure, sometimes when the sales were on they would take the red omnibus at the corner of Carlington Road and drive for a penny to Kensington High Street. But nobody in our street made a habit of shopping in Kensington High Street all the time. The others might so easily have thought it pretentious, and they would certainly have thought it unpatriotic; for we were proud of the Terrace. We often said how convenient it was that on a wet day you could get all your shopping done within a hundred yards of pavement. That was the distance between Castlemaine Road and Beresford Road, though General Brackenbury vowed it was no more than eighty. The General, however, took exceptionally long strides. To be sure, from the corner of our street to the Terrace was well on the way to being half a mile; but we were glad it was so far, because nobody wanted to be living absolutely among the shops. We should have thought that terribly noisy in those days, noisy and not without a slight suggestion of vulgarity. As it was, we used to greet one another along the wide pavement of the Terrace like dignified merchants on the Rialto of Venice.

The corner shop of the Terrace belonged to Offenbacher the confectioner, who actually had another shop in the most select part of South Kensington. To be candid, we found Offenbacher's a little expensive; but there was such style about it, and really the perfume of warm bread and chocolate it delicately diffused upon the outer air could not have been surpassed in Regent Street itself. Being a corner shop, Offenbacher's had a window which loooked out on the unimpeachable gentility of Beresford Road, and in this window there stood always a wedding cake which would have graced the most fashionable wedding breakfast in Mayfair. Offenbacher's would no more have been Offenbacher's without that wedding cake than Paris would have been Paris without the Eiffel Tower. As for the young women who served the customers, with their complexions like pink fondant, their elaborately built-up coiffures resilient and blonde as the finest sponge cake, and their fingers like sugar icing, they seemed animated confectionery themselves.

Next door to Offenbacher's was Pearson the greengrocer, and to pass from the solemnity of the one shop to the racket and confusion of the other was a severe test of the shopper's presence of mind. Indeed, I have seen Miss Lockett buffeted round Pearson's by excited fruit and vegetable buyers until there seemed a chance that her marketing would end in her being put in a paper bag herself and swung round like a toy acrobat by one of Mr Pearson's assistants, who all to my juvenile fancy looked and smelt like beetroots. Luckily the jovial and loud-voiced Mr Pearson himself always came to the rescue of Miss Lockett just in time by asking her what she wanted that morning.

'A cauliflower, Miss Lockett? Quite right. You noticed them at once. And you noticed the finest lot of cauliflowers we've had in this season. What an eye you have, if you'll pardon the liberty. I always say, "Trust Miss Lockett to pick out the best." '

With this Mr Pearson would snatch a cauliflower from the basket, fling it up in the air, catch it again, spin it round, and finally offer it to Miss Lockett as if he were a conductor handing a superb bouquet to a prima donna.

'And what else this morning, Miss Lockett? Plums, gages, rasps . . . ?'

'Nothing else, thank you, this morning, Mr Pearson.'

'Nothing else, thank *you*,' the greengrocer would reply with a bow.

Then Mr Pearson would shout 'Tommy,' or 'Joe,' or 'Willy,' at the top of his brazen voice, and when the diminutive errand boy appeared from the green depths of the shop he would say:

'Take this cauliflower round at once to Three Booclerk. Miss Lockett wants it very particular.'

Thus it was that Mr Pearson always managed to rescue customers like Miss Lockett from the hurlyburly of his shop and convince them that in spite of what he called his progressive methods of salesmanship his real interest was concentrated upon individuals who were not equipped to spend lavishly. At one moment Mr Pearson was slapping an enormous vegetable marrow to show off its points as some Arabian slave driver might treat his human merchandise. A moment later the marrow sold by these methods would be hurtling across the shop into the arms of an assistant, and Mr Pearson would be consigning Miss Lockett's cauliflower to one of his squeaky-voiced errand boys with as much personal anxiety as he would have devoted to the dispatch of a rajah's wedding present.

Eardley's dairy was next to the greengrocer's, a great contrast. Mr Eardley was as pale as the milk from one of his cans, whereas Mr Pearson by living with ruddy-cheeked apples was become himself as round and rosy as any of them. Nor was it only Mr Eardley who was pallid. Mrs Eardley was just as pallid, and when she sat in her little glass sentry box of an office adding up her accounts she used to look as unreal as a wax figure from which the pigment had faded. Did Mr and Mrs Eardley grow to look milky because they sold milk, or had he and she felt irresistibly drawn towards milk-selling by a natural affinity with the commodity itself?

Of the Castlemaine Stores where we bought our groceries there is little to say except that, in spite of its grand name, Mr Williams the owner was really just an old-fashioned grocer who leaned over the counter with both hands and inquired with a dry grave courtesy, 'What can I get for you this morning, Miss Lockett?'

He used to remind me of one of those thin oblong furrowed coconut biscuits which he always recommended as particularly wholesome. Notwithstanding his dryness he was a hospitable grocer. He would never forget to offer his youthful customers the freedom of one of his big bags of currants or dried apricots, to which he would sometimes add a couple of chocolate creams.

Beyond the Castlemaine Stores was Holt the butcher, and next to him Hargreaves the fishmonger and poulterer. Then came Rawdon's, whose drapery business had quickly expanded enough to require two shops. The peculiar attraction of Rawdon's for the young was an overhead railway in which the bill travelled to and the change travelled back from the counting house in a wooden ball. When I think of Rawdon's now, I see Miss Lockett perched upon a high chair beside the counter (and how she ever climbed up on it I cannot imagine), beside

16

her an array of cardboard drums wound round with bright velvet ribbons, and above the rustle of customers' skirts, above the thud of lengths of stuff being flung down upon the counter by enthusiastic assistants, I hear the miniature rumbling of those wooden balls travelling overhead all round the shop between the counter and the counting house.

Next door to Rawdon's large premises was a tiny toyshop presided over by the plump and genial Mrs Barlow who could hardly move without bringing down from her crowded shelves a shower of dolls and those ball frames for arithmetical beginners, so massive was she for her tiny shop. Next door to Mrs Barlow's was another tiny shop where Miss Voss sold stationery, using the shop parlour at the back as a circulating library. Winter and summer, Miss Voss was never to be seen without a red woollen shawl round her shoulders, and she used always to be knitting when a customer entered. In several other respects she resembled the Sheep in *Alice Through the Looking Glass*, and she had the same stupid and rather large pale face. What would people do with her circulating library nowadays? Nothing but tattered three-volume novels of uniform dullness and demerit, which Miss Voss lent out at twopence a volume for three days. How well I remember turning over the pages of some of them and asking myself in bewilderment why grown-up people read these stupid books called novels when they might read *Roderick Random* or *Peregrine Pickle*. These to my youthful notions were stories. It never struck me that Smollett, or Dickens himself for that matter, wrote novels.

Next to Miss Voss's dingy little stationery shop was Mr Sime the chemist, whose shop was a favourite one with the youth of the neighbourhood partly on account of a jar of leeches he kept on one of his shelves, a regular aquarium, and partly because Mr Sime himself, a large, fair, untidy man with a curiously distraught pair of very blue eyes, never failed to offer us a black-currant jujube when we fetched something for the family medicine chest. When I think of Mr Sime's eyes I wonder that our parents and guardians were not more chary of the prescriptions he made up, for the distraction of his aspect might have suggested that he was capable of mixing with them the deadliest of poisons.

Beyond the chemist's was the ironmonger, Mr Pickford, with his pincer-like figure and conspicuous rustiness among so much bright metal; and beyond him again was a tobacconist and hairdresser who had the absurdly appropriate name of Cutbeard. In nothing is our modern loss of taste so evident as in our cigarettes. Although advertisements of cigarettes have almost excluded the news from our newspapers, there is no cigarette smoker alive who could tell the difference between one brand and another if he had not read the name first. In those days every packet, even of Virginia cigarettes, was unmistakably itself. It was genuinely worth while to pause and debate whether one should parsimoniously invest threepence in a packet of Old Gold or Guinea Gold or blow five pence on a packet of Cameo or Richmond Gem. Not for us sufficed a few shreds of chopped straw faintly impregnated with nicotine from the breath of somebody who had been smoking tobacco even as the legendary salad is reputed to be blown upon by a garlic-eating cook. Well do the Americans call Virginia cigarettes domestic cigarettes nowadays.

Finally, in a shop which looked much more like the office of an old firm of solicitors than a shop, Messrs. Wingfield & Son sold wines and spirits and choice brands of cigars. I look back to that solemn window in which there was nothing to be seen but a keg of sherry with some grand sonorous Portuguese title and I reconjure the picture of General Brackenbury coming out of the shop, ushered by old Mr Wingfield and young Mr Wingfield.

'A fine morning, Wingfield,' he observes, as he pauses for a moment to twist his moustaches at the sun.

'A very fine morning indeed, General,' Mr Wingfield agrees. 'And you'll not broach the keg for a day or two after we get it round to you?'

'Certainly not,' General Brackenbury promises. 'Oh, and by the way, Wingfield, you can send me twenty-five of those Cabanas.'

'Ah!' says Mr Wingfield, rubbing his hands, 'I'm delighted to hear you've decided to give them a good trial. In my opinion that is an altogether exceptional cigar. A cigar of real character, General. You will never regret having purchased that cigar.'

Then Mr Wingfield turns to his son, 'Walter, you'll remember about the Cabanas General Brackenbury has picked out. Good-morning, General, and thank you.'

I do not know what the General paid for those cigars, but

I doubt if it was more than sixpence apiece. We could not buy their equal today at six times the price, because those Cabanas that the General bought on a fine morning in the Terrace forty full years ago were rolled before the Spanish-American War of 1898 made it improbable to find really good Cuban cigars and absolutely impossible to find really good Manila cheroots.

I walked along the Terrace recently, being curious to know if any of our old shops had survived the competition of departmental stores. Not one remained. Oh, there are still shops in the Terrace as garish and as shoddy as the wares they sell; but had I lingered there all day, I should have seen nobody like Miss Lockett or General Brackenbury. So what does it matter?

NUMBER 9

WHEN I first went to stay with my Aunt Adelaide in our street, it must have been as long ago as the Jubilee of Queen Victoria in 1887, for I well remember walking up Kensington High Street with her on a hot summer's day and seeing great crowns and stars above the shops and being told that they were the decoration for the Jubilee. And I remember what was then the incredible adventure of riding on top of an omnibus at dusk and seeing all the gas jets being lighted up by lamplighters with long poles and the scintillating crowns and stars that succeeded the operation. And I remember a big illuminated portrait of the Queen herself which no doubt through some failure of a jet showed her with mouth wide open like a salmon's about to take a fly instead of closed as it should have been in prim regal obstinacy. I know the bus driver made a joke about the old lady's having lost a tooth, which I think must have shocked all the passengers, because only the driver himself laughed at it. I remember too that the crossing sweeper at the corner of our street suddenly shouted 'God save our gracious Queen,' and stood on his head in a heap of dust he had swept into the gutter. Young as I was then, I was old enough to apprehend that it was most unusual to see a crossing sweeper standing on his head, and when I went back to our house in the country it was the chief impression of London I took home with me. It seemed to amuse the Vicar particularly, and for months afterwards he never failed when he met me to ask what I had enjoyed most of all I had seen in London. But I am not going to try to date my memories of our street, for this is not an autobiography, and over a decade visits sometimes at long intervals become merged after many years, so that the story of our street presents itself to my mind now as continuous.

Ah, those visits to stay with my aunt in London! The enchantment they cast upon me! She was my father's younger sister, and it was considered in the family that her behaviour in taking a house in London and going to live there with a friend was most extraordinary. I once heard my father say that God alone knew where Adelaide got her notions from. My aunt could hardly have been more than twenty-eight when I first went to stay with her and her friend Miss Culham, whom I always knew as Aunt Emily, though of course she was actually no relation. Aunt Adelaide was tall and slim with large grey eyes and chestnut hair and slanting eyebrows that always reminded me of a picture of one of the goddesses in Kingsley's *Heroes*; but Aunt Emily was small and very fair with cheeks like a wild rose, and a fairy princess look to my youthful fancy, though like my real aunt she too must have been nearing thirty. Women of nearly thirty were very much women in the late 'eighties; but in spite of that in old-fashioned country households unmarried daughters of that age, even if they were considered well advanced along the road to spinsterhood, were not encouraged to suppose that by setting up house on their own they were behaving in anything but a dangerously modern way.

It was through Mr Lockett that Aunt Adelaide and Aunt Emily bought Number 9 in our street. Aunt Emily had been a pupil of his before she went to study singing in Italy. She and my Aunt Adelaide had met in Milan, and there began the friendship which was to endure for the rest of their lives. There had been tragedy in both those lives. Aunt Emily had been betrothed to an officer, and during the interval at her very first concert, when she had been singing with triumphant success, a telegram had reached her to say that he had been killed in Egypt. The first song she was to sing in the second part of the programme was *She Is Far From the Land Where Her Young Hero Sleeps*, and halfway through she fell unconscious upon the platform. The shock affected her nerves in some way, and from that moment she had never sung another note. I did not find out much about Aunt Adelaide's tragedy for a long time, though I guessed from the severe way in which Janet, my aunt's elderly maid, spoke about the behaviour of men that it was an unhappy love affair. I was not less inquisitive than most children, and I suppose I could have been called romantic as well. I really longed to know the true history of that love affair.

One afternoon in mid-May when I was by myself upstairs I found that the small glass-fronted bookcase above my aunt's shiny black bureau was unlocked. Her sitting room was full of books, and I was allowed to read any book on the shelves, my favourite being a volume of Cuvier's reconstructions of pre-historic landscapes. I used to spend hours gloating upon the pictures of pterodactyls flying about over forests of unfamiliar vegetation; and there was one engraving of a fight between a plesiosaurus and a dinosaurus which outdid all the pictures of dragons in fairy tales put together. That and a big volume of one of Flammarion's astronomical works with many illustrations were my favourites. The Cuvier in particular had an ex-quisitely earthy smell which added to the thrill of turning over the pages and completed the illusion of having been taken back into that dim antediluvian past.

However, fond as I was of these books and of many others in my aunt's library, that locked bookcase had always be-witched my fancy. I wanted to ask my aunt to open it and let me look at the small volumes within; but I feared lest she might refuse, and I was always hoping that the fortunate moment would arrive when I should find it open. I wished to avoid any-thing like a direct command not to touch these particular books, for I argued with myself that if I had never been told not to open the bookcase I could not be blamed if I took ad-vantage of the first opportunity to do so. On this May after-noon my aunts had gone to a Joachiim concert at the St James's Hall, and in my solitary wanderings round the deserted room I noticed that the key was in the bookcase. I remember that as I turned the key a puff of wind sent the blind bellying into the room with a noise that fetched my heart into my mouth and made me fall off the fragile chair with back inlaid with mother o' pearl and painted with blue and green parroquets and seat of gilded cane on which I was standing to reach the bookcase. I pulled myself together and went out on the landing to peer down over the balusters for any sign of interruption. The house was still except for Aunt Emily's canaries, which were singing loudly in the dining room below. Janet would be nodding over the *Family Herald* down in the morning room, I decided, and Hetty the cook was having her afternoon out, I knew. So I went back on tiptoe into my Aunt Adelaide's room conscious that it was ridiculous to be walking about it on tiptoe, and yet, because I was going to open that bookcase, quite unable to tread boldly. The flapping of the blind still made me jump, but

I could not bring myself to pull it up and let the sunshine stream in, because the tempered light seemed to give me an assurance of secrecy and security for the enterprise I was undertaking.

The first volume I took out was a Baedeker Guide to Southern Italy, and as I hastily put it back in disgust at such a wretchedly dull reward for my audacity a pressed blossom slipped from between the pages and fluttered down upon the slanting lid of my aunt's shiny black lacquer bureau and clung to the smooth surface like a moth. It was not a flower that I recognised, and its colour had faded to a diaphanous ghostly grey; but the pages between which it had been pressed were still faintly stained with blue, and it was so thin that I could not pick it up without running the risk of crushing it into nothingness. So I blew it carefully down the lid of the bureau into my hand and replaced it in the Baedeker.

The next book I took out was a small volume of Browning's poems bound in a worn crushed morocco. I thought at first by the binding that it was a prayer book. There were many pressed flowers between the pages, and so brightly were some of them stained with crimson and blue and yellow petals that they seemed like the pages of an illuminated missal. Beside almost every poem the names of places and dates were written in my aunt's small and beautifully shaped hand, as thus: *Vallambrosa, April 15, '81*. Frequently verses had been underlined. I remember one vividly: *How the March Sun Feels Like May;* beside which was written minutely: *Read to me by O. at Amalfi, March 20th, '82.* And then I read that verse:

> *I wonder do you feel today*
> *As I have felt since, hand in hand,*
> *We sat down on the grass, to stray*
> *In spirit better through the land,*
> *This morn of Rome and May?*

At the bottom of the page was written in red ink: *May 17, 82. O. told me today. E. was so sweet. Can this wild happiness of Rome and May and us be true?* When I read this I looked up at the calendar on the mantelpiece and saw in big scarlet letters MAY 17. I was wondering if O. was perhaps the man whose behaviour had made Janet speak for evermore with such scorn of men and I was telling myself that E. must stand of course for Aunt Emily, when the door opened suddenly and Janet herself came in. I am sure I turned as white as Janet's apron, and as I jumped instinctively to replace the book I let half a dozen of the blossoms pressed between the pages go fluttering down upon the carpet. Janet asked me sharply if I had opened my aunt's bureau, and when I assured her that I had only been looking at the books I noticed for the first time that the key was in the lid of the bureau. Even had I observed this earlier, I should certainly not have dreamed of trying to explore my aunt's bureau. That would have seemed an odious thing to do; but the curiosity about her books I regarded as perfectly legitimate in spite of being so nervous over my gratification of it.

'Your aunt sent a messenger boy all the way from Piccadilly with a note telling me she'd gone off to the concert and left her desk unlocked. If she thinks you've been poking about in it, that's the last time you'll ever be asked to stay with her in London.'

'But, Janet, I haven't. I really didn't even touch the lid of the desk. I only looked at some of the books. You made me jump. You came in so quietly. That's why I let these flowers fall out. Don't tell Aunt Adelaide, will you, Janet? Please, don't.'

Janet lifted the lid of the bureau and, after a stern glance to ascertain if my aunt's neatness of arrangement showed any sign of having been disturbed, she apparently accepted my assurances and looked less sternly.

I picked up the pressed flowers and replaced them between the pages, though I felt that I must have been changing all their original resting places, which pricked my conscience badly when I thought about this adventure in bed that night.

On my Aunt Adelaide's return from the concert, she went up to lie down in her bedroom with a bad headache, and I heard Aunt Emily in the passage say to Janet:

'I hoped that the music would have kept her mind away from thoughts of the seventeenth of May; but she had been reading through his letters, and she was upset by leaving her bureau open like that.'

I held my breath, fearing for Janet's reply.

To my profound relief she said not a word about discovering me with the book.

Instead she muttered fiercely:

'He ought to see her now, poor lamb; perhaps he'd understand then what it has meant to her all these years.'

'Janet, Janet,' said Aunt Emily with gentle reproach, 'you know Miss Adelaide does not like to hear you talk like that. You know she cannot bear not to take her full share of the blame for what happened.'

I have no doubt Janet flicked her nose with her forefinger at this, for that was the gesture with which she always expressed a right to maintain her own opinion without being disrespectful. Anyway, she was silent, and though I longed to know now what name O. stood for I decided I would not risk the inquiry, lest Janet should fancy after all that I had been poking about inside my aunt's desk, in which case I was sure she would see to it that I was never invited to stay in our street again. And what a catastrophe in my life that would have been! Our house on the borders of Gloucestershire and Worcestershire was buried in remote orchards. The beauty of it was great, but as an only child I longed for the company of other children. Moreover, after my mother's death my father had devoted himself to pomology with such absorption that he could talk of nothing else. Walks were monologues by him about the obscure plums and apples he was restoring to cultivation.

'By the way, your aunt wants you to go up to London for a month on Wednesday.'

The message would reach me from far away at the other end of the breakfast table at which my father and I took our meals as ceremoniously as a couple of royalties, and for the rest of the day I would be longing for bedtime that I might fall asleep in a luxury of expectation.

OUR STREET

PERHAPS it was in winter that the pleasure of arriving at Paddington used to be sharpest. That squalid approach of the railway which has cast a gloom over so many people was to me a delicious closing in of comfortable and cosy houses, and if it were late afternoon with fog swirling about the frore dusk so much the better. And then the excitement of stumbling over the footwarmers to reach the compartment window and recognising the tall form of my aunt in her mantle of fur coming along the platform to welcome me. There would follow the joy of driving home in a hansom, and I doubt if Sir Walter Raleigh felt as proud when he flung his cloak down in front of Queen Elizabeth as I used to feel when I put out an arm to shield my aunt from the muddy wheel as she got into the hansom. If it was nearing Christmas the shops in Kensington High Street would appear like Aladdin's cave, with all that superior warmth and richness of illumination which gas could provide before it was debauched by incandescent burners and finally supplanted by that enemy of the human eye, electric light. In those days Christmas shopping was not yet become a melancholy orgy imposed hysterically upon the public through the desire of the press to help its advertisers. No doubt many of us were very sentimental over Christmas, but at least we did not surrender to sentiment in the way people surrender to community singing.

As soon as the glittering shops were left behind, we would reach Holland House, the wooded grounds of which used to loom behind the orange street lamps like a magic forest. Even in those days I fancy Olympia was already built, the last expression of that passion for megahyaline architecture which began with the Crystal Palace and prevailed during the third quarter of the nineteenth century; but regretfully and aplogetically I have to admit that in those days, perhaps because of its association with wonders like Venice in London or Barnum and Bailey's Circus, Olympia seemed to me a building of supreme beauty. It was soon after that monstrous conservatory appeared in sight that the turning off the main road into our street was to be expected.

What quickened heartbeats turnings have provided for humanity! A crooked old signpost pointing down a narrow lane has meant so much to so many; but to just as many the weather-worn name of a by-street off some wide London thoroughfare has meant just as much. The motorcar has not succeeded in robbing us of that thrill, sadly though it may have abbreviated it. Man will lose it of course when all mankind is flying; but there will be compensation, and I envy posterity the joy of dropping directly down upon a well-loved spot. To turn a corner in the country a high dogcart provided the perfect motion and pace, but to turn a corner in London nothing has ever equalled the hansom cab. To swing round out of Hammersmith Road and hear the different sound of the horse's hooves and the hansom's wheels as they left the wooden pavement and took the macadam stored my memory with a sound that I should like to rhapsodise over as old men rhapsodise over the singers they heard in youth, for that sound is the music of our street, and it still plays in the recesses of my consciousness a tune of yesterday.

Our street had houses on only one side. The opposite pavement was bounded by a high wall in which were set two or three mysterious green doors leading into the great gardens of The Grange, an early Georgian house which belonged to a famous portrait painter, and Sheba Lodge, a big bow-windowed Regency house, which was now an exclusive private asylum, if such a paradoxical epithet may be used. Where the wall of the Sheba Lodge garden began it was covered with broken glass and we children used to imagine that this had been done to deter the lunatics from trying to escape. In spite of the glass we were always hearing rumours of escaped lunatics, and these shared with burglars and murderers the chief place in our nightly fears. Houses and gardens have both gone now. Two or three years ago when I passed by The Grange housebreakers were stripping it of a wistaria two centuries old, with no more reverence than they would have shown for the bunting of yesterday's bazaar. The mellow red brick pile itself must have been pulled down soon afterward. The cedars, be-

27

neath whose shade the aristocratic lunatics, prisoners as much of their own oppressive thoughts as of the high asylum walls, used to wander or sometimes play their childish solitary games, no longer spread those dark green fans. The lawns which were once thronged with the actual and potential sitters of the famous portrait painter at his garden parties no longer shimmer in the sunlight. Huge honeycombs of flats have obliterated lawns and cedars, and where once the thrushes sang and blackbirds fluted and fluttered through the dusky shrubberies people are saying what a difference wireless has made to their evenings.

None of us in our street, not even Lady Marjorie Doyle, ever went to those garden parties; but we could hardly help taking a good deal of interest in them. Many of the carriages used to drive along our street to reach the famous portrait painter's house, and on such occasions there was a tendency to water the flowers on our balconies earlier in the afternoon than usual. Moreover, from our balconies we could stare across to the lawns and wonder if we were not recognising some of the distinguished men and beautiful women with whose faces we were familiar through cabinet photographs of them by Elliot & Fry or Russell, which in those days were sold in the shops of booksellers and stationers and were always on view to the curious, rows of them in the windows. And they *were* photographs. None of your artistic blurs of today. You could count the petals in a statesman's buttonhole and the ostrich plumes in a professional beauty's fan. Indeed, the only detail hidden was the brass clamp, which held the sitter's head at the exact angle the photographer desired. But after all, though a visit to the photographer was as much of an undertaking then as a visit to the dentist now, what did it matter to a generation of men prepared to throttle themselves with high collars or of women willing to squeeze themselves into tight stays? But while we did not pity the human beings who put themselves to so much discomfort to present the picture we expected, we did feel very sorry for the horses who were compelled to endure the bearing rein.

'I'd like to put a bearing rein on that horrid old frump herself,' Miss Lockett was heard to declare when a pair of foam-flecked high-stepping bays came superbly round the corner of our street one afternoon, drawing a landau in which a withered dowager was bobbing about in the June sunlight under a lace parasol. 'If I knew who she was, I'd send her a copy of *Black Beauty* marked in red ink. I wouldn't care who she was. She's old and ugly enough to know better.'

However, fortunately for Miss Lockett's peace of mind foam-flecked bays driven on the bearing rein were rare in our street except on the afternoons of the portrait painter's garden parties. The principal traffic consisted of perambulators wheeled by nursemaids, and of tradesmen's carts driven at such a dashing speed that it was a wonder the youths on the boxes of them were not bounced off like indiarubber balls. There was, too, passing at intervals of half an hour a green omnibus, which in the course of a long devious journey across London did nothing quite so eccentric as to go jolting down our street. Where its journey began and where it ended I no longer remember; but people who lived in our street used sometimes to mention having caught sight of our omnibus in some odd nook of London as ornithologists bring home the news of a bird they have identified in some unexpected locality.

I have said that our street was only one-sided, but I forgot to add that the numbers of the houses were all odd – from Number 1 to Number 25. As you might anticipate, Mr Lockett made many a joke about this, and often talked of founding a club to be called the Odd Numbers.

'By George, General, the man who numbered our street must have known who were going to live in it,' Mr Lockett might say in his brazen voice.

And General Brackenbury, who was as conventional a figure of a British general as may be imagined, was so fond of Mr Lockett that he usually did not object to being called an odd number in order not to spoil Mr Lockett's joke, although when he was liverish he was inclined to criticise Mr Lockett for making so many bad puns.

Of the thirteen houses in our street Number 25 remained empty over a long term of years. Some attributed this to its being haunted, though by what such a comparatively recent building without any kind of history attached to it should be haunted nobody explained. Others said there had always been trouble with the drains there. One or two had observed it was a thirteenth house and predicted ill luck for it in consequence. To the children in our street Number 25 became an object of awe, and they would dare one another to go up the unswept steps and sound a rat-tat with the knocker covered with verdigris or even more recklessly to lift up the dislustred flap of the letter box and peer through into the dim dusty hall. Legends accumulated round that empty house in the savage folklore of childhood. It was said to be the secret resort of a gang of burglars who issued forth thence at night to prey upon the neighbourhood. And of course it was often said that a lunatic had escaped from Sheba Lodge and concealed himself in the coal cellar of Number 25. I do not think that I wanted any of these accessories to make the unlet house horrific. The emptiness and dust and silence of it were enough, and the way it stood by itself at the end of a row, destroying the symmetry of our street by introducing a flight of front door steps which had no companion steps next door and which were bounded by the wall of the back garden of the corner house in Burton Road into which our street ran at right angles.

Presumably those big gardens had induced a hope in the builders of our street that one day they would be able to acquire enough ground to erect houses with even numbers opposite; but they were too sanguine, and to this day the even numbers are wanting.

Beauclerk Street was built – just before red bricks became so fashionable again after a lapse of years – of those characteristic dirty yellow bricks which the London air darkens to a uniform and indescribable colour seen in no other city of the world that I know. Apparently they are no longer used; but they were used so extensively at one time that when one thinks of London it is always of a city built with those bricks, as one thinks of the honey-brown travertine of Rome or the granite of Aberdeen. The architecture of our street was completely typical of its period. It did not, in despair of achieving originality, attempt to imitate the houses of a fairer period, and in its favour was a lack of excess in the use of meaningless and fidgety decoration to which the architecture of that date was too often unhappily addicted. The front steps of Number 1 and Number 3 rose in amiable juxtaposition to their respective front doors, which were wider than most of the front doors in roads round about. The windows of Number 3 and Number 5 confronted the world without side by side. Every house had three stories, an attic, and a basement. Every area had a laburnum, two lilac bushes, and a dustbin. Every oblong back garden had three poplar trees to screen us in summer from the back gardens of Carlington Road. A square porch supported by three pillars sheltered every pair of front doors, and this porch was divided above by a heavy green trellis between a pair of balconies. We thought them much pleasanter than the narrow balconies with railings of wrought iron which were a characteristic of the houses in the neighbourhood, and we were positive that they were much more dignified.

To a superficial glance the houses of our street would undoubtedly have presented a markedly uniform appearance. I realise that now, when I walk past any row of London houses without ever bothering to note how different each one really is. But if at this date a person had suggested to me that all the houses in our street looked exactly like one another, I should have been amazed at his blindness. Why, for me the mere numbers over the doors had significance and in many cases were inseparably associated with the inmates.

NUMBER 1

WHO else but Doctor Arden could have lived at Number 1? He was himself an incarnate Number 1. He looked so tall and spare when in his short frock coat or rather riding coat, for I believe that would have been a more accurate name for it, he used to set out with springy steps upon his daily round of visits. In all the years I knew him Doctor Arden was never seen in any other dress but that black riding coat which by constant exposure to the weather had taken on the greenish hue of sea-weed. It might snow or blow. It might pour with rain. It might freeze. The only concession Doctor Arden ever made to the weather was to carry an umbrella. I do not believe that he possessed an overcoat. Perpetual exercise had kept his figure as trim as an athletic young subaltern's. Long service in India had turned his complexion to parchment, and like parchment his skin was stretched tight across his high cheekbones. He had a nose like the great Duke of Wellington's, and indeed in many respects he bore a remarkable resemblance to the Iron Duke. He was a widower, and his only daughter, Minnie, kept house for him in what for me was an atmosphere of mystery, because my visists to Doctor Arden were always connected with matters of medicine such as the patching up of a cut finger or the lancing of an abscess or the prescribing of a tonic. Thus my impression of the inside of Number 1 was concentrated upon the surgery.

To begin with, these two extra rooms at the side of the corner house which served as dispensary and surgery were unique. Though the rest of Number 1 might conform to the familiar pattern of our street, these two extra rooms made it as different as a house in Harley Street itself. It was always a matter of speculation how the rest of Number 1 was reached from the surgery. Apart altogether from its architectural distinction the surgery itself fascinated me by the variety of its contents when I was waiting in it for the purpose of some unpleasant minor matter of medicine. It was a tiny room, but it was so crowded with objects of interest that I never noticed how long the doctor kept me waiting. I would still be wondering what everything was for, and pondering the yellowing photographs of regimental groups and Indian scenes, the curious weapons and fans, and of course the surgical instruments. What after many years I remember best were the two framed coloured prints of officers, noncommissioned officers and men of the Royal Inniskilling Fusiliers and the Highland Light Infantry. These must have been the two regiments to which the doctor had been attached. It was odd that I should be standing on the hearthrug and staring up at those two prints when the doctor came bustling in from his dispensary, nearly always drying his hands on a small towel, for to dry his hands on the way from the dispensary to the surgery would have saved him quite thirty seconds, and to a man as busy as the doctor thirty seconds were a valuable economy. He had beautiful slim hands, the colour of old ivory; and the lightness of his touch as he felt the side of one's neck to detect the presence of swollen glands was immensely reassuring.

There is little to tell about the doctor's daughter Minnie. I never remember meeting her at home, but I sometimes met her at the Locketts' next door, when she was always kind and pleasant but detached from the ordinary life of us young people in our street. I suppose that to her we were all her father's patients and that such a relation made her chary of intimacy. Even at the home of the Locketts whom she had known all her life Minnie Arden always seemed like a visitor, and it comes back to me that when she spoke of our street it was with a hint of self-consciousness as if the too familiar method of address embarrassed her. Yes, what between the cool remote Minnie, those two small additional rooms, that third entrance marked Surgery, and Doctor Arden's own air of Wellingtonian authority Number 1 looms in my mind with as much impressive superiority to the other twelve houses in our street as Buckingham Palace establishes its preëminence above any other residence in Buckingham Palace Road.

NUMBER 3

AT Number 3, where the Locketts lived, once again the numeral seemed to express perfectly the appearance of Mr Lockett himself as with the tails of his frock coat flying he hurried off to some service at St Jude's, for his grizzled carroty curls puffed out beneath his curly-brimmed silk hat in such a very three-like way, and even the curly-brimmed silk hat itself had a sort of threeness about it. Mr Lockett and his sister I have already introduced; but Mrs Lockett must not be forgotten. I always heard her spoken of as a motherly woman, and if to see that her juvenile visitors were kept well supplied at tea with what they wanted, was motherly, then indeed Mrs Lockett deserved the epithet. She probably had had a beautiful complexion in youth, but like so many beautiful complexions of youth it had turned in middle age to a network of small crimson veins. There was no such number as four in the whole of our street; but had there been, I should have found in Mrs Lockett an effect of fourness. There was a calm solidity about her like the number four, and beside the general curliness of her husband her appearance was all straight lines. Even her bonnets were somehow more oblong than the bonnets of the other ladies in our street. Mr and Mrs Lockett had a son and a daughter. Clara, the younger, was a stolid good-natured girl with rather a pasty face. She and I took tea together fairly often; but throughout our social intercourse I can recall nothing about her of the very slightest interest. In distinction to Clara, her elder brother George, who was a medical student in the days I am writing of, was as fond of noisy jokes as his father; and when George was at home tea parties with Clara were pleasantly exciting, for he would juggle first with the scones, then with the scones and buns, and finally with the big cakes themselves. So to get a second helping of anything one had to leap for it, while Clara in a brown velvet dress with a point lace collar and indefinite hair, all rats' tails, munched

34

away stolidly at the bread and butter with which her brother never juggled.

One other occupant of Number 3 there was, and that was Snuff, Miss Lockett's pug dog. His mistress declared that he was the most intelligent creature she had ever known. He may have been; but visitors to Number 3 found him as unresponsive as Diogenes, for Snuff spent all his time growling into the depths of the cushion on which he was lying, and if to curry favour with him we offered him a lump of sugar he would not even stop growling while he was chewing it up. However, Miss Lockett loved him and used always to buy a little bit more ribbon than she wanted for her cap so that her 'Snuffy-body', as she fondly and I must add rather foolishly called him, might be smart, or as Miss Lockett used to say, elegant.

FULL though my aunt's house was of books, they only increased my desire for books of my own, and one day when out for a walk by myself I found a second-hand bookshop in Hammersmith Road which afforded me a chance of beginning to buy books for myself, because outside on the pavement there were various shelves and stalls labelled 'All in this row, one penny,' or 'All in this row, twopence.' Whatever treasures the inside of the shop held there was not a volume outside which cost more than sixpence. The moment I discovered Elson's bookshop I used to spend hours in the company of various seedy-looking men of all ages grubbing about among those bargains. To be sure, about seventy-five per cent of those bargains were bound volumes of sermons or tattered treatises on old-fashioned agriculture; but from time to time I found a volume which after turning over the pennies in my pocket half a dozen times in economical meditation I at last decided to purchase.

One dank November afternoon I came across a work on the language of flowers illustrated by Birket Foster. The price was fourpence, for it was in the last stages of decay, and there were several pages missing. But in that tristful November twilight under the flaring naphtha jets which illuminated the outside wares in the bookstalls the bright posies and gay birds of Birket Foster's illustrations kindled in me a thought of spring, and, though I had only fourpence left of my pocket money for that week, I resolved to acquire the volume. Yet again I hesitated, telling myself that the purchase of this volume was just the whim of a moment and that I should probably find a book I wanted much more presently and then be without the means to buy it. While I stood thus in dubiety I heard a deep voice behind me say:

'If you don't buy that book, young man, I shall.'

Turning round, I perceived a burly man with pointed grey

beard who looked to me about sixty and who was standing under a very large dark green umbrella and leaning heavily on a rubber-tipped stick. I recognised him at once as the solitary eccentric who lived at Number 5 in our street, and with the naïve egotism of childhood I supposed that he must recognise me. I told him that I should like to have the book, but that I was not perfectly sure whether I liked it enough to spend the whole of my money on it.

'Fourpence!' the burly gentleman ejaculated. 'Yes, that's a large sum.'

He said it so gravely that I never suspected he might be laughing, and I agreed with him earnestly that it was.

'Why do you seek instruction in the language of flowers?' the burly gentleman asked. 'If you propose to communicate with the young lady of your choice through such a medium at this season of the year, you will find your investment even more expensive than you had supposed.'

'Well, it was the pictures I liked.'

'Ah, you like pictures, do you? In that case you'd better come back to tea with me and I will show you pictures in every stage from the virgin canvas to the framed article. My name is Granby Mellor, and I live at 5 Beauclerk Street about ten minutes away.'

I told him that I was staying with my aunt at Number 9 in the same street and asked him if he minded my obtaining her permission to go and have tea with him.

'Ask away,' said Mr Mellor, 'as long as she doesn't expect me to invite *her*.'

I daresay I looked a little shocked by such a disrespectful reference to my Aunt Adelaide, for he tugged at his beard and rumbled out a hoarse laugh.

'Bachelor ways, bachelor ways,' he told me. 'No reflection on your aunt. Except she's a very good aunt. So far as aunts go. But that usually ain't far.'

With this Mr Mellor put a forefinger to his nose and slowly winked a heavily lidded eye.

'Well, I'm sure she won't be offended if you don't invite her too,' I assured him.

'Sensible woman, eh? Bravo! There are damned few of 'em. Well, young man, are you going to buy that keepsake literature you've been gloating over for the last half-hour or are you not?'

The prospect of having tea with my new friend was so exciting that I was beginning to feel less urgently impelled to risk the whole of my wealth on that little volume, and I turned over the four pennies in my pocket yet once again.

'Tell you what I'll do,' Mr Mellor offered. 'All I want is one page of it. I'll blow fourpence on the volume, tear out the page I want, and give you the rest.'

I probably grinned approval of his solution. Anyway a minute or two later I was walking back towards our street beside my new acquaintance, the volume covered against the drizzle by my overcoat. We did not move over the ground quickly, because Mr Mellor was continually stopping in the middle of the pavement and talking with so much emphasis that the passers-by seemed inclined to stay and listen to what he had to say, perhaps supposing him for a moment to be a cheapjack about to conduct a sale of water-colours, the subject of his discourse.

At last we reached Number 5.

'Well, you cut along and get leave to eat with the ogre,' said the painter. 'And I'll go and rally the buns.'

Aunt Adelaide was a little dubious at first about letting me accept Mr Mellor's invitation. He had a reputation in our street for eccentricity, and the prudence of allowing me to go to tea alone with an elderly bachelor was much debated. Luckily Aunt Emily came to my rescue and intervened between me and the tales Janet was telling Aunt Adelaide about the tales current in the kitchen at Number 7 next door about the odd goings on occasionally at Number 5.

'Oh, well,' I protested, 'Lady Marjorie Doyle's cook always exaggerates everything most frightfully.'

'No such thing,' Janet contradicted sharply. 'A most reliable woman.'

And then Aunt Emily said quietly:

'Really, dearest Adelaide, are you and I going to allow ourselves mental gooseflesh over the habits of painters?'

My Aunt Adelaide looked quickly across at Aunt Emily and then said that I might go, but that I must be home at six o'clock at latest.

I did not wait for any afterthoughts, but hurried off as soon as possible.

The door of Number 5 was opened by Mr Mellor himself,

now in a much stained brown velveteen jacket.

'Come in, come in,' he shouted, his bulk filling even one of the exceptionally wide front doors of our street. The door closed behind me. The darkness and drizzle of the November afternoon were banished. I looked round me and fancied I was bewitched, for the inside of Number 5 was like a mixture of a museum, an old curiosity shop, and a robbers' cave. From outside it had always seemed one of the least interesting houses in our street, because the window of the front room which corresponded with our dining room (and indeed with the dining room of every house in our street except the Locketts' at Number 3 and the Spinks' at Number 13) was obscured by what looked like a screen of opaque glass and thus presented to the eyes of the passer-by the bleak and dingy exterior of an office. Now, when Mr Mellor opened the front door on the left of the hall and ushered me into his dining room, I saw that the screen of glass was really an inner window of small leaded panes some of which were filled with green bottle glass. They might have been magic casements opening on perilous seas instead of the sober pavement of our street. A brass chandelier like one of those the Dutch painters loved to hang in their immortal rooms hung from the ceiling, and the flames of a dozen wax candles were reflected in every pane, while in some the miniature of a leaping fire gleamed opalescent against the last dim sapphires of the November twilight.

Then Mr Mellor shut out the window with heavy black curtains at the top of which two golden dragons eyed one another serenely in the glowing room. Over the mantelpiece was a large oil painting of a knight in sea-green armour standing beside a gloomy mere from which a mist was rising to enfold him, and it shaped vaguely like the contours of a woman's form.

'La Belle Dame sans merci,' observed Mr Mellor. 'Sit down and tuck in at the grub.'

He pointed to a faldstool of embossed leather on one side of the fireplace and seated himself in a high-backed Gothic chair on the other. Between us was a low table covered with the material for tea, prominent among which was a large pot of shrimp paste.

'What's the difference between a piece of new bread thickly spread with shrimp paste and a caterpillar walking across a bathroom ceiling?' my host asked.

I could never guess riddles and gave this one up immediately.

'You don't know?' Mr Mellor repeated in apparent amazement.

I shook my head.

'You really don't know the difference?' he pressed.

'No, I really don't.'

'Then I'm bothered if you're safe to be trusted at a tea table,' Mr Mellor roared out.

The success of his catch so much delighted my burly host that I thought he would fall off his chair with laughing at me.

'By the holy poker, I must tell that to Mrs Jutsom,' he gurgled. 'I'll say, "Look here, Mrs Jutsom, it's no use your providing shrimp paste for this young man. He doesn't know the difference between it and a caterpillar walking across a bathroom ceiling. It's wasted on him." '

'But I thought it was a riddle,' I protested.

This excuse of mine only made Mr Mellor laugh louder than ever, and he became so wheezy at last that I began to think he would choke. Finally he got up, went over to the big oak ambry that nearly covered one wall of the room, and took out a bottle of port, a glass of which seemed to settle the disturbance in his lungs, though he was still gasping when he took his seat again at the tea table.

'Here's another one,' he said presently. 'Why is a cream jug like a whale?'

Although I could not perceive any cause for excessive mirth if I replied that I did not know, I was chary of committing myself again.

'Give it up?' my host asked.

I nodded, still cautious of uttering a word which might involve me in his boisterous laughter.

'Because neither of 'em can climb a tree,' Mr Mellor announced. 'Not bad, eh? Get that off on your friends.'

I promised that I would. Indeed, I had already resolved to get the other off on my friends too, and enjoy their discomfiture as much as Mr Mellor had enjoyed mine.

'Who painted that picture?' I asked presently, for the knight in sea-green armour beside the mere was filling me with romantic fancies and I was feeling in this medieval room as far from our street as he from home, and in these surroundings I was as liable as he to dream fantastic dreams.

'That picture was painted by a promising young joker called Granby Mellor about ten years ago. Unfortunately he had been a promising young joker for a quarter of a century before that, and it came too late to be recognised as the fulfilment of his promise. And let me tell you it was Dante Gabriel himself who first declared that Granby Mellor was a promising young joker. But I lay you don't know who Dante Gabriel was?'

'Dante Gabriel Rossetti?' I said quickly.

'By the holy poker, the boy guessed right the very first time. He doesn't know the difference between shrimp paste and a caterpillar, but he has heard of Rossetti. *The blessed damozel leaned out . . .* go on.'

'*From the gold bar of Heaven,*' I continued.

'*Her eyes were deeper than the depth,*' he challenged.

'*Of waters stilled at even,*' I replied.

'*She had three lilies in her hand,*' he challenged again.

'*And the stars in her hair were seven,*' I replied.

And line by line, answering one another like the stichomythia of a Greek play, we went through the poem, until my host came to the tragic parenthesis:

> '*Yet now, and in this place*
> *Surely she leaned o'er me – her hair*
> *Fell all about my face. . . .*
> *Nothing: the autumn fall of leaves.*
> *The whole year sets apace.*'

In saying these five lines he did not wait for me to take any of them up, but murmured them all to himself as if in truth he spoke for his actual self.

A silence fell. I sat embarrassed on the faldstool, watching the knight in sea-green armour and the misty shape of womanhood that clung round him beside that desolate mere. And my host sat staring into the fire.

'The whole year sets apace,' he muttered after a while, 'and not so many more of them to set.'

Then he returned to his silent brooding, and I noticed for the first time that on a corner of the mantelpiece the sands of an hourglass were trickling the time away.

At last my host sprang up and shouted to me that we would go up to his den. And indeed as he led the way from the dining room he reminded me so much of some great shaggy animal

41

that to be commanded to his den seemed the most appropriate place imaginable. However, before going upstairs he took me farther along the hall to show me what he called his workshop, which was the comparatively big room at the back that everybody else in our street except the Locketts and the Spinks used as a drawing room.

The reason by the way that the Locketts used the big room for their dining room was that they had a dining table which could be converted into a billiard table, on which we played every game except true billiards.

I had never seen a painter's studio before, and when Mr Mellor lit the gas, revealing the easels and canvases and palettes, I was filled with awe. A large piece of cheese with a penknife stuck in it on the mantelpiece caught my eye.

'Always eat cheese when I'm working,' Mr Mellor explained. 'Nothing like it. But come along up to my den. A painter's studio at night is the dreariest place on God's earth. It's haunted by the ghosts of abortive masterpieces.'

He abruptly turned out the gas as he spoke, and as I made my way towards the dimly lighted hall I stepped into a soft mess of something which turned out to be one of his palettes he had not bothered to clean and scrape.

'What's the matter?' he cried, as I uttered an apologetic exclamation. 'Trodden in the paint? Never mind. I'm always doing it myself. Rub your boots on this mat. I keep it specially for the purpose.'

And sure enough by the door of the studio there was a mat which from the amount of paint wiped upon it looked like patchwork. I got rid of the Chinese white and cadmium and cobalt which were smeared upon my soles, and followed Mr Mellor upstairs to his den which turned out to be the back room on the first floor and corresponded in Number 9 to my Aunt Adelaide's sitting room, where I had had the adventure with the unlocked bookcase.

The walls of the staircase up, and of the passage above, were hung with pictures and plates and plaques and old weapons, and all the way upstairs antique calf-bound folios were kept upright by the balusters, so that it was difficult to go up without knocking into something. How the bulky owner of all this bric-à-brac managed it was another riddle.

'I don't allow Mrs Jutsom upstairs,' my host explained. 'So

it's a bit dusty. She has strict orders to keep to the basement, though I let her clear the dining room sometimes as a favour. But all the rooms upstairs are full of books and pictures and all sorts of odds and ends I haven't had time to arrange yet. And you know what women are.'

I was wondering where he slept, when he seemed to divine my thought and told me that he had a shakedown in the bathroom. I knew well the size of the bathrooms in our street, and how he managed to find space for even the smallest bed in one of them did puzzle me.

'Quite simple,' he said, divining my thought again. 'I've got my bed alongside the bath. I turn my bath full on and if I go to sleep again it overflows and drives me out of bed. Getting up has been the curse of my life, and damme, a painter must get up in the morning, you know.'

By this time we were steering our way through the heaps of books that were strewn about the floor of his den toward a couple of very deep armchairs covered with a much worn and faded piece of tambour work in a design of blue and red birds and fruiting boughs. After fumbling in a brass box on which was engraved a crude biblical rebus my host produced two long thin cigars with straws through them.

'You smoke?'

'Only cigarettes,' I explained cautiously.

He took the lid from an exquisite porcelain patchbox on which Cupids were dancing with wreaths of roses and offered me a strange cigarette of black tobacco wrapped in what looked like grass.

'Brazilian,' he explained. 'Wrapped in maize. You can taste *them*.'

I certainly could; but somehow I managed not to splutter, and in consequence I began to feel as bold as a buccaneer in his glory, as I drew hard at my pungent cigarette, the maize round which seemed to crackle like a fuse of gunpowder every time I took a whiff.

Mr Mellor rummaged about among the books on the floor and showed me some volumes illustrated with woodcuts by masters like Fred Walker and Millais.

'Ever do anything in that line?' he asked. 'They'll go up in value every year.'

Remembering the shilling a week from which I had had to

buy whatever books I collected, I thought he was pulling my leg; but the fumes of the Brazilian tobacco filled me with hardihood, and I gave him a negative of the same kind as Mr Winkle's when he was asked by Mr Jingle if he kept dogs, a negative which implied that for the moment my collecting energies were too much absorbed in other directions to devote myself as much as I should like to the illustrators of the 'sixties and early 'seventies.

'Hullo,' Mr Mellor exclaimed presently, 'here's a bookmarker that will interest you.' He took from one of the volumes a strip of figured velvet, the colour of damson juice. 'Do you know who put that in there for a bookmarker? Rossetti himself. No other. I lent him the volume once, and it came back with this strip of velvet in it. That thrills you, doesn't it? By the way, who put you on to Rossetti?'

I told him that my Aunt Adelaide had once given me *Sister Helen* to read, and that I had learnt it by heart.

'Here high up on the balcony the moon flies face to face with me, eh?' Mr Mellor chuckled. 'Well, I knew Rossetti. Knew them all in fact. Swinburne, Meredith, Morris, Burne-Jones, Millais. In fact you're looking at one of the minor pre-Raphaelites. An antediluvian survival, young man, of whom not even a coprolite will survive him. Private means. That ruined me. Enough to get along comfortably without working too hard. Fatal! Look at Georgio Griffin opposite.'

Sir George Griffin was the famous portrait painter whose wistaria-clad mellow house dreamed among the trees beyond those wide lawns and whose stately garden parties we could watch from the upper stories of our street.

'I knew Georgio Griffin when he was glad to earn a guinea by sketching for some weekly rag the actors and actresses in a burlesque. Georgio *had* to work. And look at him now. Georgio isn't making a penny less than £10,000 a year. Georgio is a success, and I'm a complete failure. But don't let me go jawing on about myself. Rossetti was the man. Bigger than all the rest of 'em put together. But a dark strange creature. He was born too late. You remember Swinburne? Wasn't it in *Félise*? *This thin-faced time of ours*. It was too much for poor Dante Gabriel.'

And then suddenly he told me a horrifying story about Rossetti and his wife, which I will not set down because it may not have been true, though as my host related it to me it burnt itself upon the imagination like some scene in a tragedy by Webster or Ford.

'And that was why he buried the manuscript of his poems in poor Lizzie's grave,' Mr Mellor concluded. 'Have another cigarette?'

But I declined, for I was sure that it was long after six, when I had promised to be home. I tried to puzzle out the time from the queer clock with a single hand; but at last I gave it up and asked my host what the time was.

'The time?' he repeated, pulling from his waistcoat the thinnest watch I had ever seen. 'The time is exactly seventeen minutes to eight.'

'Not really?' I stammered, gasping.

'Seventeen minutes to eight. This old Ponsevret watch of mine never loses or gains a second in a month.'

'I'm afraid I must go. I never thought it was as late as that.'

'Late?' Mr Mellor exclaimed. 'Did you say "late"? My dear young man, I've only been out of bed five hours. I was just taking my after-breakfast stroll when I had the pleasure of making your acquaintance over a book as so many pleasant acquaintances have been made over a book. Mrs Justom will be expecting you to stay to supper. I always have supper about half-past nine – '

'No, really,' I interrupted. 'I'm afraid I must go now. I said I'd be back by six.'

I tried to put into this statement an implication that the promise was a voluntary one on my part, but I doubt if I succeeded in conveying a very sharp impression of independence. Anyway, Mr Mellor sped me on my way, exhorting me to come to terms with my aunt and name a day for supper.

'If your aunt is sensible enough to cultivate a taste for Rossetti in her nephew, she can't be a completely normal aunt. I'll write her a polite letter and request the honour of your company some evening soon. These chill November nights lie heavily upon the spirit. Good cheer is medicinal. We must eat and drink. December will be with us in a week or two. *In a drear-nighted December, too happy, happy tree, thy branches ne'er remember their green felicity*. Isn't that the way it goes? And then, *Ah! would that 'twere so with many a gentle girl and boy!* . . . which reminds me. Who is the buxom young creature next door? Dark wavy hair and round crimson cheeks. Oh, quite a sparkling young creature with eyes like sloes and all the rest of it, don't you know. I see her swinging in the garden next door. Scarlet sash flying in the wind. *Rarely, rarely com'st thou, spirit of delight* And she rejoices my antique bones with her pretty volatile ways. In fact she is quite authentically a stunner.'

'I expect you mean Olive Doyle. Her mother is Lady Marjorie Doyle.'

'Is she, by gad, and all? Never mind, it's not her fault. Do you know her?'

I told him I knew Olive rather well.

'Bring her to tea. I won't steal your sweetheart. No, no, she shall sit on a cushion and sew a fine seam. Beauty and the Beast. But you shall be the fairy prince. I'll remain in my bestiarium. But tell her to put on her scarlet sash when she comes, and I'll play the guitar for her.'

I was just promising to do my best to bring Olive to see Mr Mellor and had worked my way nervously out of his den on to the landing lit by a rubied sanctuary lamp when the sound of a bell shrilled upward through the dim house.

'The front door,' Mr Mellor shouted. 'A tucket without! A challenge to the ogre! Wait. Let Mrs Jutsom grapple with the outer world.'

A presentiment weighed heavily upon me that this bell was concerned with myself. And I was justified, for when the front door was opened I heard my name on Janet's severe lips prefixed with a ceremonious 'Master' which only served to call special attention to my humiliating nonage, as no doubt Janet intended it should.

I called down to her over the balusters that I was just coming.

'And so you'd better be,' she snapped back. 'Your aunts are in a terrible state about you.'

I resented this on behalf of Aunt Adelaide and Aunt Emily, for I thought that Janet's description would convey a false impression of them to Mr Mellor who already was so much prejudiced against aunts. I had never seen either of them in a 'state,' which was the kind of emotional condition indulged in by Hetty our cook when one of the tradesmen forgot to send some vital condiment.

However, it would have done more harm than good to argue with Janet over the balusters the accuracy of her description. And I made my grateful farewells to Mr Mellor, promising to bring Olive Doyle to tea with him if her mother would let her come.

My aunt Adelaide was in her sitting room when I got back, and it struck me as rather absurd that such a fuss could be made about my spending a couple of hours beyond my leave in a room of exactly the same size and shape separated from this room by only another room of the same size and shape. It had the same kind of absurdity as many of Euclid's demonstrations.

'But I only allowed you to visit Mr Mellor on the understanding that you would be home by six o'clock,' Aunt Adelaide was saying.

I assured her this was a genuine case of not knowing the time.

'There was only an hourglass in the dining room, and in Mr Mellor's den.' I might have added, 'only separated from this room we are in by nothing but Lady Marjorie Doyle's bedroom,' but refrained. 'There was only a clock with one hand.'

'But you could have asked what the time was,' my aunt reminded me austerely.

'Well, he was telling me stories about Rossetti and William Morris and Burne-Jones, and I couldn't very well interrupt him to ask the time.'

'About Rossetti?' she repeated.

I pressed my advantage home.

'Yes, he knew him awfully well and thinks he was awfully great. He was awfully interested when I told him you had made me read Rossetti. We said quite a lot of his poetry together. He was really awfully – '

'Not "awfully" in front of everything,' Aunt Adelaide begged with a disapproving shake of the head.

I always thought my aunt's dislike of 'awfully' pedantic and could never bring myself to say 'very' without sounding to myself affected; but I felt the occasion still demanded tact, and I surrendered to her prejudice by calling Mr Mellor 'Very nice' instead of 'awfully decent'. It was, to my ears, a mincing conclusion, and I was glad that Mr Mellor himself was not present to jeer at such a desiccation of his exuberant personality.

Just then Janet came in to say that supper was ready, and we went downstairs.

Supper at my aunts' house was probably the simplest evening meal of any taken in our street, though in none of the houses was there as a rule anything as elaborate as late dinner except at Number 19, where General Brackenbury dined alone solemnly every evening chiefly, it was said, on curries. Late dinner at that date was still essentially a modish affair, and it was considered a symptom of the time's increasing rapidity that people in what we called society were taking to dining as late as eight o'clock and even half-past. To be sure, we occasionally gave dinner parties, when the ladies wore long white kid gloves and were taken in on gentlemen's arms. As a rule, however, in our street we preferred to call any meal eaten among ourselves later than seven o'clock supper. The Locketts still dined at half-past five, for it was one of Mr Lockett's peculiarities to preserve in the amber of a rich conservatism the social habits to which he had been accustomed in his boyhood. Simple though supper was in my aunts' house, it always seemed to me that, compared with such suppers as I had caught glimpses of in the houses of neighbours, it was a magnificently distinguished meal. The old Worcester bowl which held the salad, the silver, the light foreign dishes, the absence of a tablecloth, and most of all the Japanese arrangement of the flowers gave our suppers a charm with which other people's dinner parties could not compete. In most of the houses in our street there was a rigid conviction that rice pudding on weekdays and on Sundays a heavy amalgam called trifle were the foundations of English sweetness, and alternating cold roast beef and cold boiled beef the source of English strength. No doubt omelettes were to be eaten in other houses besides my aunts', but they were such excessively Britannic omelettes as hardly to be distinguishable, except by their slightly more solid weight, from the Yorkshire pudding to which we all sat down every Sunday after church. Not even my aunts ventured to abolish Yorkshire pudding completely, for even their foreign habits were awed by roast beef and Yorkshire pudding.

But why do I enlarge upon this subject? Time has dealt ruthlessly with our timid excursions into the unusual at the end of the nineteenth century. Good Queen Victoria was soon to die, and within ten years the belated modernity of King Edward's reign would have so completely readjusted the standards of taste (though the credit or discredit of that will probably always be given to the war) that a household like my aunts' will probably only irritate the contemporary reader. Cranford is perfumed with bundles of dry lavender; but our street in West Kensington may just be seeming a little musty. I look back to the bundles of peacocks' feathers in vases on the mantelpiece of the drawing room at Number 9. I look back to the Morris wall papers and curtains, to the Arundel prints and the photogravures of early Millais and early Holman Hunt, to my Aunt Adelaide's loose full-sleeved sage-green dress embroidered with dull yellow marguerites, to my Aunt Emily's smocked gown of faded rose; and I remember that they would have been aesthetic young women of the early 'eighties, love-sick maidens of *Patience*, the butt of Gilbert's sterling vulgarity. I ask myself if the highbrows who have replaced the aesthetes are impressing themselves upon the children of the moment, and if forty years hence some sentimental retrospector will evoke for them and their Bloomsbury superiority as tender a mood of reminiscence as I should like to evoke for my Aunt Adelaide and Aunt Emily.

I think my reporting of Mr Mellor's tales of Rossetti must have impressed my Aunt Adelaide, and that my description of the sea-green knight beside the mere must have pleased her, for when I was in bed she sat beside me for a little while and read aloud *La Belle Dame sans merci*. It was a pleasant custom at Number 9 to use night lights, and never had the picture of Sir Isumbras at the Ford glimmered above my washstand with richer promise of romance as I faded into sleep on that November night.

NUMBER 7

THE number over the door of this house certainly did not symbolise any of the inmates. However, Number 7 was always so very much next door to us that I never thought of it as Number 7 at all, but always as next door; and in walking down our street when I saw the brass cage from which Lady Marjorie's bullfinch surveyed with secure impunity the cats of the neighbourhood I was already home. Lady Marjorie herself always reminded me of her own bullfinch, for she was short and plump, dressed usually in reddish brown, and had a pair of dark and bright bird's eyes. I believe she was the daughter of an Irish earl, and I seem to remember that she married a singer. But who the Irish earl was and what was the status of the singer have passed from my recollection, though I have a vague impression of hearing once that Mr Doyle and she had separated before he died. Certainly I do not recall that Olive ever mentioned her father to me.

Olive was my greatest friend. Her reputation was that of being an incurable tomboy. Janet alluded to her several times in my hearing as a young limb, and she even expressed amazement once that her ladyship could be the mother of such a disorderly girl. This was when Olive and I drank a full mould of lemon sponge which had been put by Hetty to set on the sill of our kitchen window in preparation for a small dinner party my aunts were giving, a rare occasion in our household and one of those that kept Hetty in a 'state' for a couple of days beforehand. Either for the pleasure of contradicting Janet or with a chivalry I must have learnt from Sir Isumbras I insisted on taking the blame; but actually it was Olive who conceived the crime and it was Olive who drank at least four fifths of the foamy liquid. It was she who, sitting astraddle the wall between our gardens, observed Hetty whipping away at the sponge for half an hour of a fine summer's morning, and it was her deep authoritative voice which bade me seize the mould and bring it to her on the wall that we might retire to a decayed summer-house in a corner of the Doyle garden and imbibe it in luxurious seclusion. Probably like Don José I protested weakly for a moment or two, and probably like Carmen she overcame my scruples or fears. Anyway, we drank the unset lemon sponge, and as I cautiously replaced the empty mould upon the kitchen window sill, hoping the disappearance of the contents would remain a mystery, Hetty sprang out at me like a wildcat with young.

'You dare start fiddling with my lemon sponge,' she challenged shrilly.

I determined on a bold line of defence.

'There's nothing to fiddle with,' I said. 'It's empty.'

'Empty your grandmother,' Hetty snapped. Then she looked. 'The Lord be good to me,' she gasped, 'if he hasn't gone and gobbled the blessed lot! And your aunt with a dinner party to-night!'

My line of defence had broken down at once.

'I'm sorry, Hetty, I only tasted it,' I confessed. 'And it tasted so good I went on.'

'But I never heard of such gormandising,' Hetty exclaimed. 'A whole lemon sponge gone in the twinkling of a bedpost. Why, a laughing hyena would think twice before it gormandised a whole lemon sponge. You must have an inside like a boiler. Don't you feel sick?'

'But it was so jolly good,' I declared fervidly. 'It was so lovely and light.'

Hetty could not resist such a tribute to her skill. She bridled pleasantly.

'Well, it was light, I daresay. I know I whipped it till my arms ached.'

'If you'd tasted it yourself you'd have drunk it all,' I hazarded.

She was not proof against this flattery. No doubt Don José had a way with him when Carmen was not there.

'Well, if you'll promise me never to do such a thing again, I'll not tell your aunts this once. I'll have to tell them it just wouldn't set.'

It was then that Janet appeared on the scene to proclaim that she had seen me carrying the mould across to Olive astraddle our garden wall, and it was then that she condemned her as a disorderly girl.

That decayed summerhouse in a corner of the Doyles' garden, the intimacy of which I was privileged to share with Olive, still enchants my memory. I can still smell the acrid scent of the privet bushes around it and the dusty sickliness of the aucubas. I can still see the filmy wings of the small black and yellow flies that hovered in the sunlight beyond its shadowy drouthy interior, and the Virginia creeper in a tangle over the garden wall, and the backs of the houses along our street, and the line of poplars planted in groups of three at the end of every garden, their leaves trembling and whispering in the light summer breeze. There was a lattice window on either side of the summerhouse; but the cobwebs within and the lanky London shrubs without made them viewless. Sparrows had built in the roof of the mouldering thatch, and in a locker that ran along the back lingered an old-fashioned croquet set. We sometimes played croquet on the miniature lawn, and these games were liable to end in a fight if one of us should maintain that the other had not rung the bell in going through the crossed hoops in the middle. Finally, after an unusually fierce battle, when Olive had laid open my forehead with a mallet and I had punctured her leg with the end of a hoop, croquet was forbidden.

There were fights between us over other matters besides croquet; but they were not serious, though on one occasion Olive managed to knock me off the horizontal bar of her outdoor gymnasium with such suddenness that I fell on my head and was unconscious for a quarter of an hour. When I came to, I was lying on my back and looking up into the anxious faces of the Doyle maids while tears from Olive's dark eyes were dropping down upon my cheeks like thunderdrops. Later on Olive denied that she had wept over my unconscious form, and there was no surer way of enraging her than to remind her that she had. Yet I would not suggest that there was even the hint of a tender emotion in either of us for the other. I remember resenting strongly being told by a new parlourmaid of Lady Marjorie's that my sweetheart was waiting for me out in the garden, and I remember when I told Olive what the new parlourmaid had said she was so indignant that she dropped a paper bomb of ink upon the poor girl from an upper landing, ruining her cap and apron. The secret of making these paper bombs of ink had been imparted to Olive by some boy cousins in whose house she had stayed, and there was a period during which we seemed to spend all our time making and loading them and then trying to drop them down on passers-by from the attic windows of Number 7. We had had a long series of successful assaults when one day an elderly gentleman at whose top hat we were aiming happened to look up suddenly and detect us watching from our window the downward course of the nasty little bomb which was to burst with a great blob of ink on the pavement at his feet.

'He's coming up the steps, Olive,' I exclaimed in horror.

'The summerhouse! The summerhouse!' she cried.

We fled downstairs as an angry bell shrilled through the house and a double rat-tat thundered upon the front door.

'Don't open the door,' we gasped to Alice, the new parlour-maid.

'It's a tramp trying to sell ferns,' Olive added with brilliant inventiveness.

The bell shrilled again. The knocker beat an urgent tattoo.

'A tramp would never be so daring as that,' Alice objected.

'Well, you're jolly well not to open the door,' Olive commanded, her crimson cheeks glowing with excitement, her dark eyes flashing. 'Hold her, hold her, you idiot,' she ordered me. 'Hold her, and I'll tie her to the banister with my sash.'

'You'll do no such thing, Miss Olive, or I'll tell her ladyship when she comes in.'

Once more the bell shrilled; once more the knocker resounded. Alice, spurred by the impulse to perform her duty which animates the breast of every good parlourmaid, broke away from us and opened the front door. My impression is that the hall of Number 7 was immediately filled with the bulk of an infuriated elderly gentleman who was demanding the name of the owner of the house; but neither Olive nor I waited to hear more. We fled to the summerhouse and left him to Alice.

'You'll catch it,' she told us presently. 'He's going to complain at the police station.'

So that afternoon when Lady Marjorie sat primly in her drawing room waiting for callers, because it was her day at home (do people still have At Home days?), the first visitor was a large policeman bringing the tale of our misdeed that morning. And that was the end of paper bombs of ink.

54

Mention of Olive's brilliant invention of that tramp with ferns to sell reminds me how much the itinerant vendors and craftsmen added to the colour of life in our street. No doubt men still sell ferns and flowers along the street which was once ours; but do the lavender girls go crying their bunches along it at summer's end, crying them with that old tune as fragrant as lavender itself? And do fine flaunting gypsy women with plumed hats and richly coloured shawls squat on the front door steps, deftly plaiting the cane seats of broken chairs? And does some sharp-featured gypsy man beside a caravan call, 'Any chairs to mend?' Does the knife grinder still wheel before him his fascinating barrow with treadle and grindstone and cry hoarsely, 'Any knives or scissors to grind?'

I heard the other day a disreputable old man somewhere in North London shouting, 'Old iron! Any old iron?' but it is long since I heard equally disreputable old men bent double beneath bulging disreputable sacks wheezing out, 'Any rags, bottles, or bones?' And it is long since I saw the tousled hair of the tinker's children, an eager swarm seeking custom all the way down our street while their father stood in the middle of the road and shouted, 'Any pots, pans, or kettles to mend?' and their mother wheeled the barrow with the furnace and the swinging tools.

Does the sweep still go whooping along that street which was once ours? And on May mornings do a company of sweeps dance round one of their craft in a wicker framework covered with boughs? Could you see a Jack-in-the-Green anywhere in London now? Have not he and the May Queen followed the fairies? Do girls carrying their baskets on a yoke and with aprons stained with juice cry, 'Fine strawberries!' or 'Cherry ripe!' Does even the milkman still yodel, 'Milk-ho!' as he passes along our street, his barrow clanking with cans? Does the cats-meat man call 'Meat! Meat! Catsmeat!' with half a dozen cats at his heels, sniffing the air of his fragrant wake? Does the muffin man's clear bell go ringing by in the November dusk and, when at the corner he pauses for a moment and carefully turns his head, on which is balanced his load wrapped in green baize, to see if some hesitating purchasers do after all want muffins and crumpets for tea that afternoon, does the lamp-lighter come busily round the corner to illuminate with his glimmering wand the street lamps one by one?

I fancy that most of those colourful people have passed along our street for the last time. They come back to my memory like the figures of a bygone harlequinade. They are as obsolete as old valentines.

Valentines? It is hardly imaginable now that February 14th had once such portentous significance as a date, and that for a week before it came round Miss Voss's shop in the Terrace was full of frilled cards with true lover's knots and pierced hearts and disconsolate Cupids. Already at this date, the habit of sending valentines was confined to children and the servants' hall, and presently the vulgarity of them was to destroy the last vestige of romance and lead through a rapid desuetude to the complete abandonment of the celebration. Still, I am glad to be able to remember the end of it, and the way it used to stand out flushed with the dawn of spring.

I have denied any tender emotion for Olive; but in spite of our severely unsentimental relationship it was my habit to send her a valentine, and I suspect that I received one or two from her, though of course neither of us admitted the dispatch.

The day after my meeting with Mr Mellor I called next door upon Olive to present his invitation. Tomboy though she was, my great friend was not without the normal feelings of girlhood, and she was evidently flattered by Mr Mellor's interest in her.

'It was only because he can see you swinging,' I pointed out.

'But he liked my sash.'

'He only said it was flying in the wind.'

'But he wouldn't have said anything about it at all if he hadn't liked it,' Olive insisted.

I congratulated myself on having kept quiet about the admiration of Mr Mellor for her crimson cheeks and dark eyes and sparkling personality. If a little notice paid to a sash was going to turn her head like this, what would be the effect of the remarks he had made about her looks?

Lady Marjorie said she must consult my Aunt Adelaide before she gave her permission for Olive to go to tea with Mr Mellor; but when my aunt seemed inclined to demur at the notion Lady Marjorie argued in favour of letting us both go.

'After all, we cannot expect an elderly bachelor to be bothered with a lot of women,' she declared. And there was a kind of prim assurance in Lady Marjorie's quiet rather deep voice when she made an observation like this which gave it an axiomatic quality and deterred even Aunt Adelaide from further argument or demur.

So Olive and I had to leave to accept Mr Mellor's next invitation, which I took care to secure by haunting the bookshop at which we had first made friends, and soon Number 5 shared with that decayed summerhouse the monopoly of according to Olive and myself a perpetual refuge from the commonplace of existence in our street.

NUMBER 11

Next door on the other side of our house was never so much next door as Olive's house, though in one way Number 11 was our real partner, because the front doors of Number 9 and Number 11 adjoined, which meant that when we were sitting on the balcony above our porch we were only separated from our neighbours by a trellis. Moreover, it was some time before we got to know Mr and Mrs Bond, and when they ceased to be the new people next door they became Number 11, because by then the Doyles' house was definitely and unalterably next door itself.

Our street took a great interest in the Bonds some time before the Bonds met any of the residents, for they were a young newly married couple, and even in these days we may hope that young newly married couples are still capable of arousing a certain amount of curiosity among their neighbours. The Bonds were extremely conscious of their state, and they were so shy at first that they gave an impression of wishing to be left to themselves. I daresay that when they first moved in they did wish to be left alone. It was Mr Lockett who resolved to destroy this exaggerated privacy. Not that he bore the least ill will to the Bonds. Far from it. He was immensely prejudiced in their favour by the fact that they had bought Number 11. It was impossible for Mr Lockett not to feel that the people in our street who owned their houses were finer Londoners than those who merely rented them on a lease. We were all as citizens of the empire on an equality; but as Londoners he could not but respect those who had bought their houses a little more deeply than those who had not. Not that any of us were genuine freeholders, and it was only a ninety-nine years' lease that was counting with Mr Lockett as absolute ownership. A lease of even seven years, however, roused his contempt. Such timid creatures would not share in the great rise in the value of property round our Neighbourhood which he so confidently expected. Such timid creatures had so little belief in their own judgment that they were able to contemplate leaving our street at the end of a few years and exchanging the serene comfort of it for an unknown and possibly wretched future in another street where the value of property was likely to fall.

'I'm delighted to learn that those two very pleasant-looking young people have bought Number 11,' he used to say. 'It's a sign of the way the neighbourhood is catching on. They evidently know what's what and don't intend to be left high and dry. They mean to spend the rest of their lives in our street. Bravo! I only hope those noisy Spinks next door will allow them to have a little peace. Mrs Clyburn was telling me the other day that Spink starts knocking his pipe out at all hours of the night, and that last week he was actually hanging pictures at three o'clock in the morning. Yes, we must get to know this young couple. I hear they've had the whole house done up and furnished by Maple's.'

The suggestion of exclusive information which Mr Lockett conveyed was hardly justified by the facts. For weeks before the Bonds arrived large boards all over Number 11 had proclaimed DECORATIONS BY MAPLE & Co. Indeed Maple's must have brooded over them from the moment that Edward Bond placed the engagement ring upon the third finger of Ethel Vicker's left hand. And when the decorators were finished large vans inscribed with the name of MAPLE & Co made our street almost impassable for that eccentric green omnibus. For several days we watched a quantity of white curly-legged furniture being carried up the steps of Number 11, and there was such a litter of straw all round our house that my Aunt Adelaide was driven to write a parody of Shelley's poem, which was called *Stanzas Written in Dejection Near Maple's*. I was not old enough at the time to appreciate its wit, but Aunt Emily was delighted with it and told Aunt Adelaide that it was too utterly amusing. After that Aunt Adelaide and Aunt Emily used to call the Bonds our Meapolitan neighbours, and I fear I must add with a hint of slightly priggish superiority, for those who had been the aesthetic young ladies of the early 'eighties did not approve of the way that Tottenham Court Road was debasing the taste of the period ten years later.

Mr Lockett, however, had never entered the Grosvenor Gallery, and if he had he might have cracked the glass of every

59

picture with his contemptuous guffaws. Mr Lockett would have considered Oscar Wilde an affected nincompoop and William Morris an insincere agitator. To him the airy extravagance of Maple's bedroom suites and the floral excesses of Maple's toilet sets represented the claims of youth to follow its own taste. He was himself content with the furniture he had known all his life; but he was no hidebound conservative, he used to protest.

'I don't pretend to be artistic myself,' he would say. 'But I can sympathise with new ideas. A lot of this modern stuff is morbid. But I was visiting at a friend's house the other day, and he had had his place done up by Maple's, and by George, I quite liked it.'

And I must admit that in those days I quite liked it myself. I thought the Bonds' drawing room the loveliest room I had ever seen. The walls were covered with lincrusta of pale salmon pink and cream. The furniture was nearly all of a light satin-wood, except the armchairs, which were so heavily upholstered that the wood of which their legs were made was hardly visible. The curtains of a rose and silvery damask seemed to me the very perfection of beauty and splendour, and to this beautiful splendour was added the interest of the large and brightly coloured insects stuffed with cotton wool which were hooked on to the curtains – spiders a foot across predominating. I liked, too, the tall vases of milky-green fluted glass or voluted and gilded glass in which stood bunches of pampas-grass plumes. The pink and green Axminster carpet caressed the feet, and a glass fire screen, inside which a dozen humming-birds displayed their jewelled wings, lent the final touch; no, not quite the final touch. That was provided by the Cosy Corner which occupied the rectangular space between the window and the fireplace. The Cosy Corner was a divan of delicious resilience, and the cosiness was emphasised by the coldness of the wall above being warmed with curtains of rosy silk. These were crowned by a rectangular shelf glossily enamelled in cream, with a fretted front to keep the plates which stood up on end from falling down upon the heads of those who were luxuriating in the cosiness of it all.

I must admit that the drawing room of my aunts' house looked sadly dingy when I went back to it after basking in the radiant flush diffused through the Bonds' pink glass shades by the incandescent gas which about this time first shone like some starry promise of a better and cheaper world. The plain green wall paper was dull after the salmon-pink lincrusta. The cretonne curtains and covers of Morris's Strawberry Thief design seemed faded. The mats of Abingdon rushes seemed dusty. I remember that I had once heard Mr Lockett observe to his wife when they were coming down our steps after paying a call:

'It's queer how these artistic advanced women revel in gloomy surroundings. And those pictures! Did you ever see anything so hideous in a frame as those three gawky females with necks like cranes? When you asked Miss Culham who it was by and she told us "Burne-Jones," I nearly said "Thanks very much, I should like to." I can't understand this mania for stuffs that look as if all the colour had been washed out of them. It may be artistic, but I'm sure it's not healthy.'

I thought of the Locketts' drawing room with its alabaster ornaments and tinkling candlesticks, its beaded mats and anti-macassars and mirror painted with bullrushes and swans. There the walls were hung with Highland scenes by Landseer, and dear little Miss Lockett herself, hardly distinguishable from one of the drawing-room ornaments, would be quivering industriously over her needlework, the Monarch of the Glen gazing down upon her handiwork and Snuff breathing stertorously in an adjacent chair.

Mr Lockett's desire to make the acquaintance of the newly married couple was gratified without having to fall back on the rural method of calling upon them and leaving cards. Had he taken such a step merely to satisfy his own curiosity the rest of our street would have been definitely shocked. We considered ourselves urban; we would not admit even to being suburban. The suburbs to us were a bleak limbo beyond which stretched the inferno of the slums. It might be that the senior residents called upon their new neighbours in the suburbs. We were not going to. The notion was preposterous. After all, a newcomer even to our street might by Anybody. And Anybody is not a desirable neighbour. If Anybody came to live in our street, it should be at his own risk. He should receive no encouragement from the rest of us.

Mr Lockett's interest in the furniture and decorations of Number 11 became so lively that we began to fear he actually would call upon the newly married couple. And when Doctor Arden was summoned in to attend Mrs Bond for one of those trifling ailments which rend with anxiety the heart of the young husband, Mr Lockett could hardly contain his impatience.

I happened to be standing by our front door when Doctor Arden went up the steps of Number 11, and as he was being admitted I caught a glimpse of the hall and particularly of a blue china umbrella stand round which gulls were flying. Doctor Arden had scarcely disappeared inside Number 11 when Mr Lockett came hurrying along, dressed as usual in his frock coat, but without his hat and wearing an antique pair of blue and yellow carpet slippers. He was dragging behind him on a lead the unwilling Snuff, who was trying to turn himself into a kid of obstinate sleigh by refusing to use his legs.

'Your aunt's not ill, I hope,' he said to me.

'No, she's very well, thank you.'

'Oh, I was just giving poor old Snuff a little run, and I thought I saw Doctor Arden going up your steps.'

I told Mr Lockett that Doctor Arden was paying a visit at Number 11, though I was pretty sure he knew that all the time. Anyway, he dragged Snuff slowly along to the pillar box at the corner, and spent five minutes talking to the crossing sweeper, with his eye in our direction throughout the conversation. Then he saw Mrs Gurney coming out of Number 23 and engaged her in conversation for another five minutes. Then he tried to persuade Snuff to make friends with Bingo, the Clyburns' fox terrier, which nearly ended seriously for Snuff, and finally he managed to arrive outside Number 11 just as Doctor Arden reached the pavement and the front door closed behind him.

'Good-morning, Doctor. Nothing serious, I hope, in there?'

'No, no, nothing at all serious,' Doctor Arden assured him.

'I was just giving my sister's dog a run, and I happened to notice you going in.'

It was perfectly obvious that Mr Lockett was longing to be given some news of the young married couple; but there was something about that pale chiselled countenance and Wellingtonian nose of Doctor Arden which forbade Mr Lockett to display his curiosity too blatantly, old friend though he was of the Doctor.

'By the way, the wife and I were hoping you and Minnie

would come in and have supper with us this evening.'

'Hah, I believe we will,' said the Doctor.

'That's capital,' said Mr Lockett. 'I've got a Dickens letter which will interest you, I think. It was written just after he had gone down to his new house at Gadshill.'

'We shall be with you at . . . ?'

'Half-past seven, if that suits you?' said Mr Lockett.

'Excellently. Hah, young man,' Doctor Arden called up to me. 'How's the broken crown?'

This was an allusion to the cut I received from Olive's mallet, which Doctor Arden had patched up.

'It's almost gone,' I told him.

'Splendid. Jack and Jill went up the hill, eh, Lockett? Did you hear of the Amazonian contest at Number 7? Well, I mustn't stay gossiping here. Good-day to you, young man. Good-day to you, Lockett.'

With this, the Doctor waved his ebony cane with a kind of pastoral benediction and strode off along our street on his daily round, a fine figure of a man with those trousers cut nearly as close to the legs as overalls and that tightly buttoned short riding coat.

I do not know whether Mr Lockett made that letter of Dickens about his new house at Gadshill an excuse to pump Doctor Arden less shamelessly about the new arrivals at Number 11; but I fancy he did, for the next day I heard him say to General Brackenbury that he thought it would be only civil if some of us looked up this young couple.

'Do you mean call on 'em?' the General asked, standing very upright with his arms behind him and tapping the back of his head with the ivory knob of his malacca cane. The tone of disgusted astonishment in which he asked the question was discouraging, so discouraging indeed that Mr Lockett hastily declared he had not meant anything so definite as that.

'Well, what the devil did you mean?' the General pressed. He must have been liverish that morning, and when the General was liverish his courtliness was less marked.

'Oh, I'm just mildly interested in them,' Mr Lockett explained. 'You know my keenness, General, about our street. And when I see a couple of young people buying a ninety-nine years' lease and evidently intending to settle down here for the rest of their lives, well, by George, I don't mind admitting that it gives me an uncommon amount of pleasure.'

'Well, I don't like this confounded east wind we've been getting for the last week,' the General grumbled. 'I'm beginning to wonder whether this neighbourhood is quite so devilish healthy as you pretend.'

'Gravel sub-soil,' Mr Lockett reminded him sharply.

'What the deuce has that got to do with east wind? I'll tell you what it is, Lockett, you're getting faddy.'

'Faddy? There's no man less faddy than I am.'

'All this belief in sub-soils is just bunkum in my opinion,' General Brackenbury declared. 'As long as the air is good I don't believe the sub-soil matters a damn.'

'Then why don't you go and live in a marsh?' demanded Mr Lockett warmly, his grizzled carroty curls beginning to bristle under his curly-brimmed silk hat.

'Why the devil should I go and live in a marsh? Marsh air is mephitic. So, by gad, is this infernal east wind.'

'Well, I must be getting along,' said Mr Lockett. 'I've got a choir practice.'

'Thank God, I *haven't*,' the General barked. And with this the conversation came to an abrupt close.

Perhaps it was just after this meeting I heard Mr Lockett remark to somebody that the General ought to eat less curry and give up those Grand Mogul airs he was inclined to assume nowadays.

But there was a speedy term to Mr Lockett's curiosity about the Bonds, for being invited to dine with the Worshipful Company of Greengrocers he met Mr Bond, Senior, who turned out to be quite an important man in the City. This meeting gave a different aspect to the question of calling on the young Bonds. It now became an imperative social duty, and that duty was performed with gusto.

Mr Lockett was so much delighted by the enthusiasm which the newly married couple displayed for our street that he persuaded his wife to give a dinner party for them; after which Mrs Clyburn gave a dinner party for them; and then Mrs Gurney gave one. Finally, even General Brackenbury, who had met pretty little Mrs Bond at Mrs Gurney's rather to Mr Lockett's annoyance, gave a dinner party for them himself, at which all his favourite Indian dishes were trotted out, until his guests were nearly curried themselves, and Mr Lockett for the first time in the chronicles of our street was compelled to mop his forehead with the crimson silk handkerchief that Mrs Lockett always arranged so neatly for him in his waistcoat on grand occasions.

'If we'd had snapdragon for dessert,' Mr Lockett used to say in describing the inward furnace which the General's curries and chutneys had kindled, 'I should have gone out and rung the fire alarm at the corner. I must say I pitied poor little Mrs Bond on the General's right. Every morsel was an agony after that second curry. And he fed her like a stoker. By George, I nearly asked him why he didn't give us pokers and tongs instead of knives and forks.'

It was indeed some time before Mr Lockett forgave General Brackenbury for that conversation I overheard, when the General had been so discouraging about the young Bonds. But after that spell of east wind the weather turned mild and balmy, and the General became his courtly self again.

Mr Lockett could not resist for long the charm of his old friend's manner, and there was not a hint of disagreement between them until they both leant simultaneously over the perambulator to chuck the Bond baby under the chin and their top hats knocked one another off their heads.

'Steady,' the General commanded in his parade-ground voice.

'Steady yourself,' Mr Lockett replied sharply.

The arrival of the Bond baby stirred our street profoundly. Even if we had not already made friends with the young parents, we must have made friends with them over that baby. At the same time, both Olive and I thought this baby attracted much more attention than its beauty or intelligence or even its behaviour warranted. The fact that it was the only baby in our street was not enough, we felt, to justify such an outburst of adult imbecility. There were babies by the dozen to be seen all round. They were as common in the neighbourhood as fox terriers. To be sure, the Bond baby had a more elaborate perambulator than most of those tiresome vehicles which were for ever driving one from the pavement into the gutter; but after all the most elaborate perambulator could not excite our interest in the way a bicycle could, and how dull were the solid tires compared with those exciting pneumatic tires which had just appeared in the world with all the magic of seven-league boots.

However, in spite of the contempt Olive and I felt for the gush which the grown-ups of our street gurgled out over the Bond baby, the infant itself continued to be as much flattered and fussed over as if it were the future ruler of an empire.

'And he's such a good baby, isn't he, nurse?' some feminine admirer would exclaim rapturously, gazing down at the infant lying asleep in his perambulator as still as a raspberry on a plate.

'Yes, he's a very good baby indeed, ma'am,' the nurse could complacently agree.

I longed to tell the fond female sycophant that only an hour ago this tranquilly sleeping infant had been yelling in the garden at the back until the very sparrows had forsaken the poplar trees in dismay. Yes, that baby was a curse to those of us who had been used to making in our gardens the noise we could not always make indoors. Olive and I would perhaps be playing battledore and shuttlecock, when over the garden wall that divided our garden from Number 11 the face of the Bond nurse would appear like some Aunt Sally in a fair and invite us to make a little less noise in case we woke up poor Baby. She had even the self-assurance to attempt to quell the Spinks on the other side with the same tactics; but half a dozen of them rushed at her like young Zulus, and she did not venture to show her face again over the wall on that side of the garden.

Considering the ridiculous amount of attention their baby received, the Bonds themselves were wonderfully unspoilt. They were really a dear little couple, and the Eleven over their front door symbolized them perfectly for me when I wandered up and down our street, contemplating the characteristic variety of the houses.

A year or two ago I wandered down our street after a long interval of time. The houses looked sadly shrunken and shabby. No doubt they were just as small when I first came to visit my aunts there; but I am sure they were not so shabby then. I was glad that Mr Lockett was no longer alive to see his belief in a rise in the value of property round about our Neighbourhood shattered. Something had gone wrong with the middle age of our street. The great blocks of flats which had been heaped up on Sir George Griffin's garden cast a gloom upon it. From an open window on the upper story of Number 9, the window of my own playroom once upon a time, came the sound of a child playing with laborious tinkles *Le Carnival de Venise*. I had sat thus and practised the same tune; but in those days I could swing round on the piano stool and gaze out across the gardens opposite to the wide western sky. That poor child now playing the second simple variation of that simple old tune could only gaze out at the pretentious concrete honeycomb opposite. Along what was once our sedate roadway cars were hooting, and presently a motor omnibus, presumably the heir of that eccentric old green horse omnibus, came roaring past.

Then a brief silence fell upon the street that was once ours, one of those brief silences when the traffic seems to pause for breath before it begins to belch and hoot and clang more furiously than ever. Even the child's performance of *Le Carnival de Venise* had tinkled out. I listened for the sound of some distant piano organ to float into this quietness as surely forty years ago I should have heard it. But I heard none. It was a Saturday, and the time was ten o'clock. Where was the German band that used always to gather at the corner of our street every Saturday at this hour? Years had passed since the band of plump and blond Teutons had set out their music stands for the last time. How cheerfully they had played in the holiday! What a sense of leisure their music had diffused upon our street! How jovially they had blown away all thoughts of lessons until Monday morning! Every week for years they had played in rain or shine at the same hour on the same day for fifteen minutes, and while they were playing one of the instruments had called politely at every house in turn for their reward. How pleasant it had been to present the penny and perhaps have a chance to touch the euphonium! And with what pomp we had marched up and down our street to those martial strains!

While I was meditating thus in the approved fashion upon all our yesterdays and the way we strutted and fretted our hour and then were heard no more, neither we nor the German band, down the steps of Number 11 came a perambulator wheeled by a nurse in bonnet and cloak and flowing ribbons. I played with the fancy that this was the baby of the Bond baby, and later on having had the curiosity to look up the names of the present residents in that street which was once ours I discovered that it actually was. At any rate, at Number

11 according to the directory lived Arthur Vickers Bond, and Arthur had been the name of the Bond baby, Vickers the maiden name of his mother. Edward and Ethel, the original 11, must have moved on to the paternal house at Highbury when old Mr Bond died; and when the Bond baby grew up and married he must have entered upon his share of that ninety-nine years' lease. How right Mr Lockett had been to feel so much enthusiasm for that newly married couple! His confidence in their loyalty to our street had been justified indeed.

I HAVE already written of the excitement with which I used to arrive in London about Christmas to stay with my Aunt Adelaide; but, wonderful though Christmas was, the pleasure of it was almost eclipsed by the gaiety of January. I do hope that children's parties have not disappeared from that street which was once ours together with the street cries and the crossing sweeper at each corner and the German band and the old green omnibus and that luminous expanse of western sky. I do hope that they still exist like the pillar box and the fire alarm at the corner which used to stare at one another from opposite sides of the street like a fat fusilier and a thin light-infantryman, and which with a laudable military devotion to their duty are still staring at one another today.

As soon as Christmas was over one might expect by any post to see beside one's plate at breakfast a small envelope with that scarlet halfpenny stamp, the withdrawal of which from circulation was one of the first omens of imperial decline. Inside the small envelope would be an invitation card headed probably by a little Kate Greenaway boy bowing low to a little Kate Greenaway girl, and underneath that one might read the names of the hosts inviting the gilded freehand guests whose names would be filled in with sprawling childish letters as thus:

15, Beauclerk Street
West Kensington,
W.
The Misses Enid and Gwendolen Clyburn
and Master Harry Clyburn
request the pleasure of
the MISSES AND MASTER GURNEY'S *company*
on Wednesday, January 7th.
R.S.V.P.   *7 p.m. – 11 p.m.*

I have chosen one of the invitations from the Clyburns because Enid and Gwendolen themselves much resembled the
Kate Greenaway children whose quaint courtesy and old-
fashioned grace were so often illustrated on the invitation cards.

Enid and Gwendolen were twins, and their mother used to
dress them in long high-waisted dresses and frame their cherry-
ripe faces in poke bonnets. Looking back now to the picture
of those twins walking demurely down our street on a blue and
white April morning, I could fancy that their progress was
watched by Captain Brown and dear Miss Matty, and that Miss
Jenkyn herself noted with austere approval their well-behaved
progress; but, to be candid, I must confess that in those days a
little less remote than Cranford, I and the rest of the young
people in our street used to think their mother's choice of
clothes displayed an outrageous lack of consideration for the
feelings of her twin daughters, whom we pitied as martyrs to
parental indiscretion. We thanked heaven that our parents and
guardians showed on the whole a nicer appreciation of our
desire to escape notice by the least eccentricity of costume.
Not that dear Mrs Clyburn herself had a trace of pretentiousness
about her. She was, when I first remember her, still in widow's
weeds, and a kinder, more generous woman never lived. We
realised this and because of her kindness and generosity we
forgave her treatment of Enid and Gwendolen who, incident-
ally, seemed completely unaware that by dressing them like
that their mother was making them appear idiotic.

It was no doubt this innocent unworldliness which led Enid
and Gwendolen, after their brother Harry had passed out into
the *Britannia*, to include him as a host with themselves for
their children's party that year, and what was worse, call a Naval
Cadet *Master Harry Clyburn*. I believe there was quite a scene
at Number 15 when Cadet Clyburn, R.N., heard of it, for one of
his shipmates, Cadet Riggs, R.N., was staying with him at the
time and Cadet Riggs, a plump boy with a rich humour, teased
Cadet Clyburn about it so hardly that Harry began to fear he
would divulge the painful domestic secret to their shipmates in
the *Britannia*. However, I do not think Riggs would have done
that, for he was a good-natured if boisterous youth, and was
definitely an asset to that party, being devoid of self-consciousness and willing to play games like Oranges and Lemons and
Spinning the Platter with as much respect for the rigour of

those games as if they had been cricket or football. Harry Clyburn on the other hand was aloof and melancholy all the evening and seemed anxious to demonstrate to the young guests that the Master Harry Clyburn who appeared on the cards as a host was a figment of his twin sisters' foolish feminine brains.

Cadet Riggs was much to the fore in a game called Postman's Knock, and he had such a success with the girls that he was Postman almost throughout the game, for when he knocked at the door and announced a letter for one of the blushful misses, with some preposterous sum like one and twopence to pay on it, the blushful miss, dazzled by his uniform, skipped out with a simper to be kissed fourteen times, and moreover as often as not would announce a letter for Gordon Riggs by return of post on which there was seldom less than threepence to pay, after which Riggs of course would be Postman again. It was left to Gladys, the eldest of the three Gurney girls, to express the full measure of feminine susceptibility to the magic of a uniform, and a shocked murmur went round the Clyburns' drawing room when she put her head round the door to announce a letter for Cadet Gordon Riggs with half-a-crown to pay. Gladys always had a reputation for boldness, but this was beyond everything, and we were not surprised when such a gross excess of dues brought the game of Postman's Knock to a swift end to be succeeded by Hunt the Slipper. However, Riggs's triumphs that evening did not finish with Postman's Knock. At Hissing and Clapping he was always chosen by the prettiest girls, and when forfeits were cried it was usually he who was kissed as the one loved best, for Gladys Gurney's boldness seemed to have affected every other girl at the party.

And did it fall to one of us boys to pay that forfeit which commands bowing to the prettiest, kneeling to the wittiest, and kissing the one loved best we invariably showed our respect for the brains of the royal navy by kneeling to Riggs. At Oranges and Lemons we thirsted to find ourselves in the line behind Riggs; and the tug of war at the end was a fiasco, because Riggs had a tail of children behind him like the Pied Piper of Hamelin, whereas his opponent had hardly half a dozen, and them only because they had been bluffed away from the other side by being asked to choose between peaches and strawberries or plums and cherries instead of oranges and lemons. At Nuts in May we longed for the moment when we would be pulled over

71

to the side which Riggs captained, and dreaded the pain of being torn from him by an incorruptible and sturdier adversary. Nelson was not a greater hero to England after Trafalgar than Riggs was to us that January night.

I fear that with so many other things over which I have been sentimentalising our games have vanished from juvenile parties and that their place has been taken by dancing. We never wanted to interrupt our games by dancing. The girls may have wanted to dance; but the boys always voted steadily unanimously against it. Dancing in truth involved us males in too much ceremony. We by no means relished having to walk across a room, bow formally to some fluffy-headed girl, and request from her the pleasure of the next dance. Besides, there was not too much space in the average West Kensington house for the square dances of that period.

Not that we were without opportunities to test the teaching of the dancing class in the school of hard experience, for there were usually two or three juvenile balls during the Christmas holidays. Such grand affairs, however, were given in the local church hall where it was easier to escape the criticism of one's friends. The younger children were not invited on these occasions, at which we wore white gloves and buttonholes, carried programmes, and often did not career round the hall in the final gallop until well after midnight.

One benefit which the Bond baby did confer upon us was an extra party, for six months after he was born we received an invitation from Master Arthur Vickers Bond on some night in January to a party at Number 11. Master Bond himself had been in bed long before we arrived, and left his parents to act as deputy hosts for him. The suppers at these children's parties always offered a delicious opportunity to be greedy, but none offered such a chance as those at the Bond baby's yearly parties. Strawberry, vanilla, and lemon ices were to be found in most houses. At Number 11 pineapple, raspberry, and pistachio were added to the repertory of flavours, and though the average child's stomach has the capacity of a Nansen for facing extreme cold, even that capacity was severely tested at the Bonds'. When I say that there were several boys who were boasting at that first party of having eaten over twenty ices in the course of the evening, the profusion of the Bond baby's hospitality will be appreciated.

Besides the ices and the repertory of jellies, shapes, and trifles which was no less remarkable, the Bond baby provided a conjurer and a palmist at one party, a Punch and Judy show and a thought reader at another, and a mesmerist at a third. How the maids in our street must have cursed the advent of that mesmerist, for there was not one of us that came away from that party who was not firmly convinced that he possessed hypnotic powers himself, and who did not try to demonstrate those powers in the kitchen.

THE maid-of-all-work at Number 13 was probably the one who suffered most, for the eldest of the Spink boys persuaded Polly to submit to his hypnotic influence and take a large gulp from a bottle of ink. The girl threatened to pack her boxes and leave the house within an hour of the outrage, and incredible though it might seem, her departure was likely to make that barrack of a house just a little more uncomfortable than it was already. This roused the apprehensive wrath of Mr Spink. Almeric was summoned before him to pay the just penalty by being thrashed, and pleaded in defense of his deed that he had clearly told the girl that it was ink when he exercised his hypnotic power by commanding her to drink it.

'But I never thought it really was ink,' the weeping Polly bemoaned. 'I never thought as any young gentleman would play such a dirty trick on a poor girl.'

'But I'd mesmerised you,' protested Almeric. 'You wouldn't have known it was ink if you hadn't gone out of your trance too soon.'

'It's my turn to do a little mesmerism now,' Mr Spink proclaimed wrathfully. 'And I'll begin by mesmerising you, my lad, in a way you won't enjoy. Bend over that desk.'

Our authority for the details of this grim scene was Almeric's younger brother Aylmer, who was listening outside his father's study door, which was ajar.

'But you haven't mesmerised me,' objected Almeric, whose mind was earnestly scientific and who deplored his father's disinclination to take mesmerism seriously. 'You haven't made passes over my face.'

'No, but I'll make more passes than you'll like over the other end of you,' Mr Spink vowed. 'Bend down, and I'll soon teach you not to waste my best ink like that.'

Even the severe thrashing which Almeric received did not cure his empirical zeal, and he actually persuaded Polly to submit herself once again to his influence, inviting several of us to view the experiment.

'But if you make me swallow more ink, Master Ricky, I'll tell your father on you,' she warned him.

'All right, all right,' Almeric agreed impatiently. 'Stare into my eyes. Don't squint. Stare right into my eyes without squinting like a dying duck in a thunderstorm. That's the way. Now! Have you surrendered your will to mine?'

'I haven't got no will,' Polly answered sullenly. 'What's a poor girl like me want with a will?'

'Not that kind of will,' Almeric scoffed. 'Surrendering your will means that you'll do anything I tell you.'

'But I won't,' said Polly firmly. 'No fear, I won't.'

'But you must,' Almeric insisted. 'Or else I can't mesmerise you.'

'It's you as wants to mesmerise me, isn't it?' Polly asked. 'I never asked to be mesmerised or nothing.'

'All right. Just look into my eyes. Don't start giggling, you stupid.'

'Well, it's enough to make anybody giggle when you go stroking my face like that. It don't half tickle.'

But in the end Almeric's ruthless devotion to science prevailed. Polly ceased to giggle and did at last appear to the audience like a creature in a trance. Indeed, there was something in the farouche Almeric's appearance, with his mop of jet-black curly hair, which recalled the methods of an African medicine man.

'Now, Polly,' he proclaimed in a solemn voice, 'you have surrendered your will to me, and you will feel nothing when I stick this pin into you.'

Polly's reply was a wild shriek, and that not an anticipatory one, for Almeric had plunged the pin into her leg even as he spoke, and by the sound of it the anaesthetic powers of mesmerism had been exaggerated.

Fortunately for Almeric his father was not in the house that afternoon, and we were able to soothe Polly down before he came home from the editorial office. Rather I should say that Annie Spink offered to be mesmerised by her younger brother and to let him run a pin into her leg. This he did with the single-minded enthusiasm of a vivisectionist or witch finder. It was a big pin, and the devoted Annie never winced in order to prove to Polly that her brother sincerely believed in the efficacy of his mesmeric passes.

Annie was of the stuff of which heroines are made. By inclination she must have been as wild and feckless as the rest of her family; but by sheer goodness of nature she had kept the whole of that sprawling family from utter disintegration, for I never saw her but that she was occupied in helping one or other of them. I remember her best when she would have been about sixteen or seventeen, a long gawk of a girl dressed in a stained and faded tartan frock, her curly black hair piled up on the top of her head, her stockings wrinkled round her ankles, a couple of fingers usually wound up with grubby rags, and half the buttons off her boots. She helped Polly in the kitchen. She mended her brothers' clothes. She waited on her foolish mother who spent the whole time chattering about the house in bright silks and who had brought nine children into the world with less sense of responsibility for their welfare than a little girl would have felt for nine dolls. Annie fended off duns. If her father ever gave her any money which was not instantly required to propitiate tradesmen, she would walk nearly as far as Walham Green in order to do her marketing cheaply and walk all the way home again loaded with parcels. When her brothers' school fees were unpaid she would try to teach them herself, and when they were at school she would sit up till all hours to do jobs she had neglected in order to help them with their homework. In addition to her other tasks she acted as her father's amanuensis and endeavoured to extract from the disorder of his study without worrying him the material for his daily outpourings. Luckily for her Mr Spink spent a great deal of his time in the office of the rather disreputable paper of which he was editor; but less luckily, he also spent a good deal of time in the taverns of Fleet Street, from which he would sometimes be driven home in a hansom and wake the whole household to find the necessary silver to pay the cabman. Yet in spite of it all Annie was the most continuously cheerful person in our street, and to the rest of us young people in our conventional homes an invitation to tea at Number 13 was an escape from ordinary life into the glorious freedom of a gypsy camp.

We usually had tea in the kitchen, because Annie would not have had time to clear the table in the morning room next to it after the mid-day meal; and if, as it usually was, the kitchen table was laden with the unwashed dishes and plates of yesterday, tea was laid on the dresser. In summer we often picnicked out in the garden in a tent which Almeric and Aylmer had built from curtains, the absence of which from the windows of the house made the outside of Number 13 so characteristic of its ravaged interior.

The room which in nearly every other house along our street was the dining room, and the windows of which being immediately beside the front door revealed more than any others, was completely empty except for a dressmaker's bust, a rusty knife on the mantelpiece, a grandfather's clock which always gave the time as five-and-twenty minutes to three, and a large oil painting, much cracked and torn, of a Greek temple by moonlight, though much of the charm of the landscape was spoilt by a cup of cocoa's having once been upset over the moon, which gave it the look of a large paregoric lozenge. The drawing room, in which the restless Mrs Spink sat more frequently than anywhere else in the house, was somewhat oriental, for the walls were hung with draperies sewn with tinsel arabesques and there were two squat octagonal tables, the metal tops of which were inlaid with Arabic writing, the kind of tables you see in a pseudo-oriental café. There was also in a corner of the room a large palm, many of the fronds of which were dead, and two or three extremely decrepit divans on which Mrs Spink used to recline with the languor of an odalisque and smoke innumerable Turkish cigarettes, which her neighbours thought a pity; for though by this date it was no longer considered actually immoral for women to smoke, such a habit was still one to be deplored. It was in this room that Mrs Spink received such callers as she had; but they were not many.

On the first floor was Mr Spink's study, and to this day I am inclined to regard that room as representative of authorship at home. Untidy is an epithet which miserably fails to express the condition of that room. Owing to Mr Spink's conviction that if anybody touched one of his papers the work of a lifetime would go for nothing, nobody did touch any of his papers, which were strewn inches deep all over the floor like a drift of dead leaves in a wood. Then, owing to another conviction of his that if anybody touched a book of reference he would never again find what he wanted, the books he took down from his shelves to consult had to remain upon his desk, where they stood about like cairns, some of which presumably collapsed from time to time, for there were many books embedded among the papers on the floor. The difficulty of finding a memorandum or engagement book amid such confusion would have been acute; but Mr Spink had avoided the trouble of such a hopeless search by using the walls of his room as a record of his projects, his fancies, his friends' addresses, his engagement, and his accounts. He wrote with a quill pen, and the discarded quills flung down on the floor crackled beneath the feet like twigs. There was this to be said on behalf of Mr Spink's study: it did conform to the popular conception of an author's sanctum, and those of us young people who were privileged to visit Mr Spink's study felt that we had had a glimpse of a mystical world never beheld by the average person.

Above the first-floor landing there were no carpets at Number 13, and as with all these children in the house there would always be somebody going upstairs or downstairs I cannot remember ever being inside the portals of Number 13 without hearing the sound of thunder in the upper regions of the house, where the bare boards would be responding to the boots of a Spink clattering over them.

As I have described it Number 13 may sound to the fastidious reader a little uncomfortable. I suppose by the ordinary standards of urban existence it was uncomfortable; but we young people had a great affection for it. I never knew a house that was so completely exempt from the thraldom of adult fads. So long as Mrs Spink had cigarettes to smoke and somebody to sit and hear, though not necessarily listen to, her chatter, she did not care what we did. Mr Spink himself was rarely indoors during the afternoon and evening, and though he sometimes chastised his sons when he was interrupted by a domestic scene which they had provoked, as when Almeric tried to mesmerise Polly, he did not otherwise bother his head what happened.

So Number 13 was ours. Most houses demand a measure of self-sacrifice from their inmates and visitors. WELCOME may be printed on the mat inside the front door; but the presence of that suggests that boots should pause and free themselves of mud. The WELCOME on the mat at Number 13 came sincerely from the hearts of the inmates. It did not expect those to whom it was offered to wipe their boots in gratitude. When the mat disappeared from the hall of Number 13 nobody bothered. It was carried upstairs to his bed by one of the younger Spinks who had suffered from a lack of blankets in cold weather, and there it remained, for it was obviously more useful as a coverlet than as a doormat. Its departure from the hall was really a convenience, for it saved the trouble of even a pretense of wiping one's boots upon it. I have alluded to the curtains which Almeric and Aylmer took down to build a tent in the garden. The average house would have insisted that other curtains should veil its windows. Not so Number 13. It recognised that curtains could be put to better use than that of giving people the trouble of drawing them across windows. And if assegais or rifles were required for some game of war, why should balusters which could be removed to serve as such stay where they were less serviceably employed? The rail did not require the support of so many balusters; but the beleaguered garrison did require arms. Thus it was in everything. Number 13 was compelled to serve those who dwelt within it, and the sense of freedom, once the front door closed behind one, was intoxicating. The house was ours as the corrie belongs to the deer, as the cliff to the seabird, as Eden once upon a time to Adam and Eve. And though the Spinks could not afford to give parties in the Christmas holidays with jellies and ices and conjurers, every visit we paid them was a glorious party, even if there was sometimes nothing to eat for tea except bread and dripping. More interesting than food would be the aquarium into which the bath had been turned, or the water chute in imitation of Captain Boyton's at Earl's Court, created by arranging for the cistern at the top of the house to overflow and pour down the top flight of stairs, down which we tobogganed on planks to which had been screwed castors taken from the first chairs that presented themselves. And if there had been nothing but stale bread and dripping last time, next time there might easily be a grand making of toffee poured into the first plates that came to hand, to which it usually stuck so fast when set that the plate had to be broken from it with a hammer, as little regret being wasted over the plate as over the shell of a dead crab.

The grown-ups in our street used to say that the Spinks were a terrible example of improvidence, and there was at one time a move to keep the young people from frequenting Number 13 so much; but it never succeeded, for a house like that open to us at any hour was too difficult to put out of bounds, and perhaps the notion that we were out of the way of mischief in our own houses was not distasteful. Moreover, as the Spinks viewed with disgust the prospect of coming to tea with us we never felt that we lacked hospitality in not being allowed to invite them. To be sure, they were invited to the parties in the Christmas holidays, and to these they came; and from these I know they always went away with lots of cake and chocolates, by the gift of which the grown-ups atoned for not allowing us to invite them to tea.

Annie herself never came to these parties, for she never had a party frock, and I suppose I must have told my Aunt Adelaide about this, because one Christmas Eve she sent me round to Number 13 with a cardboard box addressed to Miss Annie Spink, inside which was a lovely yellow silk dress. Although Annie had always declared she did not enjoy parties I think she enjoyed herself more than any of us when she did come. And all the grown-ups agreed that they had never realised how pretty poor Annie Spink was, for none of them had ever seen her in anything except that old frock of soiled and faded tartan.

Annie was too shy to come and thank my aunt for her present, and how well I remember the letter she wrote her, with four blots and a teacup ring on it.

'Didn't you tell us that Annie Spinks always helps her father with his literary work?' my aunt asked me.

And when I assured her that she often sat up very late copying out what he had written, my aunt murmured, 'Poor man!'

And then presently she sighed and murmured, 'Poor child! Poor children!'

Perhaps my Aunt Adelaide had some prevision of trouble in store for the Spinks, because in truth soon after she sent Annie that yellow silk dress trouble came upon them fast enough.

One afternoon I went round to call at Number 13 and found the house strangely quiet.

'Come downstairs to the kitchen,' Christabel told me. She was one of Annie's younger sisters, aged about ten. 'And don't make a noise,' she added in a whisper, 'because Father's upstairs writing a book.'

When I got downstairs to the kitchen I found the children sitting in a circle round the range, looking as gloomy as crows.

'Father's paper has stopped,' I was told. 'And he's writing a book to try and get some money. So we can't make a row.'

'He can't think if we make a row,' Aylmer explained.

I asked where Annie was and was told that she was sitting with her mother, because Mother would keep going up to Father's study and talking to him, which made him waxy.

Presently there was a ring.

'Area door,' said Almeric. 'Go and squint through the morning-room window, Aylmer, and if it's a tradesman don't open the door.'

I asked where Polly was.

'She went this morning. We couldn't pay her wages,' Almeric explained. 'Father gave her that dressmaker's thing in the dining room. She blubbed a good deal. She didn't want to go a bit.'

The bell sounded again.

'It's the butcher,' Aylmer came back to announce.

'That's the third time he's been today,' said Almeric.

'What's your father's book about?' I asked, to change the subject.

'Oh, love, I expect, or some rot like that,' Almeric said wearily.

I fear the public must have felt much the same way about Mr Spink's book as his eldest son, for I never heard that it had been a success. Indeed I never heard that it was even published. Probably Mr Spink managed to scrape together something every week by writing odd articles; but of course at that time I knew nothing about journalism, and I doubt if anybody else in our street knew much more than I did. We used to see a couple of the smaller Spinks like Christabel or Ferdinand emerge continually from Number 13 to spy out the land at the corner of our street and look if there were any loiterers who might be duns. Then if they returned and reported all clear, Mr Spink used to run down the steps of Number 13 and go hurrying along either to the left for West Kensington Station or to the right for the omnibuses going along the Hammersmith Road. He was still wearing his full-skirted frock coat and dark sombrero hat and black satin Ascot tie; but we no longer saw the sardonyx pin with the head of Medusa, which I had once thought was a portrait of Mrs Spink. I suppose it had been pawned.

The duns became more and more persistent, and Mr Spink had to find a new ruse to escape them and reach Fleet Street in safety. One of the smaller Spinks was now sent out to watch when that eccentric green omnibus turned the corner. Then he would signal to his father who would be waiting in the hall of Number 13, and as the omnibus went jogging past Number 17 Mr Spink would come dashing down his steps just as it drew abreast of Number 13. This method of getting away from the house was successful for a while, but presently the duns got wise to it, and when the omnibus came round the corner they used to gather in a bunch at the foot of the steps of Number 13, so that Mr Spink became a fast prisoner in the house.

We heard now that it would not be long before the bailiffs would enter and take possession, and neither of the doors at Number 13 was ever opened by so much as a crack. What a thrill it was to hear that the two dumpy men in bowler hats and bobtailed coats, one of whom was leaning against the portico pillar which belonged exclusively to Number 13 and the other against the pillar which was shared with Number 15, were sheriff's officers waiting a chance to get in through an open door or open window of Number 13 and take possession. I used to stand and gaze up at the beleaguered house as if it were a castle in a fairy tale, and how well I remember the contrast between the dirty grey steps of Number 13 and the trim white steps of Number 15.

Mrs Clyburn had always been a little severe on Mr Spink, partly because of that habit of knocking out his pipe at all hours of the night in that study of his which was next her own bedroom and partly because she could not bear the casual way in which the children were being allowed to grow up; but when the Spinks were in these straits Mrs Clyburn's kind heart was touched, and she used to send food to them over the wall of the back garden. She even allowed various junior members of the family to use her own front door for going out, and I fancy that most of the smaller articles at Number 13 were taken out to pawn this way.

MOST of the residents in our street were not as sympathetic as Mrs Clyburn with the troubles of the Spinks. Naturally one would not have expected General Brackenbury to feel anything except irritated by the scandal they were causing; but Mr Lockett should have been less bitter, for the situation at Number 13 had much about it that was Dickensian, and there was a want of logic in lavishing so much emotion upon Mr Micawber, yet so little upon poor Mr Spink. Of course, what upset Mr Lockett was the lowering of the tone of our street by having one of the houses thus invested by bailiffs. He felt that every road in the neighbourhood was superciliously condoling with our street, and that on the Terrace our financial stability was being sapped. Miss Lockett, probably without in the least meaning to do so, aggravated her brother's resentment by continually coming back from her visits to the tradesmen with further disgraceful particulars of the Spink insolvency. I remember once calling at Number 3 with my Aunt Adelaide and finding Miss Lockett full of the topic.

'Mr Pearson told me this morning that the butcher's bill had been owing for seven months, and when I asked Mr Holt if this could possibly be true he actually told me himself that it certainly was and that, though he could give a reasonable amount of credit, he did think that seven months was beyond reason. And poor Mrs Eardley says she hasn't had a penny for nine months and that knowing what a regular supply of milk means to any family she hadn't liked to refuse to supply them with any more until last month, when really, as she said, she felt she had to think about themselves a bit more, particularly as poor Mr Eardley has been having a lot of trouble with his teeth lately.'

I hoped that my Aunt Adelaide would not agree too cordially with Miss Lockett about the disgraceful behaviour of the Spinks; but to my regret she did, and while Miss Lockett sat holding a thin piece of bread and butter in her trembling hand, my aunt nodded a grave and austere agreement with her condemnation.

'And my brother says it *is* so bad for the reputation of our street,' Miss Lockett continued, her pale blue eyes popping further out than ever, her many beads and bugles rattling with emotion. 'He has as you know such a belief in the future of this neighbourhood and he feels that one family like the Spinks can set the clock back years. Those were his very words to me. Years! And what *would* a stranger think who passed along our street and saw those dreadful grimy steps and those bare grubby windows? He would never dream that there were nice people living in our street at all. It's always been such a grief to my brother the way Number 25 has stood empty all this time. And now with Number 13 looking like another empty house! Oh, dear, it's most distressing, and the lovely sunshine we've been having lately does show up every little speck and spot. Have you had your spring cleaning yet? Not yet? Well, I always say that spring cleaning is a sad trial, but really with this fine spring weather one cannot grudge it to the house. And so – ' at this point in the excitement of what she was going to announce Miss Lockett trembled so much that her teacup seemed likely to walk over the edge of the saucer – 'and so my sister-in-law and I have definitely made up our minds to begin ours on Monday. But really, when one passes Number 13, half the pleasure of having one's own house nice and dainty is spoilt. And those uncomfortable-looking men lounging outside Number 13 and smoking away all day long like two real loafers, what a name they will give our street in the neighbourhood. Mrs Clyburn says that Bingo, their fox-terrier, simply cannot bear the sight of them. In fact she has to let him out at the back now unless he's on the lead, for she feels sure he wouldn't hesitate to bite one of those bailiffs. And my dear old Snuff is just the same. He growled at them this morning most ferociously. Most ferociously. In fact I had to cross over and walk on the opposite pavement for fear he would fly at them. And I do not like walking on the opposite side of our street, because I find that my mantle is apt to gather quite a lot of unpleasantness from the wall. And all through not paying one's just debts. Life can really be very sad on occasions. May I tempt you with a mustard and cress sandwich? I think we should all take a little more green in spring. Mr Pearson was telling me this morning we may really begin to expect that asparagus will soon be cheaper, and I always feel it is wrong to anticipate; and to buy vegetables before they are really in season, apart from being very expensive, is apt, I always think, to seem a little presumptuous. I do feel so very distressed about the poor tradesmen in the Terrace, and I'm sure the Spinks must have a lot of foreign blood. So black. Their hair, I mean. But really I do think Mr Spink has behaved badly.'

I had never heard Miss Lockett speak at such length before, and I never heard her do so again. The crisis at Number 13 must have been preying upon her mind. My Aunt Adelaide too must evidently have resented strongly the position in which the unpaid debts of the Spinks placed all the rest of us, for she listened to that long speech of Miss Lockett's with every appearance of attention, and usually when people talked at such length before my aunt she would jingle her chatelaine as an impatient horse jingles its bridle. I could not understand how she who had thought of giving Annie Spink that yellow silk dress could look on so coldly and disdainfully at the family's misfortunes.

NUMBER 9

IT WAS over the Spink business that my Aunt Adelaide and Aunt Emily had the only argument I ever heard between them in which there was a hint of mutual irritation.

'I cannot understand, dear Adelaide, why you should align yourself with all those rather silly people in their attitude towards the wretched Spinks. I was delighted that Lady Marjorie kept out of it, and I wish you would. What on earth do the affairs of Number 13 matter to us?'

Thus Aunt Emily challenged my Aunt Adelaide one afternoon when there had been something in the nature of a committee meeting in the drawing room at Number 9, with Mrs Lockett and Miss Lockett, and Mrs Clyburn and Mrs Bond and Mrs Gurney and Minnie Arden devoting the whole of their conversation at tea to the crisis at Number 13. I had been handing round the cakes and bread and butter, and so deeply engaged were all present upon the solution of the problem that I could hardly persuade any of them to pay the least attention to the food I was bringing before their notice.

In the middle of the discussion Aunt Emily jumped up suddenly from her chair and went out of the room, returning only, when the front door had closed on the last visitor, to make the observation above.

When Aunt Emily was put out, her fair hair always expressed her ruffled feelings, and now as she criticised her friend's descent from dignity, she tossed it back from her screwed-up speedwell eyes. She was wearing, I remember, an apple-green linen overall above which her delicate cheeks seemed more than usually flowerlike. And my Aunt Adelaide was in a severe gown of peacock blue girdled loosely with a rope of twisted silk. Her chestnut hair was done in two coils over each ear. Her high forehead was serene; but those always slightly slanting full grey eyes were slanted a little more sharply when she replied to her friend's challenge:

'Really, dearest Emily, you must allow me a few opinions of my own.'

'Of your own as many as you like,' Aunt Emily agreed quickly. 'But are they your own? Are you not surrendering to the poor little conventions of struggling gentility? Dearest Adelaide, it hurts me to see you of all people being – I am afraid I must say it – being just a little undignified.'

My Aunt Adelaide's eyes and eyebrows slanted yet more sharply up in displeased astonishment.

'Not even by you will I be called undignified,' she said coldly.

'Hasn't your pride made you suffer enough!' exclaimed her friend. 'You shan't be proud with me. We who have both genuinely suffered, are we going to sit here and pretend that we suffer because people like the Spinks are disgracing our neighbourhood with unpaid bills? Be fair to yourself, Adelaide.'

And just when my heart was beginning to beat fast with apprehension and embarrassment my aunts remembered that I was in the room, and a silence fell, after which Aunt Adelaide asked me if I had forgotten that the history of ancient Rome had claims upon my attention.

So I was able to escape from the room, and glad I was to find myself in our hall with those cool Japanese landscapes and bright Chinese birds painted on rice paper. Such pictures seemed to forbid anything like a terrible quarrel between two friends. I do not know what Aunt Emily said after I left them; but about an hour later when I was feeling much stirred by the tale of Cornelia, the mother of the two Gracchi, Aunt Adelaide came in with a letter in her hand.

'I want you to slip this into the letter box at Number 13,' she told me, and looking at the envelope I saw that it was addressed to Mrs Spink.

I was tempted when I reached Number 13 to ring the bell of Number 15 and ask Mrs Clyburn if I might go through and climb over their garden wall so as to reach the beleaguered Spinks and deliver the letter in person. I was curious to learn what the letter was about, and I was sure I should not have the least difficulty in finding out from Mrs Spink, who did not know the meaning of secrecy. However, I was afraid my Aunt Adelaide would be annoyed if I did not carry out her orders exactly. So I slipped the note into the letter box, hoping the poor Spinks would not assume that it was one more bill.

The sequel was exciting. We were sitting in the drawing room of Number 9 after dinner, and Aunt Adelaide was reading aloud *Goblin Market*, which was one of my favourite poems and to hear which I had asked to be allowed to stay up a little longer than usual. I divined, I think, at the time that it was to have the pleasure of reading the lines:

> *For there is no friend like a sister*
> *In calm or stormy weather;*
> *To cheer one if one goes astray,*
> *To lift one if one totters down,*
> *To strengthen whilst one stands;*

which had led Aunt Adelaide to choose *Goblin Market* that evening, for when she came to them her deep voice grew husky for a moment and as she paused I saw that her grey eyes were starry and that she put out a hand to clasp the hand of that friend who was to her a sister of sisters. The thought that nothing remained of their disagreement lulled me into a state of dreaming felicity in which the words of Christina Rossetti's poem spun like catherine-wheels of coloured flame.

Suddenly there was a tap on the French windows that opened on to the balcony whence a flight of steps led down into the small garden. The curtains were fast drawn, and we all three looked up to stare at the maze of Morris's pattern in which the same wise-eyed thrush pecked the same strawberry over and over again. As we looked up, the travelling clock on Aunt Emily's desk struck ten with that silvery tinkle which always reminded me of Aunt Emily herself. And then the tap was repeated.

It was Aunt Emily who rose and pulled back the curtains. A big moon, already slightly humped, was rising over the houses at the back of our street, and we could see a large figure in black silhouetted upon the balcony.

'It's Mr Spink,' I said.

'Can he be sober?' my Aunt Adelaide asked.

It had been too much of a relief to evolve Mr Spink from that black shape, which might have been the burglar whom all of us had been expecting for years, for the condition of Mr Spink to trouble me. A drunken Mr Spink was better than a sober burglar.

'We'd better open the window and see what he wants,' Aunt

Emily suggested. She did not wait for Aunt Adelaide to question her advice, but drew the bolts and turned the handle. Not a breath of whisky entered with Mr Spink, nothing except that peculiar acrid fragrance of a London garden in spring when lilac and privet contend with bricks and mortar.

'Ladies,' said Mr Spink, bowing ceremoniously, 'I beg you will forgive this somewhat unconventional way of calling upon you, but there are reasons of which you are doubtless aware for my not following the ordinary procedure of the formal visit.'

I fancy Mr Spink must have rehearsed this preliminary speech during his negotiation of the two walls which lay between our garden and his, for he delivered it like an oration, and when it was finished he did not seem to know what to say next, but stood twisting his black sombrero, looking as sheepish as a schoolboy without an excuse.

'Won't you take a chair, Mr Spink?' my Aunt Adelaide suggested.

'Well, I don't think I ought to sit down,' our visitor replied; and having thus replied he at once sat down heavily in a low armchair.

I was expecting every moment that my Aunt Adelaide would dismiss me to bed; but in the surprise of Mr Spink's visit she forgot about me, and I was able to withdraw into comparative obscurity beyond the glowing emerald globe of her reading lamp.

'I cannot express without appearing fulsome,' Mr Spink began, 'I cannot express the gratitude of myself and Mrs Spink for the gift which you so generously conveyed to us this afternoon. Words should be my strong point, for I live by words and not by deeds, if I may so put it. But on this occasion words fail me. Mrs Spink would have written to you herself, for I can assure you that if there was anything that Mrs Spink appreciated even more than the munificent gift, it was the delicacy which prompted you to address the envelope to herself. Mrs Spink has the blood of old Castile in her veins. Hence Carlo and Ferdinand as the names of two of our boys. The Spanish blood in Mrs Spink's veins coursed with impetuous warmth when she opened that envelope, for she expected nothing but a repetition of that stale phrase "to account rendered." Mrs Spink, as I say, would have written herself to thank you . . . but . . . *mañana!* Her Spanish blood is too much for her sometimes. She is racially incapable of resisting the temptation to put off until tomorrow what should be done today.'

'There is really no need for you to apologise, Mr Spink,' said my aunt. 'The letter was sent without any desire for it to be acknowledged. Indeed, I am at a loss to know how you knew it was sent by me at all.'

'My daughter Annie, to whom you were so kind as to send a yellow silk dress once, recognised the handwriting. And that brings me to the explanation of my present intrusion upon your privacy. When Mrs Spink informed me about the precious enclosure I felt as if my prayers were answered. The entire absence of anything in the nature of ready money from which we have been suffering for the past week, ever since the last portable article in the house was pledged, had thrown my poor wife into a state of mind bordering upon despair. Generous Mrs Clyburn next door has been providing us with meals; but I could not trespass upon her kindness indefinitely, and it was imperative for me to escape somehow and endeavour to earn my family's daily bread. But the house was beset. I cannot blame my creditors. Poor souls, they have every right to get their money by any means open to them. So when your five-pound note lay before me I realised that here at last was the opportunity to escape. With five pounds I could take my family elsewhere, leaving behind me in partial satisfaction for my creditors, among whom must be numbered the land-lord of Number 13, those heavier pieces of furniture which I was not in a position at the moment to dispose of. I knew that were I once more a relatively free man, I could earn enough to maintain my family. And now comes the real reason for my disturbing you at this hour of the night. Almost immediately on receipt of your banknote I sent my eldest daughter out to change it. This, I regret to say, she was entirely unable to do. At shops where she was known, delicacy forbade her to change a five-pound note without offering to settle the account at the same time. At shops where she was not known, apparently something in her appearance or manner provoked an unworthy suspicion that she had stolen the note. When she returned home just now, worn out with her long quest, I resolved to take the bold step of approaching our benefactress by this unconventional route in order to thank her from the very depths of my being and ask to increase still further the obligation under which we lay by changing the five-pound note into gold and silver. Let me add in conclusion that my daughter Annie would have come herself, but owing to her long walk in quest of change on top of a not absolutely adequate tea she fainted on arriving back home.'

'Ah, poor child,' exclaimed both my aunts impulsively.

'Thank you, thank you,' said Mr Spink, 'thank you for so quickly understanding why I was compelled to impose my inappropriate self upon you in this extremely inappropriate fashion.'

I do not know whether my Aunt Adelaide felt any scruples over being the chief agent in helping Mr Spink to escape from his creditors. If she did, they were not apparent, for she at once set about the business of gathering together the necessary change. This involved her going off to draw upon Janet and Hetty to make up the full amount.

While she was out of the room, Mr Spink kept up a ridiculous monologue of small talk for the benefit of Aunt Emily, all about the weather we had been having lately and the weather we were having now and the weather we might expect with the rapid approach of summer. He might have been a farmer whose livelihood depended upon the weather instead of a penniless journalist unable to move out of his front door for fear of his creditors, to whom sunshine and rain were equally unprofitable.

At last my Aunt Adelaide came back with the change, which she poured so abruptly into Mr Spink's hand that as he jumped up from the low armchair he dropped half the coins on the floor. Thus it fell out that he had to count them.

'You've made a mistake,' he told my aunt. 'There are seven pounds ten shillings here.'

'Oh, you must have had some money of your own,' she murmured.

'Not a farthing. There was not one farthing in the whole house,' he insisted.

'Well, well,' she said, 'we won't argue about it. The money is yours.'

I can see now the expression on Mr Spink's big face as he stood there, his full lips working and one grubby hand pushing back the hair from his forehead. The green light from the reading lamp made his already sallow countenance look almost livid, and I could see two large tears gather in the corner of his eyes and trickle slowly down through the bristles of ten days' growth like marbles working their way among the spikelets of the game called German billiards.

Then he shook his head slowly, bowed, and went out through the French windows to make his way back over the two garden walls to Number 13.

'My dear child, haven't you gone to bed?' my Aunt Adelaide exclaimed, turning to me.

So I had to be off and did not hear what she and Aunt Emily had to say to each other about that strange visit.

Two days later, we heard the Spinks had successfully flitted, though of course all their dilapidated furniture was left behind and was seized by the landlord in default of rent. The tradesmen were indignant over this, for they felt they had a right to their share of what was owing.

It would be pleasant to be able to tell my readers that a year later Mr Spink wrote such a popular book that he came back to our street and paid off all his debts. But the truth is that we never heard anything more of him or of that mopheaded family of his. Perhaps they all emigrated.

NUMBER 13 *To Be Let or Sold*

IN SPITE of the unanimous opinion of the grown-ups in our street that the departure of the Spinks was a good riddance, we younger people missed them very much. Outwardly, except for the big TO LET board over the portico, Number 13 looked almost exactly the same as when it was inhabited, and we could hardly believe that if we rang the area-door bell we should not at once be admitted by Aylmer, or Carlo, or Christabel, or Ferdinand, or dear Annie herself, and that when the area door closed behind us we should never again experience that delicious security from the cares of conventional childhood.

Olive and I and the Clyburn twins clambered over from the garden of Number 15 one day and managed to get into Number 13, where as we wandered from empty room to empty room we grew sentimental over the chips and stains and burns which recalled various great occasions when the very fabric of the house had been compelled to serve our purpose, was it never so exacting. That grate had been removed from one of the bedrooms when we played at the last days of Pompeii and when Almeric arranged such a superb eruption on the top landing with showers of soot for noxious volcanic fumes, with hot marbles fired from a decapitated Jack-in-the-box for lava, and for Vesuvius itself a roaring bonfire in the grate which set light to some of the balusters. That strip of wall paper had come away after being soaked in the flood let loose from the top cistern to represent a burst dam in some adventure story. That skylight had been cracked by the rocket sent up as a signal of distress from a sinking ship. And that heap of soil in the garden represented the labour of several afternoons on a secret passage which was to emerge in a piece of waste ground a quarter of a mile away and enable us all to carry on a series of highway robberies without the least risk of discovery or capture.

Then one of us, wandering into that room which was always

93

without the least justification known as the dining room, found upon the mantelpiece that rusty knife which had been lying in the same place ever since we had known the Spinks. We gathered round to stare at this miserable relic with profound emotion, and because the Clyburn twins had a museum Olive and I felt they were entitled to the knife. So it was taken back to Number 15 to be placed upon one of the museum shelves between the lower jawbone of a sheep discovered on Beachy Head the previous summer and an emu's egg which the Clyburn twins had always believed to be a thunderbolt until an ornithological uncle had undeceived them.

Number 13 remained to let for some time, much to the displeasure of Mr Lockett, who in spite of being well rid of the Spinks could not bear the spectacle of two vacant houses in our street. Then the landlords, realising that perhaps the interior of Number 13 was discouraging to prospective tenants, decided to do it up, and so all the many signs of the Spinks' occupation vanished.

GLOSSY new paint soon beamed invitingly from all the external woodwork of Number 13. Missing balusters were now replaced. Windows were glazed. A new bath was installed. Whitewash obliterated the murk from ceilings. The enterprise of the landlords was justified, and the house was taken for a term of years by a Jewish couple called Rosenthal, the jolliest and most hospitable people, whose one object in life seemed to be to cram everybody old and young with delicious food.

I must confess that when the Rosenthals first arrived at Number 13 we all thought they were a little vulgar. If we had censured the Spinks for their lack of money, we censured the Rosenthals for their excess of it. They actually kept a ralli car, and we wondered what was happening to our street when on a fine Sunday morning it pulled up outside Number 13 and waited for Mr and Mrs Rosenthal to go off driving in it to Richmond, the smart groom balanced behind with arms crossed and Mr Rosenthal taking the reins. We thought the cigars Mr Rosenthal smoked were too large. We thought Mrs Rosenthal's fur coat was too ostentatious. We disliked the heavy gold Albert chain across Mr Rosenthal's well-filled waistcoat. We objected to his lemon-yellow gloves and to the big diamond that flashed in his bright cravat. Nor did we approve of the way Mrs Rosenthal powdered her face and always wore half a dozen jewelled bracelets.

'People like that would be more in their element in Bayswater,' General Brackenbury observed to Mr Lockett. 'However, I suppose this is what you mean by the neighbourhood's going up.'

'Well,' said Mr Lockett, 'apart of course from the fact that it would be more gentlemanly if they didn't make a point of gadding off in that showy-looking dogcart just when the rest of us are starting for church, I see no reason why people in our street should *not* keep a private carriage. No reason at all, General.'

It was evident that General Brackenbury's implied criticism had touched Mr Lockett's pride of belief in our street's future. He was not prepared to admit that it was incapable of sustaining a ralli car. And I think it was a slight resentment against the General's remark about the neighbourhood's going up which led Mr Lockett to restore in person an Angora kitten which had strayed from Number 13 to Number 3. I think if the General had not made that remark Mr Lockett would probably have sent the kitten back by one of the maids.

I happened to see Mr Lockett when he came down the steps of Number 13 after taking back the kitten, and he was smoking one of Mr Rosenthal's largest cigars, smoking it too with every appearance of relish and without the least embarrassment at his own vulgarity.

'Ah, young man,' he said to me, 'I've just been making the acquaintance of our new neighbours. They're simple, unpretentious, good-hearted people.'

And exhaling a terrific cloud of fragrant smoke Mr Lockett passed jauntily on, humming to himself Mendelssohn's *Oh, for the Wings of a Dove* which was to be his anthem next Sunday and which I had the pleasure of hearing from the organ loft at St Jude's Church. I am sure I was invited to accompany Mr Lockett that Sunday in order that he might tell me all about the Rosenthals, for he would know that I should not criticise his change of attitude over the newcomers and I believe he was still a little nervous what some of his older friends might say.

The ralli car overtook us just as we turned the corner into the main road, and Mr Rosenthal, reining in the chestnut cob, bade us jump up and let him drive us to church.

'Mrs Rosenthal was feeling a bit under the weather this morning. So there's plenty of room.'

Mr Lockett looked round. There was nobody he knew in sight. Then he looked at me, and I have no doubt that my countenance expressed the liveliest anxiety to do as Mr Rosenthal had suggested.

'Come on, by George, we will!' Mr Lockett vowed, and he got up beside Mr Rosenthal and up I clambered beside the groom. And as we went spinning along that wide empty Sabbath thoroughfare I felt that we were driving over the top of the world instead of to church.

'I'll take you for a spin as far as the Park,' Mr Rosenthal wheezed amiably to Mr Lockett.

'We must be in church by a quarter to eleven,' Mr Lockett warned him.

'That's all right, my boy. I'll see you there with five minutes to spare.'

And so we were.

'Here, take a couple of these. You'll want one after dinner and another to wind up your day,' said Mr Rosenthal, pressing two enormous cigars on Mr Lockett who did not refuse them. 'Sorry I've nothing to offer you,' our genial friend went on, turning to me. 'But come in and have tea with us this afternoon, and we'll see what we can do in your line.'

'That's a hospitable, kindly, straightforward, thoroughly decent fellow,' Mr Lockett declared as we paused for a moment outside the vestry door to watch the ralli car go spinning westward.

And I warmly agreed with him.

Tea with the Rosenthals that afternoon was memorable for the quantity and variety of the cakes I ate and for a box of fondants which Mrs Rosenthal pressed upon me before I left. It was impossible to imagine any longer that the Spinks had once inhabited this house crowded with heavy comfortable furniture, this house whose windows were hung with figured velvet curtains, whose walls were covered with the kind of oil paintings you might see in the Royal Academy Exhibition.

The Rosenthals had no children of their own, and their advent in our street was the dawn of a golden age for all of us younger people. Nor could our parents and guardians object to the expensive toys with which we were always being presented, because they themselves were accepting presents of cigars and scent. Scent-making by the way was Mr Rosenthals's business. Most of us after that first drive to St Jude's were given drives in the ralli car by Mr Rosenthal, and we soon forgot how unsuitable a private vehicle had looked in our street. Even General Brackenbury's reserve was melted by the Rosenthals' ability to do justice to his curries.

Those two people seemed to live for nothing except trying to give pleasure to other people, and one day after I had told them the story of their predecessors at Number 13 Mr Rosenthall set all sorts of inquiries on foot to see if he could not find out where they had gone so that he might be able to help them. I wish for the sake of the poor Spinks he had been successful.

Before the Rosenthals came to live in our street we were most of us lucky if we saw one pantomime during the Christmas holidays, and that usually from the upper circle. Mr Rosenthal used to book a couple of large boxes at Drury Lane, one on each side of the stage, hire a big railway omnibus, and arrive with a party of sixteen, half of us sitting in one box with Mrs Rosenthal and the other half in the other with himself. He used to laugh so loudly at Herbert Campbell and Dan Leno and Harry Nicholls that he sometimes made them laugh on the stage. And when he had taken us to Drury Lane he would take us all to the Grand Theatre, Islington, and to the Standard Theatre, Shoreditch, and to the Britannia Theatre, Hoxton, and to the Surrey Theatre on the other side of the river. What audiences they were in those days!

When I had written these words I fell into a reverie, for I was hearing again the deep murmur of the pit at Drury Lane before the curtain rose on that time-honoured first scene in the smoky abode of the Demon King. I was hearing the cries of the orange girls outside and the hoarse shouts of the link boys on a night of fog and the thunder of traffic along the Strand. And then I was alighting from the train at the Temple Station and smelling the fresh air of the Embankment after the mephitic vapours of the Underground, and hurrying up Norfolk Street or Arundel Street into the Strand and lingering to look over my shoulder at the queer books in the sinister little shops of Holywell Street and being jostled in Wych Street and passing the Olympic Theatre and reaching at last the mighty colonnade of Drury Lane.

And in waking from that reverie at the hoot of a motorcar I perceive that all this book is no more than a reverie, and I feel inclined to apologise to readers for trying to communicate a dream.

Yet it is appropriate I should be dreaming of vanished theatres and of old pantomimes just at the moment when I am thinking it is high time to introduce Miss Molyneux who lived at Number 17.

I DO not remember whether it was Miss Molyneux who was the first to have her front-door steps red and so compelled General Brackenbury at Number 19 to follow her example, or whether it was the General who began it and Miss Molyneux who surrendered to his fashion. My impression is that it was Miss Molyneux, for I do not think the General would have deliberately made Number 19 so conspicuous. I think he would have felt that it was being what he so much deprecated at first in the Rosenthals. Miss Molyneux on the other hand might consider that as an actress she was as much entitled to redden the steps of her house as to rouge her cheeks on the other side of the footlights. Not that Miss Molyneux could be accused of attracting attention to herself in private life. On the contrary she was famous for her dislike of publicity, and she never stayed at any public function a moment longer than was necessary to let people know that she had been present. Even in our street, although she would always bow graciously when she met us, we could hardly consider that we knew her. As a matter of fact, unless she happened as a favour to accept an engagement to play some part in a London production we did not see much of her, because she was nearly always away on tour. She had a company of her own and was much esteemed for her refusal to lower the standard of British acting in any play written less than forty years ago.

Looking through the files of an old theatrical newspaper the other day, I came across the following letter to the editor:

> The Prince of Wales's Theatre,
> Bristol.
> November 20th, 189 –

SIR,
    May I trespass upon your valuable space to correct a serious misstatement in your last issue which has caused

much pain to myself and my friends, and to that public whose loyal support has enabled me for the last fifteen years to maintain in my own humble way the highest traditions of the British drama?

It is quite untrue that I have accepted an offer to play Mrs Alving in the forthcoming production of Ibsen's *Ghosts* for a series of matinées. It is true that the part was offered to me, but in refusing it I ventured to express astonishment that my name should ever have been mentioned in connexion with a play which is utterly foreign to all the dramatic ideals we have learned to cherish in this country and to which I have devoted my career.

Yours faithfully,
MAUD MOLYNEUX.

Miss Molyneux never used her first name on the playbill. There it was always Miss Molyneux and her Comedy Company who would appear in a repertory of Shakespeare, Sheridan, and Goldsmith, with perhaps a play like *Mask and Faces*, or *Caste*, or *The Lady of Lyons* to show that Miss Molyneux was not quite out of touch with the progress of the drama through the nineteenth century. But I always knew her name was Maud, for I remember that I associated Number 17 with the lines from Tennyson:

> *Maud is just seventeen,*
> *But she is tall and stately.*

Looking back on Miss Molyneux over nearly forty years, I confess I am a little at a loss to know how the association of ideas started. To be sure she was tall and more than stately; but she was certainly not just seventeen. I remember Mr Mellor shocked me once by exclaiming as she walked past his window on a fine afternoon in early summer, her parasol held to shield her as much from the gaze of the curious as from the rays of the sun:

'By Jingo, she's a real bouncer, eh?'

This did not seem to me a respectful way in which to describe a woman of whose fame we were so proud. After all she was the only resident in our street whose name we could read in print, for the account of Mr Lockett's last Dickens recital in the St Jude's Parish Magazine did not impress us greatly. I had even seen my own name printed in a parish magazine as the winner of a silk cushion in a raffle at a local bazaar.

My own acquaintance with Miss Molyneux was first made by as simple a device as any in one of the old plays to which she devoted her art. She dropped her handkerchief, and I summoned up the necessary courage to run after her and return it just as she was ascending her red steps (you could not use a simpler verb for that motion) to enter the portals of Number 17.

'Thank you, thank you. That was most gallant and charming,' she told me. 'Your manners are very good, young gentleman. What may be your name?'

It was the first time I had ever been complimented on my manners; but strange to say, the compliment did not abash me in the least. On the contrary I responded with perfect self-possession, told her my name, and added to it an account of my circumstances.

'And which of those two distinguished-looking women is your real aunt?' she asked.

I described my Aunt Adelaide, whereat Miss Molyneux inclined her head graciously.

'Ah, yes, I have noticed her on more than one occasion. No doubt both she and . . . Miss Culham, I think you said, both she and Miss Culham have seen me act.'

Fortunately my good manners were not tested by this indirect question. I was able to inform Miss Molyneux that my aunts had seen her as Rosalind, which part, with that of Viola, represented the extreme concession that Miss Molyneux's gentility, by donning the garb of a boy, was prepared to make to dramatic art.

'Only as Rosalind?' she murmured. 'Well, of course, it is a glorious part, and I could not resist the repeated demands of the public to play it, but . . . only as Rosalind? I shall be opening my autumn tour next month at Croydon. I wonder if I were to send your aunt and Miss Culham a box . . . ? I should so very much like them to see me as Beatrice in *Much Ado About Nothing*. I fear that I have been a little neglectful of my neighbours; but you must explain that when I am resting I am apt to retreat into my shell. And do you often go to the theatre?'

I told Miss Molyneux that I had been to the pantomime last Christmas.

'Oh, yes, the pantomime. Well, of course that is rather different. Not that I object to pantomimes, provided of course that they are not vulgar, which I fear they too often are. Still a pantomime is not quite what I meant by the theatre. Well, thank you once more for restoring my handkerchief. Pray give my compliments to your aunt and Miss Culham and say that I very much hope to have the pleasure of their company one afternoon to tea, if they will dispense with the preliminary ceremony of the formal call.'

When I told my aunts that I had made the acquaintance of the great Miss Molyneux, they were, I flattered myself, not unimpressed. I fear she will be sounding a little pompous, maybe a little absurd, as I describe her so many years later; but she was a public figure, and we still preserved a genuine reverence for the public figure at that date. We respected the right of the public figure to put on the airs of some majestic Alpine solitude. We even allowed the reputations of the famous dead to remain untarnished by the verdigris of lesser men. We believed, no doubt with excessive credulity, that there must have been something in a man if he had succeeded in imposing upon the time his personality. In our zest for the goodness possibly interred with the bones of the great villain we may have gone in for biographical whitewash. But biographical burnt cork was unknown to us.

A few days later after my chance encounter with her Miss Molyneux wrote to invite my aunts to tea and graciously included me in the invitation. We had tea in the garden, reclining in wicker chairs upon the small lawn.

'I take every opportunity of enjoying the fresh air when I am resting,' Miss Molyneux confided in us. 'That is the only complaint I have against my profession: the long hours in the theatre.'

I do not believe that Mrs Siddons could have uttered the words 'my profession' more majestically, and she was a tragedienne whereas Miss Molyneux was a comedienne. But I daresay there may have been a twinkle at the back of her lustrous eyes which I failed to catch. It will distress me if I suggest that Miss Molyneux was a little lacking in humour.

In due course Miss Molyneux kept her promise to send a box for *Much Ado About Nothing*; but I was down in the country with my father at the time and missed that performance. However, in the autumn when I was once more in our street she played for a week at the Lyric Opera House, Hammersmith, and I was invited to see her play Portia. It was an afternoon performance and the theatre was full of children, so that I felt particularly grand when between the acts Miss Molyneux's manager came along the stalls and took me through the pass door behind the scenes to visit Miss Molyneux in her dressing room.

'Well, and are you enjoying it?' she turned round from her mirror to ask.

I told her I was enjoying it very much, although I had felt sorry for Shylock.

'Ah, but I think that Shakespeare intended us to feel sorry for Shylock,' said Miss Molyneux.

'I expect he did,' I agreed, thinking of Mr Rosenthal.

'And did you enjoy my acting?' Miss Molyneux asked.

Now, one of Miss Molyneux's greatest assets was that nobody in her audience could ever have felt a momentary doubt that she was acting, and I was able to assure her with enthusiasm that I had enjoyed her acting very much. When she had risen to proclaim that the quality of mercy was not strained we had listened with the respectful admiration accorded to anything that sounds terribly difficult and over the difficulties of which human endurance finally triumphs. We had applauded out of gratitude to that tall handsome lady who, almost it seemed at the risk of her health, had been determined to get through with that speech. It had never struck us that Portia might have been conceived by Shakespeare as a real human being. To us it was a part to be acted, and we were sure that Miss Molyneux had done her duty nobly. In fact we had been as successfully spellbound by her oratory as the Doge of Venice himself. But Shylock had made us feel definitely uncomfortable. We had never been perfectly sure that he was acting.

I was bidden to wait on the stage for Miss Molyneux after the play was over in order that I might take tea with her at some local shop, and it happened that just as she came out of her dressing room, no longer Portia now but the great Miss Molyneux herself, the late Shylock also appeared as himself again, and I was greatly astonished to find that he was very like the rest of the cast, one or two of whom I had recognised as they left the theatre. Indeed, I was so much astonished at his ordinary appearance that I suspected I was being made fun of, and that the real Shylock would presently appear and laugh at my credulity.

'He doesn't believe that Shylock was you, Openshaw. How delicious!' Miss Molyneux exclaimed, with that deep musical laugh of hers I had heard from Portia and should hear from Rosalind, from Beatrice, from Lady Teazle, from Peg Woffington, and indeed within a year or two from every one of the great heroines of comedy in the repertory of Miss Molyneux.

Mr Henry Openshaw, the actor who had played Shylock, suddenly started that passionate speech which begins; *'To bait fish withal: if it will feed nothing else, it will feed my revenge.'* I vow I jumped in the air with fright and half fancied he would presently chase me round the stage with the knife I had watched him whetting on the sole of his shoe during the trial scene.

'Ah, now he's convinced,' said Miss Molyneux. 'Oh, and by the way, Openshaw, do be careful not to scrape your chair in the screen scene tonight.'

I was not acquainted with *The School for Scandal*, and the rest of the lecture on stage deportment that Joseph Surface received from Lady Teazle was lost on me. But I remember that she accused him of a tendency to clown this particular scene and that she begged him to remember that if he did this it killed her exit.

Later on I ventured to ask Miss Molyneux what 'killing an exit' meant.

'You know what an exit is?'

Yes, I believed it meant when a character left the stage.

'Very well, when the leading character has to make an exit, it is essential for the artistic effect that nothing should distract the attention of the audience from that character. This means that all the other actors on the stage should be most careful to subordinate themselves in order to make that exit as artistically effective as possible. When you see what is called the screen scene in *The School for Scandal*, which I hope you will some day, you will realise that it is what is called Lady Teazle's scene. That means to say the audience are more interested in Lady Teazle than in anybody else on the stage. Besides this, in my case, as you would expect, the audience are more interested in me than in any of my company. So when the actor Joseph Surface makes silly faces down stage, some quantity of barren spectators, as Shakespeare calls them, laugh. That's villainous, our great bard goes on, and shows a most pitiful ambition in the fool that uses it.'

You may be sure I was much impressed when I heard Miss Molyneux speak as sternly about the behaviour of one of her company as if he were a schoolboy who had been fooling in class, and I expect I looked as suitably awed as was proper.

'And now tell me,' Miss Molyneux continued, 'which scene of Portia did you like best?'

I told her that I had liked them all equally, and when egged on by Miss Molyneux I selected the trial scene, she seemed to want me to like the casket scene best; but no sooner in deference to her anxiety had I declared for that than she asked me in a somewhat hurt tone of voice if I had not liked her last act. I was too young in those days to be familiar with this sphinx-like behaviour of actors, authors, and painters, and quite unable to play the Œdipus satisfactorily.

'Well,' I repeated, 'I think I liked them all equally.'

Miss Molyneux sighed.

'I want you to learn how to appreciate acting,' she told me earnestly. 'You are an intelligent and sympathetic boy, and I don't want you to fall into the idle English habit of just knowing what you like. I want you to know why you like it.'

I was suddenly aware that the eyes of all the other people in the teashop were fixed on our table, and I rather wished Miss Molyneux would not talk so much like the way I had heard her talk as Portia. She told me to take a piece of cake at this moment, and really there was no difference in her invitation from the tone in which she had lately said to Shylock: 'Take then thy pound of flesh.' Indeed I was so much overcome by the sonority of her tone that I took another piece of bread and butter instead.

Looking back on it all now, I am tempted to believe that Miss Molyneux was aware of and enjoying the impression she was making on the other customers, most of whom had probably been at the matinée. And yet that could hardly have been so, because Miss Molyneux looked up and frowned at the inquisitive eyes regarding her and the inquisitive ears concentrated upon overhearing her lecture on acting.

'I have an idea some of these people have recognised me,'

she whispered. 'Dear me, I can't bear being stared at. I thought we had chosen such a quiet place for tea.'

I may mention that we had already caused a considerable sensation by driving up to the teashop in the brougham which Miss Molyneux always hired when she was acting within reach of her own house in our street. Those at tea already would have stared at anybody who drove up to that shop in a brougham. However, young as I was, I had enough tact not to suggest that the brougham had anything to do with the interest our arrival had aroused.

'Waitress,' Miss Molyneux called, and when the harassed little waitress had inquired her pleasure she asked if there was a private room available.

'Do you wish the cloak room, mum?'

'Cloak room?' Miss Molyneux repeated with a shudder. 'Certainly not. I wish a private room for tea.'

'I'm afraid this is the only room we have, mum,' said the waitress.

'Thank you,' she sighed like Melpomene, 'I thought you might have a private room.'

'Shall I bring you a nice fresh pot of tea?' suggested the waitress brightly. The little creature was evidently longing to oblige this unusual visitant in every way within her power.

'Yes, you may bring us some more tea,' Miss Molyneux allowed grandly. And then turning to me with that whimsical smile of hers she murmured, '*A good deed in a naughty world.*'

When we had finished tea and it was time for Miss Molyneux to be going back to the theatre to dress for the evening performance, she called up the waitress again:

'You know who I am, of course?'

'Yes, mum. You're the lady with the kerridge outside.'

Miss Molyneux laughed that deep musical laugh which had thrilled thousands.

'Well, well, do you ever go to the theatre?'

'Oh, yes, mum. Only last Saturday night I went to see *The Grip of Iron*. Oh, it was awful. I couldn't hardly sleep after it. It made me all of a trimble.'

'You have not been to the theatre this week?'

'No, mum.'

'Here are two passes for the pit tonight.'

Miss Molyneux took out a card from her bag and wrote the

equivalent of open sesame in that large hand which all leading actresses used at that date, and the shrinking of which among the leading actresses of today is a sad indication of the decline of the great figure.

'Thank you, mum. What must I do with this?' the waitress asked.

'You must present it at the entrance to the pit, and you will receive two free seats.'

'I won't have to pay nothing?'

'Nothing,' Miss Molyneux proclaimed superbly.

'Well, thank you very much, mum. I'm shore it's most kind.'

Yes, I fear I am making Miss Molyneux sound a little pompous and absurd, but we did not think that kind of charitable gesture pompous or absurd. We expected it from our great figures.

And I really do dislike making Miss Molyneux sound pompous and absurd, because she was extremely kind to me. Moreover, she was a beautiful woman. She must have been forty at the time of which I was writing, and of course to a boy every woman over thirty seems so venerable that I hesitate to say that she did not look nearly as much as that. I myself should not have been surprised to hear that she was fifty, but I heard lots of people say how astonishingly young she looked to have had such a long career of success, and I knew that Will Brackenbury, who was then about twenty-two, fell in love with her. I have not mentioned General Brackenbury's only son yet. He was always away when I first went to stay with my Aunt Adelaide in our street, and though we heard from time to time of what Will was doing in Malta and how he was expecting his regiment to be ordered to India at any moment, he was something of a legend to me, for his leave had never happened to coincide with one of my visits to London.

NUMBER 19

I HAVE already mentioned that General Brackenbury's house like the house of Miss Molyneux next door had red steps; but the two things which to my mind always distinguished it particularly from the others in our street were the large image of Buddha in his dining-room window and the unique lock on his front door. I do not know if Yale locks were invented when our street was in its prime; but this lock must have been something after the same style, and the General was very proud of it. When he was going up his front-door steps he used to swing all the rest of his keys by the key of his front door, and when he fitted it into the small aperture he used to turn the key with a click that may have reminded him of a private soldier springing to attention at the sound of his voice. Mr Lockett, whose name perhaps gave him a right to criticise, was a trifle contemptuous of the General's patent lock. I heard him express once his surprise that a man of General Brackenbury's experience should take such a childish delight in such fal-lals. He said the General had completely failed to convince him that his patent lock had a single advantage over the ordinary lock, and when Doctor Arden announced that he thought of having a similar lock fitted to the door of Number 1 Mr Lockett became almost heated.

'I'm amazed at you, Doctor,' he protested. 'I should have thought an old campaigner like you would have despised such a faddy affectation. You mark my words. The first house to be burgled in our street will be the General's. A lock like that just puts ideas into the heads of these light-fingered gentry.'

Doctor Arden never argued with Mr Lockett. He just stood silent, gently rubbing his Wellingtonian nose between his thumb and forefinger. However, perhaps he was convinced after all, or perhaps the patent lock was too expensive. Anyway, the front door of Number 1 remained like its fellows.

The big gilded image of Buddha at Number 19 had its back

to the street, but its presence in the dining-room window always suggested to me when I was walking past that it was having a colloquy with the General. And if the General himself happened to go up his steps with swinging keys, I always used to feel that the image must in another moment turn round and nod to him.

As it happened, it was a long time before I ever met the image face to face, for I was too young to be asked to the General's dinner parties when he used almost to burn out the insides of the guests with his curries, and the back of that image symbolised for me the mystery of Number 19's exterior. I would sometimes catch a glimpse of a large oriental-looking lamp in the hall as the General passed within, and once he left the front door open long enough for me to see a big temple gong and a cluster of assegais and shields on the wall. I fancied that Number 19 would be full of absorbingly interesting objects. Rumour related he had a table made out of the hide of a hippopotamus, tiger skins galore, and the tails of two elephants. The General was always pleasant with us young people; but it never seemed to strike him that he had treasures we should appreciate a great deal more than his grown-up neighbours did. We for instance would almost have given our own heads to see those desiccated Dyaks' heads which he had tossed casually into Miss Lockett's lap one evening after dinner.

Poor Miss Lockett had supposed they were some kind of tropical nut, and when she had picked them up and seen the shrivelled little monkey-like faces looking at her she had had to smell her salts for the rest of what she had called a most uncomfortable evening. And uncomfortable was a very strong word with Miss Lockett. A brutal murder in Fulham was near enough to our street to strike Miss Lockett as a most uncomfortable affair. When in a neighbouring road a servant left the gas on and blew the front of the house out by going in some hours later with a lighted match, Miss Lockett thought that a most uncomfortable business. I had been reading about this time in *Tit-Bits* a serial story by Conan Doyle called *The Sign of Four*, and I always used to think that the house where the mysterious murder took place must have been General Brackenbury's house, and I could easily imagine an Andaman Islander climbing up the drain pipe of Number 19 and shooting a poisoned arrow at the General through a blowpipe. It was not through *Tit-Bits*, however, that I first gained admittance to the General's house, but through the *Boy's Own Paper*, the monthly arrival of which, in a world where the young people had to amuse themselves for the most part, was an event of outstanding importance.

For some reason it had not been delivered that month at Number 9, and I had gone to inquire of Miss Voss what was become of my copy.

'Dear me now,' Miss Voss sighed. 'What can have happened to your copy? I'm sure it was sent. William,' she called to the small newsboy who set out every morning from the Terrace, laden with dailies and periodicals for the neighbourhood. 'William, did you leave the B.O.P. at Nine Boclerk as you should of?'

William in a squeaky voice denied that he had been given the B.O.P. this month to deliver, and Miss Voss grew so confused that she took off the red woollen shawl which she wore winter and summer and put on her strongest spectacles to investigate the matter. Finally, she found a copy of the current number and told me to take it with me.

'I'll be bound that William has left your copy at the wrong house.'

'No, I haven't,' William contradicted sulkily. 'I haven't left no copy of the B.O.P. nowhere this month.'

'Well, then you ought to of,' said Miss Voss, 'and you're an idle negleckful boy, and if your poor mother hadn't the lumbago so chronic I wouldn't keep you another minute.'

But by the time I was out of the shop with the *Boy's Own Paper* under my arm Miss Voss had put on her red shawl again and relapsed into an ovine placidity, ruminating with her false teeth the cud of William's past misdeeds. As for me, I perused the orange-buff magazine all the way back to our street, walking once into a plump old gentleman and once into a lamp-post.

It happened that this special summer number of the *Boy's Own Paper* contained a large coloured plate of the cavalry regiments of the British army. As I remember, there were thirty-one representatives: Hussars, Lancers, Dragoons, Dragoon Guards, Life Guards, and Horse Guards, and to contain them it had been necessary for the coloured plate to be folded. How many times I pulled it out to gaze entranced at that display of masculine splendour I should not care to guess, but between Miss Voss's shop and my aunts' house, I had debated with myself a dozen times to which regiment I would devote myself when grown up.

Finally, the choice was narrowed down to the 17th Lancers and the 11th Hussars; but at this point an impasse was reached. I simply could not make up my mind between them. No sooner would I have decided that the skull and crossbones on the helmets of the Death or Glory Boys must be my badge than I would find it impossible to relinquish definitely the crimson breeches of the Cherry Pickers. Just outside General Brackenbury's house I pulled out the plate once more and tried to reach a final decision. Was I to be a Dead and Glorious Lancer or a Cherry Picking Hussar?

'Hullo, young man,' a voice was heard over my shoulder, 'what's all this about?'

I turned to see General Brackenbury himself looking down at the cavalry regiments of the British army outspread in all their rich diversity of uniform.

'Let me see,' the General went on, 'where's my old regiment? Ah, here we are.'

He put his long lean forefinger on one of the Dragoon Guards.

'There you are. *That's* the regiment.'

I felt a little depressed about this, because as a matter of fact though I had dallied for a brief moment with the notion of wearing the blue uniform of the Carabineers I had ruled out all the Dragoon Guards some time before I walked into the lamp-post. I realised, however, that it would be difficult to argue the superiority of Lancers and Hussars over Dragoon Guards with one who had actually worn the uniform of a Dragoon Guard himself, perhaps in the charge of the Heavy Brigade at Balaklava.

'Were you at Balaklava, General Brackenbury?' I asked.

'I was.'

'Did you . . . were you in the charge of the Heavy Brigade?'

'I was.'

I looked at the General in awe. I had a book called *Famous Battles of the British Army*, with coloured plates of Crécy, Poitiers, Agincourt, Blenheim, Ramillies, Oudenarde, Malplaquet, Dettingen, Salamanca, Vittoria, Badajoz, Waterloo, and then of Infantry of the Line crossing the Alma under fire and plucking grapes upon the opposite bank to moisten their powder-parched throats, of the Guards in grey overcoats fighting with clubbed muskets at Inkerman, and of Dragoon Guards, Greys, and Royals thundering down upon the Russian guns at Balaklava. And this tall, straight-backed old gentleman who was looking down at me on this quiet pavement of our street had lived in one of those pictures. It would hardly have seemed more incredible to hear that he had saluted Marlborough, shouted for King Harry, or swung a battle-axe beside the Black Prince himself.

I suppose something in my expression of reverence appealed to the General, for what should he do but invite me into his house that he might show me some 'bits and pieces,' as he put it, 'from the Crimea.'

No doubt, after the souvenirs of the late war, a round shot or two from Sebastopol, a Russian bayonet, and a few faded ribbons with long unfamiliar medals attached will not seem much to be writing about. Yet in spite of all the efforts of humanitarians the old glamour still survives. In conversation with a young friend recently I happened to ask her the age of her brother.

'He was born just before the war finished,' she told me. 'Wasn't he frightfully lucky?' Then with a sigh she added: 'I wish *I* had been.'

There were plenty of other things to look at in General Brackenbury's house in addition to the relics of the Crimean War. The table of hippopotamus hide proved to be no idle rumour, and the weight of the elephants' tails was something to marvel at. As for the Dyaks' heads which had given Miss Lockett such an uncomfortable evening, they were indeed full of value, though it was disappointing to hear that the secret of reducing a full-sized human head to the size of a monkey's still belonged exclusively to the Dyaks.

I asked the General if he had any scalps; but he had none. He showed me, however, a portrait of himself as ensign in the Dragoon Guards with whiskers that rivalled the plume over his helmet. And then he showed me a photograph of his son Will, in uniform.

'He's not a Dragoon Guard,' I murmured.

'No, no, he's in the Line.'

'Why isn't he a Dragoon Guard?'

'Because his father can't afford it.'

'Is it expensive to be a Dragoon Guard?'

'Well, you want a handsome private allowance,' the General admitted.

'Is it very expensive to be a Lancer?' I asked.

'Very.'

'Or a Hussar?'

'Any cavalry regiment is expensive,' said the General.

I decided not to ask his advice over my choice between the 17th Lancers and the 11th Hussars. Recently when I was home in the country my father had turned his attention from pomology for a few moments to remind me that it would be a good idea if I were to begin to ponder the career on which I intended to embark.

'And don't think,' he had concluded, 'that I can afford to support you indefinitely.'

If General Brackenbury could not afford to let his son be a Dragoon Guard like himself, it hardly seemed probable my father would approve of my being a Lancer or a Hussar. To console myself for the disappointment I reflected that Hussar officers no longer wore those rakish sleeveless dolmans, so that I should not be missing quite so much as once upon a time.

'My boy's coming home on leave next week from Malta,' the General was saying. 'He tells me there's talk of his battalion being ordered out to India at any moment now.'

Will Brackenbury was neither so tall nor so straight as his father, and we all agreed that he would never be as typically military a figure as the General. Perhaps Will Brackenbury felt this himself, for shortly after he arrived home from Malta we heard that he wished to give up the army and go on the stage. It appeared that when he first heard of his son's proposal the General had taken him round to see Doctor Arden, not because he wished to have Will certified, but because he hoped that Doctor Arden out of his long experience of Indian life would be able to persuade Will that it was the ideal place for a young man to find himself. Mr Lockett was not long in getting out of Doctor Arden enough of what had happened to be able to produce for the rest of us a most circumstantial account of the whole business.

'The Doctor was a bit shy of saying anything at first,' he told my aunts. 'But I pointed out that he had not been consulted

professionally and that in trying to stand on his professional
dignity he was being overscrupulous. In fact I told him that
he might injure the boy's prospects for life. "After all, Doctor,"
I said, "what the deuce do you know about the stage? What
right have you to assume that you are omniscient? This is not
a question of pills from what I can gather, but bills.' The fact
is,' Mr Lockett went on in a confidential tone, 'the boy has over-
run his allowance. Polo ponies, I believe. And one or two other
little things. Then he made a great hit in some amateur
theatricals. Oh, yes, from what I can make out the youngster
has decided talent. Now, Arden is a good fellow. He's been a
friend of mine for years. As you know, when Minnie came
home from India she was with us for a long time, and I look
on her as another daughter. In fact I've always rather hoped
that she and my boy George will make a match of it one day.
But good fellow though Arden is, he's an obstinate as a mule
over some things. He actually told me I'd no more right to talk
about regimental life abroad than he had to talk about the behaviour of a choir. So, seeing that it was useless to put any sense
into him, I resolved to tackle the General himself. My wife
was a bit worried when she heard what I was intending to do.
"Now do be tactful," she begged. "Tactful? When have you
known me not tactful?" I asked. Well, I went along to Number
19, and when Dawkins, his man, opened the door I asked him
if the General was in a good mood. That's the beauty of these
old soldier servants. You *can* ask them anything like that.
"Not in one of his best moods," Dawkins told me. "A bit frac-
tious, sir, between you and me." So I said I'd look in again tomorrow, which is precisely my notion of tact. So I called the
next day, but before I had time to ask if the General was in,
Dawkins advised me not to see his master that morning. "Well,
it's like this, Mr Lockett. When I tell you he threw the bootjack
at me, a thing he hasn't done since three years ago when I
brought him up the *Morning Post* of a month before by mistake, I think you'll understand he's what I may call on the
ramp a bit." You never heard about that *Morning Post* before,
did you?' Mr Lockett paused in his narrative to ask my aunts.

They assured him that the story was entirely new to them.

'It seems that the General read it right through without
realising that it was a month old, and if Dawkins had
been less conscientious and not come up with the current

114

Morning Post, his master would probably never have known anything about it. But as soon as he found out he'd been reading news a month old he picked up the bootjack and threw it at Dawkins. I asked Dawkins how he came to make the mistake, and he told me that it was a mystery at the time and that, though he and Mrs Dawkins had talked it over frequently since, it was still a mystery. Well, to cut a long story short, it was not until this morning that Dawkins thought he could safely advise me to call on his master. Now, as you know, the General and I have our differences of opinion. I've always thought he made a great mistake in not buying Number 19. And that ridiculous patent lock he had put on his front door. Well, as you know, I've never concealed my opinion that it was a mere fal-lal. Still, we have never had a serious disagreement, and I felt that as a teacher of singing I had some right to put the other side of the case to the General. Well, I didn't beat about the bush. I went straight for him. "Look here, General," I said, "I hear your boy wants to take up the stage as a profession, and I'm taking it on myself to give you a bit of advice based on the experience of a good many years." "What's it got to do with you?" he rapped out at once. "Now, look here, General," I replied, "you're not going to play the Grand Mogul with me over this, and that's letting you have it straight from the shoulder." Well, I really thought for a moment he was going to throw one of those elephants' tails at me, and by George, if he had, I should have felt it. Nothing ever gave me such an insight into an elephant's strength as those tails, which they flick about like feathers, though they must weigh a couple of stone. However, the General thought better of it and did *not* throw the tail at me, and in the end by being firm I actually got him to see reason, and the upshot of my visit is that he's going to take his boy to interview Miss Miss Molyneux when she comes home next week.'

Aunt Emily applauded Mr Lockett's intervention, and I fancy that she who had been intending to be a professional singer herself and who had been engaged to a soldier out in Egypt had a right to feel that she was qualified to give her opinion. Perhaps General Brackenbury felt this, too, for that very afternoon he called in person and took my aunts into his confidence. I did not expect to have the luck of overhearing the General's account as well as Mr Lockett's; but it happened that when the General called my aunts were on the balcony outside the drawing room, and by sitting at the open window of the room above I was able to get the continuation of the story, to which the coming intervention of Miss Molyneux added a special interest for myself.

'You've heard, I suppose, that my son plans to become a confounded play actor?' the General began.

My aunts made no attempt to pretend that Will Brackenbury's intention was not the chief topic of the moment in our street.

'Of course, it's an unheard-of step in our family,' the General continued. 'We've all of us been soldiers except for two or three parsons. But I never heard that any of these parsons could preach a good sermon, so where this play-acting comes in God bless me if I know. It must come from his poor mother's side. She had a brother who went exploring in Africa and came back and lectured about it, which we thought rather bad form. Still, that wasn't play-acting, though I believe he was inclined to be a bit theatrical in his delivery. I never went to hear him myself. Didn't like the idea at all.'

'But we hear that your boy made a great success in some amateur theatricals at Valetta,' said Aunt Emily.

'So I understand. He's brought back a whole parcel of newspaper cuttings. Fulsome stuff. I can't think what his colonel was about to let one of his subalterns make such an exhibition of himself, but the army's not what it was. Still, he chose his profession, and I saw him through. Made an ass of himself at Wellington by failing for Sandhurst, and I had to get him in through the militia. Always a bad thing, that, you know. Still, I got him in, and now he wants to throw it all up. He's been getting into debt, too. Bought a string of polo ponies. Now, I ask you, what earthly right has a subaltern of the Line to be thinking about polo?'

'You were in the cavalry, weren't you, General?' Aunt Emily asked.

'I was, Miss Culham,' the General replied grandly.

'Perhaps your boy inherited his polo from you,' she suggested.

'If I could have afforded it, he should have gone into the cavalry,' said the General. 'But I couldn't afford it.'

'I suppose you spent a good deal in the cavalry yourself?'

Aunt Emily asked innocently. And before the General could reply to this thrust she went on: 'You know, I'm not going to sympathise one little bit with you. You see, I've had a long talk with your boy.'

'Have you, by gad?' the General exclaimed. And I may say he expressed the astonishment of myself and Aunt Adelaide as well as his own.

'Yes, we met in Kensington Gardens yesterday, and he was good enough to confide in me. So you mustn't expect any sympathy from me, General. I think if he wants to send in his papers, you ought not to oppose the step. He told me frankly that he hated the prospect of going to India and that his whole heart was set on the stage.'

'Yes, that's all very well, Miss Culham,' the General objected. 'But where is that kind of thing going to stop? One's whole heart may be in anything at my boy Will's age.'

'Isn't that his good fortune?' Aunt Emily murmured. And though from where I was sitting I could not see her face I knew by the tone of her voice just how she would be looking at the General when she murmured this question.

But who can expect to recapture for his readers the magic of a glance? We look at a shell we once carried home with us so fondly because it had seemed to hold the sunset in its shallow cup, and we find in it no more lucent vitality than a fragment of lime. And as the colours of a shell fade in air, so too in words the most subtle countenance becomes as commonplace as the face of a fashion plate. As Aunt Emily tries to speak upon my page she is not herself, for I cannot echo that faintly husky voice. I cannot paint those speedwell eyes, that hair like blown corn, nor can I flood her cheeks with the carnation of all her eager life. *And when I am dead who shall remember that beautiful lady of the West Country?* I am driven to summon Walter de la Mare to my aid, and he was singing of a beautiful lady that I have never known. Perhaps at the end of it the painter may feel more secure than the rest of us that he may bequeath to posterity what he genuinely willed.

'It seems to me,' Aunt Emily went on, 'that he's just at the age to be entitled to have his whole heart on anything. Be honest, General Brackenbury. Wouldn't you give a very great deal if you could still have your whole heart in anything?'

'Anything in reason,' the General growled. 'I don't want to

make an ass of myself now any more than I did forty years ago.'

However, I think Aunt Emily's little lecture must have had some effect on General Brackenbury, for we were soon discussing the solemn visit he and Will had paid to Miss Molyneux. None of us was present at it, but I venture to think that I could imagine the way of it better than anybody else in our street.

There was certainly no doubt that Miss Molyneux made a great impression on the General. We heard no more of the blot on the escutcheon of the Brackenburys which Will's adoption of the stage as a profession was going to splash. In fact the General was inclined to brag about Miss Molyneux's offer to give Will an engagement in her company for the tour which would open on August Bank Holiday at the Devonshire Park Theatre, Eastbourne.

'She seemed quite struck by his promise,' he told Mr Lockett, who had no hesitation in rubbing into the General that it was he who should be considered responsible for the overtures to Miss Molyneux.

I think we were all of us a little jealous of Will Brackenbury's good luck, and some of us were inclined to ask ourselves if we did not possess vocations for the stage. I know that I forgot all about my fancy to become a cavalry officer and that Olive even went so far as to deny that she had been for some weeks intending to become a teacher of swimming when she grew up. Both of us were convinced now that our real future was upon the boards. Curiously enough we did not see ourselves as comedians. Romantic melodrama was what attracted our ambition. Partly this was due to Mr Mellor's permission to make free with his collection of costumes.

OLIVE and I were telling Mr Mellor all about Will Brackenbury and Miss Molyneux one afternoon at tea. It was a particularly good tea, I remember, because Mr Mellor had been awake all night reading *Jane Eyre* to find out if it was as good a book as he had once thought it.

'And by the holy poker, young 'uns, it was better,' he roared. 'It's absolutely rumbustious. I didn't get off to sleep till eight o'clock this morning, so you won't mind if we have eggs and bacon for tea, because this is my breakfast.'

Olive and I voted that eggs and bacon were the very thing for tea, though we followed them up with strawberry jam, whereas Mr Mellor, loyal to his own meal, ate marmalade.

'I'm going on the stage as soon as I'm seventeen,' Olive announced.

'So am I, Mr Mellor,' I put in.

'Not when you're seventeen,' Olive corrected.

This habit of Olive's of trying to arrange the future for me was always rather irritating, and I told her sharply that I had as much right to go on the stage at seventeen as she had.

'You haven't,' she contradicted. 'Because girls are always much older for their age than boys. Aren't they, Mr Mellor? I'll be grown up at seventeen. But *you* won't be.'

'I will if I want to be,' I protested. 'Perhaps I don't want to be.'

'Sour grapes,' Olive jeered. 'Perhaps you won't have any grown-up clothes.'

I told Olive that she need not put on so much side about her intention to become an actress, and reminded her that only as late as last week she had been planning to become a swimming instructress and a trick diver.

'Oh, I just thought of that for a moment,' said Olive.

'Well, why did you practise holding your breath with your head under your bath water every morning? Why did you tell me that you could hold your breath for two minutes? Why did you – '

'Oh, shut up,' Olive interrupted indignantly. 'If I tell you what I do in my bath because I thought you were my friend, you needn't go yelling about it all over the place. You were going to be a Lancer, weren't you? But I didn't go yelling that out to everybody.'

'Steady, steady,' Mr Mellor intervened. 'We all blow rainbow bubbles which burst. But we needn't try to make one another swallow the soap. You've neither of you ever rummaged about in my hamper of costumes, have you? Well, after I've had my pipe we'll go upstairs and have a look at them.'

Olive and I were used to the discovery of fresh treasures every time we visited Mr Mellor; but those costumes exceeded everything we could have hoped for in the way of thrills.

'Try them all,' Mr Mellor called back over his shoulder, when he left us with the freedom of that room at the top of the house.

The dusty floor was littered with gauntlets and cuirasses, with hauberks and habergeons, with morions and cabasets and casquetels, with blades of Ferrara or Toledo, with daggers and poniards and stilettos, with halberds and partisans, and there was one huge battle-axe, at which we both made a dart to claim from the other. Standing about in the litter of old arms and armour were large wicker chairs crammed with velvets and laces and satins, with petticoats and farthingales and empearled stomachers, with garters and silk hose and doublets and tabards, with kirtles and paduasoys, with perukes and periwigs and cravats, with coifs and kerchiefs, with everything in fact to keep a couple of children dressing themselves up until even their curiosity and peacock vanity were glutted. The air was odorous with camphor and antique fabrics and musty leather. Even the great Miss Molyneux, we felt, might have been impressed by this profusion of clothes to wear. I actually had the luck to find a fur-trimmed dolman and a sabretache with which to play the hussar; and Olive was made happy by a Spanish costume of black and yellow until she was made even happier by a silvery steeple hat and a gown of aquamarine velvet which Mr Mellor told us afterwards was the dress he had given to the model who sat for his picture of *La Princesse Lointaine*.

The only fly in the amber of our joy was the impossibility of finding any complete costume that was not much too large for us. We were nearly as completely lost in some of the wigs as needles in haystacks. My dolman forfeited much of its devil-may-care look by sweeping the ground at the back, and there was not a ruff in which my face did not look like a half-eaten pie. Olive thought she could don the armour of Joan of Arc; but it was not a success. And my attempt to assume the part of the Black Prince was not a success either. In fact, the pair of us looked more like Tweedledum and Tweedledee about to have a battle than the chivalry of once upon a time.

It was while Olive and I were trying over these old costumes of Mr Mellor that Will Brackenbury must have fallen in love with Miss Molyneux. Our spare time had been so entirely pre-occupied by that romantic wardrobe that neither of us had a moment to spare for the current life of our street. We became out of date like the old clothes themselves. We emerged for meals like a couple of Rip Van Winkles, shedding upon the air of the present a faint perfume of lavender, camphor, and naphthaline mothballs. Our hands were scratched by spangles, and Olive's nose had been grazed by the abrupt descent of a visor. But that retirement from the world of today into the world of yesterday was as happy a fortnight as any two children can have spent. Moreover, it inspired us. Olive sat down to design, with a good deal of help from Mr Mellor, a series of tableaux to be performed for charity on the first suitable occasion. I retired to my room and embarked upon a play about Richard Cœur de Lion, for I was feeling that Shakespeare had missed a great opportunity there. Somehow the play did not progress to my satisfaction, and I decided to consult Miss Molyneux about it.

WILL BRACKENBURY was with Miss Molyneux in the drawing room of Number 17 when I arrived, and I cannot say he appeared to take much interest in my play. Indeed, he showed something like irritation when Miss Molyneux most kindly explained to me that there was no theatre the resources of which would allow quite such rapid changes of scene as I had planned. She was also a little critical of the briefness of some of my scenes, and thought that Saladin should have had more to say than 'Allah!'

'Well, I couldn't find what Mahomedans said except that,' was my defence.

And then she talked a good deal about poetic license and the right of the dramatist to the convention that those of his characters who might be expected to speak in their own tongues should speak English instead.

'You see, my dear boy, you have this great battle scene in which Richard and Saladin fight in single combat, and all that Richard says is, "By my halidom, have at thee, Saladin," and all that Saladin can reply is, "Allah! Allah!"'

'Must you waste the afternoon teaching this kid his alphabet, Maud?' Will Brackenbury protested.

'Oh, but we two are old friends, aren't we?' Miss Molyneux said to me.

I turned in amazement to look at Will Brackenbury. It was not that I objected to his calling me a kid. I recognised that from his point of view I was a kid. At the same time, in spite of his very high choker, in spite of his double-breasted pale green waistcoat, and in spite of his boots having lavender kid uppers, he was himself not so long grown up as to venture to call Miss Molyneux by her first name. I experienced the same kind of shock when I first heard one of the young Spinks repeat a blasphemous parody of a hymn. To be sure, in passing Miss Molyneux's I had sometimes thought absolutely to myself the words, 'Maud is just seventeen, but she is tall and stately.' I had never once gone so far, though, as even to whisper them aloud. And it was true that Mr Mellor had on one occasion asked me how my friend Maud was; but then Mr Mellor talked about Rossetti by his Christian name and about all sorts of famous people as familiarly. He even left out the 'Queen' from Queen Victoria when he mentioned her.

'What are you staring at me for?' Will Brackenbury inquired with a hint of truculence in his tone as he loosened that monstrous choker and waggled his neck and shot his cuffs in order presumably to impress me with his grandeur.

I told him I wasn't staring at him particularly, and he asked me if I had no lessons of my own this afternoon that I must be bothering Miss Molyneux with my idiotic plays.

'Will, Will,' Miss Molyneux protested, shaking her finger at him as I had seen her shake her finger on the stage at Bassanio. 'Do you mind if I entertain my guest in my own house in my own fashion?'

Will Brackenbury apparently minded very much, for he groaned.

'Maud, you promised me I should have the whole afternoon with you,' he sighed reproachfully.

'Yes, my dear boy, but I don't at all care for this possessive manner of yours,' said Miss Molyneux.

Presently she left me and Will Brackenbury alone for a few minutes.

'Look here,' he said to me, 'do you want to earn half a crown? If you'll say you can't stay to tea when Miss Molyneux comes back, I'll put this half-crown in your cap. You see,' he added, 'I'm going through all my parts with Miss Molyneux, and if you stay to tea we shan't get any work done.'

I considered the offer. It seemed to me a fair wage. I accepted it.

Presently Miss Molyneux came back. She had changed into a white frock and was wearing a big pale blue sunbonnet.

'We're going to have tea in the garden,' she announced.

There were few things so embarrassing to me at that age as declining an invitation; but the thought of the half-crown gave me courage, and I gulped out something about having promised my aunt that I would be back in good time for tea.

'Bad luck,' said Will Brackenbury cheerfully,

Miss Molyneux flashed a glance from her big deep blue eyes at the ex-subaltern, and I thought that I had never seen any human being gaze up with quite such a foolish expression at another human being. I really felt quite ashamed on his behalf, and I could not understand how somebody who had been in the army dared make such an exhibition of his feelings. It never struck me for a moment that Will Brackenbury was in love with Miss Molyneux. I should have felt that I had as much right to fall in love with her as Will Brackenbury, which would have appeared to me ridiculous.

In justice to Will Brackenbury I must mention that he added another sixpence to the half-crown when I held out against the persuasion of Miss Molyneux to stay. I still have the book on heraldry I bought with these three shillings to which a hoarded sixpence of my own had been added, and I was soon able to blazon a coat-of-arms so accurately that I gave up the notion of going on the stage and resolved to join the College of Arms, debating as between the 17th Lancers and the 11th Hussars between the dignity of Bluemantle Pursuivant and Rouge Dragon for the aim of my heraldic career.

Although I had suspected Will Brackenbury of being in love with Miss Molyneux, it was not long before his infatuation became a topic in our street.

'By George,' Mr Lockett said to my aunts, 'though you know I'm a Dickens man, I must admit Thackeray did understand the foolish side of human nature. Who'd have thought that we should have the Fotheringay and Arthur Pendennis all over again in our street? And no worldly-wise uncle, I'm afraid, to manage the young man's affairs for him. Rosenthal tells me that she sits on her balcony at the back like some tremendous Juliet and that the poor Romeo stands in the middle of the General's geraniums gazing up at her like a woebegone mooncalf.'

'I'm sure Mr Rosenthal never said anything so unkind,' Aunt Emily commented sharply. She was always a loyal supporter of Will Brackenbury. 'And I'm surprised that a Dickensian like you, Mr Lockett, should indulge in such easy cynicism.'

Mr Lockett blinked to hear his old pupil take him to task like this.

'Well, we must admit, Miss Emily, that the difference in their ages does make the whole business a little ludicrous.

Why, there are twenty years between them if there's a day.'

'I've not heard yet that they are engaged to be married,' Aunt Emily observed.

'No, no; but she must be encouraging him. And he's going out on tour in her company. It's baby-snatching, that's what it is. I had no sympathy with the General's point of view at first; but upon my word I'm beginning to think the young man had better by half have stuck to his regiment.'

And then we heard that Will Brackenbury had proposed to Miss Molyneux and been refused, and on top of that we heard that he was so utterly heartbroken that he had secured an engagement in an English company which was being taken over to New York. There was now an inclination even among those who had most loudly disapproved of the encouragement Miss Molyneux had been giving to Will Brackenbury to say that she had treated him outrageously in refusing to marry him.

However, Miss Molyneux herself was always the same, and I do not believe she gave a second thought to the possibility of being criticised by her neighbours over her behaviour to poor Will Brackenbury. I use the epithet without condescension and only because Miss Molyneux always called him that when poor Will had crossed the Atlantic to show New York audiences how a typical British subaltern spoke and dressed and behaved – so far, that is, as the author of that particular melodrama allowed him any scope for realism. And whatever some of us in our street may have thought about Miss Molyneux's treatment of Will, Will's own father apparently approved of it, for he became a frequent visitor at Number 17, and I heard it whispered by one or two that he had his eye on Miss Molyneux himself.

'Well, there's no fool like an old fool,' Mr Lockett said, shaking his grizzled carroty curls.

In fact, Mr Lockett's point of view was veering round towards Thackeray's all the time, and indeed at his next reading he left out his emotional *chef d'oeuvre*, the death of Little Nell, and read us the death of Colonel Newcome instead. At this rate we might presently expect to hear from him that in Becky Sharp Thackeray had drawn everywoman.

Our inclination to criticise Miss Molyneux was presently allayed when we heard that Will Brackenbury had married a charming American girl from Baltimore with lots of money. A year later a son was born to them, and General Bracken-bury became more upright than ever and absolutely went swaggering down our street.

'Upon my word,' Mr Lockett commented with some acer-bity, 'to see the General, one might suppose he was the first grandfather since Adam.'

NUMBER 19

GENERAL BRACKENBURY was not deterred from enjoying his new relationship by anything Mr Lockett said. He sailed away to America, enjoyed himself there thoroughly, and came back to our street with as many recipes for cocktails as he already had for curries. Mr Wingfield, the wine merchant of the Terrace, was kept busy obtaining various kinds of bitters, exotic fruit cordials, special brands of whisky, and some stuff called vermouth which he had never stocked in his life. He was much too respectful a wine merchant to point out that his best respected client's head had been turned by that visit to the United States. He went no further in criticism than referring to the General's cocktail hobby as a most interesting development. But I realised how much it must have hurt Mr Wingfield's sense of fitness to find sherry regarded as a mere ingredient in a drink called cobbler, brandy corrupted by mint and strawberries. and port disdained entirely, when I heard him talking to Doctor Arden one morning at the door of his shop in the Terrace.

'If anybody had told me a few months ago, Doctor Arden, that General Brackenbury would have started using brandy as a salad dressing I wouldn't have believed him. Do you like these mint juleps, as the General calls them?'

'Oh, yes, I think it's a capital refreshing drink in warm weather,' the Doctor replied.

'Refreshing?' Mr Wingfield echoed in pained astonishment. 'But brandy was never meant to be a substitute for lemonade. Brandy is a meditative spirit. In my opinion, Doctor Arden, to put strawberries into that '65 brandy of the General's is as — well, I would as soon try to keep goldfish in my best port.'

But no amount of implied, though always respectful, disapproval by Mr Wingfield deterred the General from his new hobby, and I am bound to say that except for a few purists we all enjoyed the General's drinks very much. I say 'we,' for though I was of course too young to get a taste of them myself I heard so much about them I felt as if I had sampled the lot.

'We had a most poetical beverage last night,' Miss Lockett might say. 'A Golden Fizz, the General called it. And I'm sure it must have been most wholesome, for I never felt better than I did last evening. Probably drinking it like that before dinner is better for the digestion. I've always heard that we should not drink and eat at the same time. Let me see, what did the General say were the principal ingredients? The yolk of an egg was the chief, I know, and of course that would be extremely wholesome. The yolk of an egg, and I believe I remember that there was a little gin in it, but naturally a very little. If the white of an egg is used, it is call a Silver Fizz, and the General has promised that I shall try that next time and see which I like better.'

Rumour said that the General had invented a new drink which he called a Piccadilly Weeper, either because it brought tears to the eyes of the strongest or because it made a man's whiskers sprout, or because it did both. It was said that Mr Lockett after being given a Piccadilly Weeper had unhooked from the wall the General's sabre, that very sabre with which he had cut down the Russian gunners at Balaklava, and had then stood upon a chair to recite *The Burial of Sir John Moore*, after which, without waiting for an encore, he had immediately gone on to *The Battle of Linden*, by which time, according to scandal, he was rolling almost as rapidly as the river Yser. And when he had been persuaded to get down from the chair and let them hook the sabre up on the wall again, he had taken two or three of the guests into a corner of the General's room and recited to them Hood's *I remember, I remember the house where I was born*, the tears pouring from his eyes in the stress of his emotion.

But then Mr Rosenthal was rather fond of telling funny stories, and perhaps he exaggerated a little. It is not quite fair to convey an impression that General Brackenbury spent his whole time in giving dinners with very hot curries and very strong cocktails.

I like to think of him best when he invited me to go for a walk with him and when he would pace up and down the sunny side of some old Kensington square, while he told me tales of a world which was even then vanishing fast and of which now there is scarcely a survivor left.

The General was particularly fond of walking round Edwards Square, and if the ghost of one of the old *émigrés* of the Revolution who lived out their exile in this square had met the General face to face he would have recognised in him a compeer of *ancien régime* and made him a courtly bow as he passed on.

The General had a friend in one of these little houses, the unmarried sister of an old comrade-in-arms, and sometimes we would pay her a visit and escort her for a turn in the garden. I fancy they must have levelled much of the garden of late years in order to make room for the tennis players; but in those days the lawns undulated like those round a country house and one had an illusion that time had stood still since that colony of exiles from France had taken snuff with one another on those same lawns; taken snuff and wondered about the news from home. They would have cursed Bonaparte and longed for him to be defeated, and yet perhaps their withered hearts would have beat a little faster with a pride that all their wrongs could not quench, when they heard of that last charge of the Old Guard at Waterloo.

I used to walk along beside the General and Miss Alington, and while they talked of people long dead and of houses long since passed into other hands I would dream the lawn alive with the figures of a still earlier age.

And when Miss Alington had walked enough we would go back with her to her little house and have tea with her in a room that would hardly have surprised with a single novelty the old *émigré* who had furnished it first. I remember the General always vowed that the only good cup of tea to be had nowadays was at Miss Alington's; and indeed it was delicious tea with a faint flavour of muscatel grapes, drunk in cups of such fine porcelain that one could see the shadow of the tea through them. The room was always scented with potpourri in Lowestoft bowls whose rosy lilac flowers matched the embalmed petals within. Miss Alington made her own potpourri from roses grown in her own London garden, old Provence roses so sweet that their fragrance hurt because there were no words to praise it meetly. In a corner of this room there was a large musical box which played six tunes. I know that *The Last Rose of Summer* was one of them; but the names of the others I forget. Only sometimes I fancy when I hear an old tune from an opera that I heard it first in Miss Alington's room in Edwardes Square nearly forty years ago. She always wore white silk mittens, and a big brooch inside the glass of which the prophet Jonah was sitting under his gourd; but what they were made of I do not know, though the gourd looked as if it were real greenery. On the other side of the mantelpiece hung silhouettes, picked out with gold, of Miss Alington's father and mother. Over the door there was the sabre of Miss Alington's brother, the Dragoon Guard, and on the window sill basking in the sun was a large white Persian cat with one blue eye and one green eye.

And I can see the General marching downstairs and Miss Alington leaning over the balustrade of the passage above and warning him that there were fourteen steps and to be sure not to think that he was safely in the front hall until he had passed the fourteenth. My cap was always hung upon the horns of an antelope, no doubt shot by that Dragoon Guard brother years ago, and I can hear the General telling me never to put on my hat until I was out of a lady's house. You may be sure there was no bustle about our exit. Miss Molyneux herself never made any more dignified exits than those the General and I made from Miss Alington's house in Edwardes Square. And when we were out on the pavement we used to look round and see Miss Alington's mittened hand waving us farewell, at which the General would take off his grey top hat and I my cap and we would both of us bow to Miss Alington with marked ceremoniousness. And nearly always when we had walked a dozen paces or so the General would say:

'I remember when Miss Alington was the prettiest gal of my acquaintance.'

It was easier for me to imagine those old *émigrés* than to imagine Miss Alington as a 'Gal'; but now that I am older myself I feel sure that General Brackenbury was quite right.

Yes, they are dearly remembered, those walks I went with the General, and I expect his old-fashioned opinions and hatred of so many things we feel nowadays it would be so narrow-minded to hate were very good for me.

WALKS AND RIDES

THOSE walks with the General bring back to my memory thoughts of so many other walks in that leisurely London of yesterday, bring back too, with a peculiar sharpness, the difference between a walk and a ride. Mark that I use the word 'ride.' Nowadays, I fancy 'ride' has almost been displaced by 'drive.' We rode on an omnibus in those days, and in doing so we implied that we consider an omnibus something better than a mere vehicle to convey us as quickly as possible to our destination. And when we went anywhere by the Underground Railway we 'travelled.'

Kew was a ride, the combination of a red omnibus to Hammersmith Broadway and an astonishingly slow green horse tram to Kew Bridge, for which as often as not we would have to wait a quarter of an hour at either end. What has happened to time? When I remember that the journey to Kew Gardens and back from our street could never have taken less than three hours, I ask myself how it was possible to extract from the afternoon enough time to make that visit to Kew Gardens the flowery epic it was. I suppose the explanation may be that we always chose a fine day for such an adventure, because to ride inside an omnibus or a tram was a sentence of imprisonment to the young, and that riding down to Kew was a flowery progress in itself when the lilacs and hawthorns were out all the way and the orchards beyond Chiswick were in full bloom.

If Kew was a ride, Richmond was a journey; and when we travelled to Richmond we were always as careful to arrive at West Kensington Station in good time to catch the train as if we had been setting out for the coast. We even looked it up beforehand in the A B C, for one might wait forty minutes in those days when trains only passed through West Kensington every twenty minutes, going alternatively to Ealing and to Richmond. It was at the station called Turnham Green that we really began to feel we had left London behind us for an afternoon. The very porters as they walked past the train warning passengers to change for somewhere or other wore an authentic rural air about them. We never went to Kew by train, though I remember a station called Gunnersbury, underneath the name of which FOR KEW GARDENS was temptingly painted. But Kew Gardens seemed too tame a destination on the days we went to Richmond. All very well the flowers of Kew; but we were bound for the vastness of Richmond Park. We should be seeing deer and perhaps getting gloriously lost in a magical woodland or perhaps catching some rare butterfly or finding some bird's nest before the sun went down.

Charles Dickens has been accused of sentimentalising the delight of driving by coach or chaise through the English countryside. We are assured by those full of confidence in the present that we should actually have much disliked the slowness and discomfort of such travel. If we use transport merely as a means of conveyance modern methods must win; but I know that I would put up with all the slowness and discomfort of it to be sitting once more on the top of an old horse omnibus, preferably in a front seat, with a descendant of Tony Weller on the box, spelling his name with a W, I fear, thanks to what is called education, but nevertheless having inherited enough of his great-grandfather's personality to be able to express himself nearly as picturesquely in spite of being so much better educated. He would be driving a pair of sleek and powerful bays, and he would never pull up the omnibus unless the road were dead level. He would have drawn on a fund of anecdotes for his front-seat passengers, who would all four of them become friendly with one another through their common enjoyment of the driver's rich humanity. When the conductor came up to collect the outside fares, he too would always have a capital tale about something which had happened inside or outside or about someone whom he had seen on the pavement to whom a capital tale was attached. The driver would be a beefy round-faced man seeming about to burst the strap that kept him in his seat like a fat baby boy in a two-wheeled perambulator, and in contrast to the driver the conductor would be sharp-featured with a store of cockney sarcasm and a slightly cynical and yet always tolerant attitude towards life developed from constantly having to deal with all classes and ages and sexes in that condition of enhanced stupidity to which travelling

132

renders the human race prone. That conductor I have in mind would be capable of reading a sharp lecture to a maiden lady on the ambiguity existing in her mind about her precise destination; but he would be incapable of not taking her arm to put her in kindly fashion safe upon the pavement. Both the driver and conductor would be in exceptionally good form, because it would be a cloudless morning at the end of May, and the watering cart crawling along in front of us would have laid the dust and be spreading that forgotten London fragrance which to attempt to recapture in words is to destroy. Those who never smelt it will not smell it from my pages. Those who smelt it long ago will smell it again at the mere words 'watering cart.' The omnibus would be passing that big bow window of Lady Burdett-Coutts's house where the china parrot used to sit upon its ring, and a moment later we outside passengers would be turning our heads to look over the wall of Devonshire House and watch a landau and pair come round from the stables to wait in front of the great portico. There would have been window boxes all the way down Piccadilly, and we should have had time to note an exceptionally fine mass of crude colour from geraniums or lobelias or calceolarias. The trees in the parks would have been wearing their brightest green. We outside fares on the top of that omnibus should all have been feeling when we alighted at Piccadilly Circus and threw away our twopenny blue tickets that the ride from Kensington High Street had not been a moment too long, and had somebody asked us if it had not been rather uncomfortable we should have wondered what on earth the fellow was talking about. No doubt, the internal combustion engine has made it easier to move about freely; but it has done so much to promote a dreary uniformity in people and places that simultaneously it has destroyed the reward of moving about.

But although we rode with a zest in the ride itself I am clear that we only rode with an object in view. If we walked it was for the sake of the walk itself, and this being stressed by our parents and guardians and governesses we were inclined to regard a walk as a kind of penal exercise. It was often necessary to cheat the mind of despair over the length of a dull street by walking only upon the cracks of the paving stones or by never walking upon the cracks, or by always stepping upon the coal plates or by never allowing the iron of a single one to ring beneath our feet. It was even necessary sometimes to adopt the desperate measure of ringing somebody's front doorbell in order to drive ourselves into running away as fast as possible and thus covering in a state of temporary excitement a long stretch of uninteresting pavement.

Yet these walks for the sake of walking were only relatively dull because time is so slow and space so long to the youthful fancy. Actually it was seldom that a walk did not produce something to stir the pulse, for the London streets were thronged with all sorts of queer characters in those days. The pavement artist still survives; but nowadays he sits in a dejected attitude beside a row of crudely framed pictures leaning against a wall or railing. He may or may not have chalked them himself. We no longer see him at work. In old days he worked before one's eyes on the paving stones and usually kept his marvellous collection of coloured chalks in a bag similar to that in which a carpenter carried his tools. He had a comparatively easy time when the weather was fine; but one shower could obliterate his work, and my impression of pavement artists in those days is that they were usually on their hands and knees, conjuring from the unsympathetic stone the illustrations of salmon on dishes or ships in distress that were such favourite subjects. The vendor of toys still survives; but his toys no longer cost a penny, and the press of foot traffic does not allow one to stand and stare at his tray for ten minutes with any degree of comfort.

There are still beggars, though I hardly like to use such a word for those respectable men and women who sit unobtrusively at quiet corners with trays of matches and bootlaces, both objects for which they have every right to expect a public demand. The beggars in those days often surpassed the wildest caricatures of Cruikshank in their *macabre* horror. It will not do to be regretting the disappearance of such ghastly creatures; but they did provide a thrill for the young. They were peripatetic too, many of them; and often did we turn round to flee in terror from their appearance, for we always associated those livid scars and fearful sores and distorted limbs with evil. These phantoms come back to my memory even passing along the prim quietude of our street. There was a woman with St Vitus's Dance dressed entirely in black crape and always wearing a pair of men's boots, to see whom come jigging by was enough to drive any of us back into the house, for her eyes had the milky blue of blindness; and yet she saw with them well enough to suppose that she saw us laughing at her, poor soul, so that she would stand twitching on the pavement, and then make a sudden dart to seize us, muttering oaths which chilled the blood. There was an old rat catcher who wore a moleskin cap and a red waistcoat, in and out of whose pockets were always crawling a couple of dozen white rats, crawling all over him and caressing his queer flat face as they squirmed round to snuggle down about his neck. There was an ancient female rag picker dressed in patchwork of all colours who used to go wandering along the gutter with her sharp pick poised like a spear to descend upon trifles she wanted for the basket she carried on her back. She was as jealous of her rights to any rubbish in her path as a miser over his gold, and one had to be careful in passing her, because she was capable of rushing at one with her pick, under the impression that some miserable relic in the gutter was going to be stolen from her under her nose. There were families of poor Irish, father, mother, and half a dozen farouche children who used to surround one and beg for a copper, the whole lot whining at once. I suppose the Germanic type of law and order by which we now are clogged has got rid of all these individualists, or perhaps they have been cut down by the relentless machine of modern life.

Does the youth of today ever find himself at war with what we used to call cads? We did, and to find ourselves cut off by a body of cads was as unpleasant an experience for us as for early American colonists to find themselves surrounded by Indians on the war path. We might not lose our scalps but we often lost our caps; and these wandering bodies of cads were a menace to any of us who ventured to walk where the confines of West Kensington merged almost imperceptibly with the dark hinterland of Fulham. For some reason cads had an implacable hostility to the straw hats we wore in summer, and if a couple of us came in sight of a largish body of cads we would always hear the war-cry in shrill cockney:

'Straw yard! Straw yard!'

Fortunately the cad was much more susceptible to pain than we were, so that a couple of us fighting back to back could usually maintain the honour of our class against as many as a dozen cads. Still, the cads were not particular in their choice of missiles, and if they disliked being punched and seldom came to close quarters they could put us in a pretty mess before we managed to retreat into our own territory. But the best fights were those on the large spaces of ground as yet unbuilt on. Those were our prairies, and for the right to roam about on them the aborigines fought us hard, especially when the snow lay thick and ammunition was plentiful.

Besides these chance encounters with cads there was open to us the adventure of walking through a slum. Actually within a few yards of our street there was an alley of old-fashioned cottages closed against wheeled traffic by a couple of posts, down which legend reported that no policeman dared venture to walk with a fellow. We dared one another continually to walk through this alley, but I cannot recall that any of us ever had the courage to take up such a challenge. Even to stand at a corner for a minute and eye the blowsy women gossiping across to one another from their windows was a severe test of our nerves. Perhaps there were more murders in that London of forty years ago, or perhaps the way 'Murder!' was shouted by the newsvendors to sell their papers at night brought murder nearer to us. Anyway, we all of us, as I remember, lived with the fear of being murdered continuously in our minds. No doubt we inherited the dark apprehensiveness that lingered from an earlier and more lawless London whose popular light reading was the Newgate Calendar and the Malefactors' Bloody Register, or the broadsheets hawked at public executions. It would not do to deplore the disappearance of what may be called domestic superstition, and yet I would argue that the imagination derives more benefit than harm from terror.

And then in the middle of what has come to seem that medieval existence the safety bicycle arrived as herald of to-day, and I can fancy now that from the moment I had a bicycle of my own the outer world became less vivid, the magic of ordinary things less potent. It would hardly be hyperbole to say I rode out of Eden on a bicycle. Still, it would not do to suggest that we were aware of the road we were taking. Indeed, if anything, we supposed that we were riding into Eden on our machines, as we significantly called them until affectionate familiarity with the new wonder evolved the de-

136

testable abbreviation 'bike.' Even my aunts took to bicycling, and I well remember the start of our first long expedition, which was Hampton Court. If my aunts had announced that we were setting out for Tokio it would not have seemed much farther to the other grown-ups in our street. I can see now my aunts' two bicycles propped against the curbstone, and their dignified mounting of them, and the way they draped their long skirts to hang decorously on either side of the saddle, and the look they gave over their shoulders to see that there was no traffic approaching from behind before they pressed the pedal firmly and glided forward the first few yards of the ten tremendous miles to Hampton Court. I can see Miss Lockett in the drawing-room window of Number 3 in more of a tremble than usual with alarm for their safety.

'Why they are called safety bicycles I do not know,' Miss Lockett used to lament. 'I cannot imagine anything more dreadfully dangerous.'

However, we did reach Hampton Court, and what is more we managed to get back home again without having so much as a skid.

But these bicycling expeditions were almost at the end of the time I spent in our street, and I do not associate it with such recent triumphs of progress as bicycles. It is an earlier Kensington of which I find myself dreaming mostly, when indeed a few people rode high bicycles for the amusement of the youthful cads who made a point of running along and yelling derisive remarks at the riders, but which, as I dream of it, seems empty of all traffic. I hear the remote tinkle of a muffin man's bell on some sad November afternoon. I hear a barrel organ in some far-away street, intangible as the wandering voice of the cuckoo about a wide countryside. I hear a hurdy-gurdy droning a hymn tune, and gaze for a moment or two at the blind man who turns the handle, a tattered cloak round his shoulders, a shade over his eyes. And when all music is still I hear the lisp of the dead leaves along the pavement on some windless golden October day. I see the pale green of the lime-tree buds bursting from their sheaths pink and delicate as shells. I see the first butterfly of the dancing year white against the blue April sky between the tall thin houses. I smell the freshly watered window boxes in the summer gloaming, and the hot potatoes on the spiked oven of the baked-potato man, when the pavement rang with frost in the swift December dusk. I taste the slightly metallic water in the chained cups of the old drinking fountains which kindly folk long dead had placed for wayfarers. There was a battered old milestone by one of them which said 4 miles to London and 9 miles to Hounslow. I taste the sweets in the shop kept by three old ladies, all of whom had heavy moustaches and beards, those sweets which would taste sadly alike nowadays, but whose flavours to the unspoilt palate of childhood required half an hour's discussion before a choice was made between them. I read old advertisements on the big hoarding just before we turned off the main thoroughfare into the road that led down our street. I look at the big blue poster of the *Daily Telegraph* and read in huge cursive letters *Circulation over half a million. Largest in the world.* I read of the wonders of Sapolio as a soap, and what could be more poignant than the thought of a soap which is no longer made, let alone used? I look at the pictures of old ballets and the bills of old farces. I gaze for a penny into a peepshow and am thrilled by the crude illustrations of a murder committed a century since. I stand in a crowd of children gathered by the reedy tune of the showman's panpipes and am absorbed in the drama of Punch and Judy. And then I watch a queer figure come slowly down our street. On his back is a big drum, with a pair of cymbals on top of that. With one hand he plays a flageolet. With the other he beats a side drum or strikes the triangle attached to it. With one foot he pulls a string which beats the drum and sounds the cymbals. He wears a white top hat with a lot of sleigh bells round it which he shakes, and as I follow this extraordinary one-man orchestra entranced, I meet another eccentric with what looks like a tall white hat, but which is really a bowler surrounded by the fly papers he is advertising and a sheaf of which he carries like newspapers and peels off for the eager maids who stand by area gates to buy them at his cry of, 'Catch 'em alive-O!' And then as these figures recede I am jumping off my bicycle to buy the first number of the *Daily Mail* and thinking, as I look at the clear uncrowded type and read for a halfpenny six times as much as I could ever find to read about in the *Daily Telegraph* for a penny, what a really good newspaper somebody has had the common sense to publish at last.

The world of today is rising.

NUMBER 21

IT MAY have occurred to some readers that my youthful existence was a perpetual holiday. This was not so by any means. I was given plenty of work to do, though my father's prejudice against schools kept me unattached to any regular educational system. Instead I had various tutors; but as this is not a conscientious account of a boy's education, of which we have had enough for the present, I shall mention but one of them, and that only because he lived in our street at Number 21. He was the only son of a retired business man of extreme plumpness, who to his father's pride had won a scholarship at Pembroke College, Oxford, from the City of London School. I forget who preceded the Joliffes at Number 21, but it was nobody who made the least mark on the life of our street. The Joliffes, however, became characteristic from the first moment we saw stout Mr Joliffe and stout Mrs Joliffe walking along our street followed by a more than stout Manchester terrier, by coming to the rescue of which in a fight with Roy, the Gurneys' Airedale, I first got to know them. They happened to hear my Aunt Adelaide mention that the tutor I was then under could not be available one July and suggested that their son Henry would be delighted to tackle the job when he came down from Oxford at the end of the summer term. They were so grateful to me for rescuing Kaffir, their obese and elderly terrier, from the ferocious Roy of the Gurneys that I think they were intending to pledge Henry's leisure without any fee. Luckily for Henry my aunt would not agree to this.

'He's a splendid scholar, my boy Henry,' Mr Joliffe declared, his little twinkling eyes orbed with admiration of his son's learning. 'He took to Latin and Greek like a duck to water, and Mrs Joliffe and me said if he could win a scholarship we'd see to it that he went to college. He's intending to be a schoolmaster, and he'll welcome any chance to get his hand in with a bit of teaching.'

I looked forward a little anxiously to my first glimpse of young Mr Joliffe. The tales of his scholastic prowess had created in my fancy the picture of a young man sicklied o'er with the pale cast of thought, and I was beginning to wonder in some trepidation how this earnest young scholar would feel about my tendency to forget the rules of *oratio obliqua* by putting an imperfect indicative where an imperfect subjunctive was required. None of my tutors hitherto had turned out to be the bogy I anticipated; but I could never get rid of the preliminary anxiety over a new one, and Mr Henry Joliffe did sound more alarmingly learned than any of them.

'Who can this young man be?' I heard my Aunt Adelaide exclaim one drizzling morning as from the dining-room window she caught a glimpse of a visitor on the way up our front-door steps.

I peeped cautiously out at an extremely plump young man, who, wearing a light Newmarket coat cut in at the waist as much as its wearer's figure allowed, was twisting the waxed ends of a small golden moustache set in the middle of an almost perfectly round face coloured a uniform pink. The door was opened, and he vanished inside our hall, whence Janet came in with the card of Mr Henry Joliffe, Pembroke College, Oxford.

'Your new tutor,' exclaimed my aunt, and though she was trying to appear as grave as the occasion demanded, her grey eyes were twinkling with merriment and she looked round instinctively for the dancing speedwell eyes of Aunt Emily to share the joke. But Aunt Emily was out, and Aunt Adelaide had to compose her mirth in order to present me with appropriate solemnity, for it was being impressed upon me about this time that my Latin verbs were inclined to exceed in irregularity the most irregular in the tables of conjugation.

In the hall she paused for a moment to glance at young Mr Joliffe's overcoat hanging upon a peg, as if to reassure herself that her eyes had not deceived her. But there it hung, almost seeming capable of laying the odds itself and looking the very antithesis to the gown of a classical scholar.

Nor was young Mr Joliffe's appearance without his overcoat less intensely sporting, for he was wearing a check suite of definite, even aggressive, individuality, the horsy suggestion of which was enhanced by an Ascot tie of white piqué and the fox's head with ruby eyes of his pin. In spite of his clothes Mr

Joliffe's manner was shy, and while he was talking to my aunt about the potter's clay he was to mould, myself to wit, his pink cheeks deepened to carmine and the tight golden curls, already thinned one had to presume by the labour of the book reader rather than that of the bookmaker, seemed to glisten with embarrassment.

Even when my aunt left us alone to discuss the course of our researches into the Latin language during the next month Mr Joliffe remained shy for some time, until in a sudden burst of confidence he ejaculated:

'I say, do you know you're my first pup?'

It did not dawn on me immediately what he meant by this remark, and the dignity which surrounds the growing boy was perhaps a little wounded for a moment. However, as he evidently did not intend to claim the grown-up privilege of insulting the defenceless young, and as his whole manner beamed with good will, I forgave the curious epithet.

'It's most awfully good of your people to let me try my hand out like this,' Mr Joliffe continued. 'I hope I shan't make an ass of myself. And now let's see where you stand in Latin.'

After he had probed my knowledge of the Latin primer as gently as a careful dentist probes his patient's teeth, Mr Joliffe declared that I was famously ahead for a boy of my age, and inquired if I did not find learning Latin the most exciting thing that ever happened to me. I could not honestly reply that I had, though I tempered his disappointment as well as I knew how by adding that I did not think any lessons particularly exciting.

'Well, it's my job to make you think all the lessons you have with me as exciting as a box of fireworks,' Mr Joliffe declared enthusiastically.

And I am glad to remember now that if any of my tutors ever did nearly succeed in making the prescribed study of dead languages not absolutely annihilatingly dull it was Mr Joliffe. Yet ultimately it was not for the Latin and Greek he managed to impart that I derived most benefit from Mr Joliffe's coaching of me at intervals over several years, but for the freedom he allowed me of his small but eminently *fin de siècle* library. From Mr Mellor I could borrow what had been the most advanced books of the 'seventies. In my Aunt Adelaide's library I could find most of the books that moved the 'eighties with their modernity. On the shelves of Mr Joliffe's study almost at the top of Number 21 I could thrill myself with the slim gilt volumes of the 'nineties when the moment arrived to be stirred by these dazzling revelations of life as it really is.

Mr Joliffe became a master at St. James's School when he left the university, and his Newmarket overcoat and check suit and Ascot tie and fox-head pin were never seen again. In tail coat and glossy silk hat and sombre black silk tie he went down the steps of Number 21 at exactly ten minutes past nine every morning, went up them again at exactly twelve minutes past one, went down them again at exactly a quarter to three, and went up them again at exactly ten minutes past five. And this he continued to do for all the rest of the time I lived in our street for nearly two hundred days every year, and for twenty-five years afterwards. I used to wonder if, during the fortnight's holiday he allowed himself every year, he ever put on again those bright garments of his youth; but I fear not. I think he had reversed the natural order and turned from a butterfly into a caterpillar. I was the first of countless private pupils, and every hour of his time out of school was occupied with coaching. Apart from that annual fortnight the long holidays of a schoolmaster were spent in private coaching or preparing his next term's work in school. I suppose he really enjoyed teaching, and I hope that most of his pupils rewarded his patience and enthusiasm more handsomely than I did. I did try my best to simulate a passionate interest in defective and deponent verbs, but I could not manage it, though a defective or deponent human being aroused my liveliest curiosity. I tried to shudder with him at a final cretic, but thought in my heart that the writers of iambic verse had laid upon themselves a quite unnecessary hardship in resolving to avoid such a useful trisyllable. I simply could not work myself up into a condition of excitement over a proleptic epithet, and the most audacious zeugma left me unmoved.

'Now, here we are,' Mr Joliffe used almost to gibber in a voice husky with emotion and the deep puffs he had taken at that huge pipe which was filled with latakia and perique. I have been driven into syllepsis myself as I try to recapture the scene!

'Here we are! You see what's coming?' Mr Joliffe would pant, his throat whistling.

I would shake my head.

142

'Oh, yes, you do, my dear fellow.'

Another shake.

'Why, a most glorious hendiadys!'

Then he would gaze lovingly at the page of Virgil as if the page were an oak tree and the hendiadys a purple-emperor butterfly, himself an entomologist rather than an etymologist.

'By Jove, it's an absolute beauty,' he would gloat.

Then he would cast his mind back to where such another splendid grammatical creature could be found, puffing hard and huskily at the huge pipe, which would wheeze back at him like a pet answering its master's whistle. The locality of the hendiadys he had been trying to remember would occur to him. The pipe would be laid down on his desk with a bump.

'Take this note,' he would command, and he would give the whereabouts of the rarity, probably in another book of Virgil's Æneid or Georgics. And if I did not start turning over the pages with the eagerness of a terrier scraping out the earth from a rabbit hole to worry and shake that other hendiadys he would sigh huskily refill his pipe, and murmur:

'I do wish you were really keen.'

When old Mr and Mrs Joliffe were still living with their son, before Henry got married and then went down into the country, old Mr Joliffe used sometimes to intercept me for a moment in the hall on my way up to his son's study and ask how I was getting on with my lessons.

'Quite well, thank you,' I used to reply, for the most truthful boy does not suppose that questions like this are meant to be answered except with formal courtesy.

'I believe you are,' old Mr Joliffe used to gurgle enthusiastically. 'I believe you're learning things you never dreamt you'd be learning, eh?'

I once informed old Mr Joliffe when he had pressed me more than usually hard on what I had been learning with his son that we had been reading Xenophon's anabasis, at which old Mr Joliffe shook his head gravely and said he could quite believe it.

Occasionally my tutor would take me with him to a large second-hand bookshop over in Paddington, his object being to acquire the standard commentaries upon the classics from which he could extract those various readings, the comparison and discussion of which so much excited him. While Mr Joliffe was digging about in the shelves to discover a cheap edition of Conington's or Papillon's Virgil, I would mount a ladder and ransack the dusty topmost shelves of the big bookshop for some bargain within my means. It was thus I found James Thomson's *City of Dreadful Night* in which I revelled as if it were a nightmare of my own. On the top shelf, too, I found Vondel's *Lucifer* to which Milton was said to have been so much indebted for *Paradise Lost*, and having a great dislike for Milton's politics I read this ponderous work with the liveliest delight in the accusations of plagiarism levelled against the great Puritan poet. And then one evening, when it was time to relinquish the pleasure of delving among books, I noticed Mr Joliffe take down from a shelf two or three volumes bound in pink of an unusual shade and ask the price of them.

'Half a crown a volume,' said the assistant, and I remember being puzzled by Mr Joliffe's manner of slightly guilty self-consciousness as he laid the money down and put the volumes under his arm. It was as if he had been caught out in an unpardonably frivolous action, and in fact I was mildly surprised when instead of leaving the shop with a portly calf-bound text of Horace or Cæsar edited by some polysyllabic German pundit he carried away with him as the only spoils of an inquisitive hour those brightly bound numbers of a quarterly magazine called the *Savoy*. He would hardly buy them today for less than ten guineas if the second-hand book catalogues I receive are to be credited. This was probably the last frivolous purchase Mr Joliffe ever made. It was perhaps the final twitch of his butterfly wings. As for me, I took an early opportunity of borrowing those pink volumes from the library at Number 21. Bewitched by the drawings of Aubrey Beardsley I craved to explore more deeply the hothouses of *fin de siècle* literature.

It was soon after this that I found on Mr Joliffe's shelves a volume bound in that shade of green which as I supposed was the Grosvenor Gallery greenery-yallery that so much revolted the beefy mind of W. S. Gilbert. *Intentions* was not an exciting title; but the name of the author was sufficiently exciting to make me decide not to ask Mr Joliffe if I might borrow this book, but to borrow it and if possible return it without his ever noticing that it had left his shelves. Why those elaborate conversations between Vivian and Cyril should have given me such an acute intellectual thrill I am at loss to explain; but I recognise that the young of today are getting comparable thrills from writers of considerably less talent than Oscar Wilde, and once more I allow myself to be perplexed by the phenomenon. I hear what seem to me now the most preposterous charlatans being acclaimed as genuinely creative forces in literature, and I wonder what is the secret of their spell over youthful taste. I have gone through the same experience myself in admiring the inferior work of Oscar Wilde and many lesser writers than him, but that does not help me to solve this problem of aesthetics, by allowing myself to ponder over which I have introduced a false note into the simple straightforward little composition of our street. Yet perhaps I have not, for though I should like to pretend to myself that our street exists as it always was, unchanged and unchangeable like a picture in a cherished picture book, I have to admit that like almost every other apparently secure entity it has been changed by the ruthless catalysis of time, and just as to my fancy the purchase of those pink volumes of the *Savoy* by Mr Joliffe celebrated his final surrender to remaining what he was where he was, the perusal of them by myself symbolised the abandonment of being what I was where I was.

I remember that, while I sat reading that green volume of Oscar Wilde, Sir George Griffin's largest garden party of that season was scattered about his lawns, and that as I read on, intoxicated by the meretricious paradoxes of *Intentions*, I looked down upon the outspread scene with a conviction that I belonged to a fresher and more potent world. Those guests seemed to me dull and old-fashioned, overburdened by the meaningless trammels of convention, and possessing, none of them, the key to reality which had just been handed to me by the glittering Vivian and the plausible Cyril.

It was as much *à la mode* in those days for the young æsthete to sneer at the Royal Academy as it is for the shell-shocked young intellectual of today, and Sir George Griffin's garden party that afternoon was apparently composed entirely of the kind of people that maintained the Royal Academy. The very strains of the Hungarian band concealed in one of the big shrubberies affected me, under the influence of Vivian and Cyril, with a nausea of the commonplace, and I turned with relief to look down at the aristocratic lunatics wandering about on the lawns of Sheba Lodge next door, each in a privacy of mad dreams. I remember one female figure in black satin hung with pinchbeck chains who was following cautiously in the wake of a peacock, ever hoping the bird would shed a feather as it strutted along. Any such feather she would leap forward and pick up to put with a small sheaf of peacock's feathers she used to carry under her arm and which after many months of following that bird about the grounds of the asylum was still slim enough. I had watched her often before, and I had never yet seen the peacock oblige her by dropping a single feather; but this afternoon he dropped two in quick succession, to the evident delight of that solitary fantastic figure. I thought of the peacock's feathers in vases on my Aunt Adelaide's mantelpiece, and of how at one time not so long ago everybody with any pretensions to an artistic interior collected peacocks' feathers in their vases. It had been Oscar Wilde himself who was supposed to have started a fashion which already the glittering Vivian and the plausible Cyril would have regarded with as much contempt as the guests of Sir George Griffin would have regarded that solitary eccentric on the other side of the glass-covered wall beyond the music of the Hungarian band. I began to meditate with rising excitement on the way I would shock the conventional world under the inspiration of such a dialogue as that on the decay of lying; and, dreaming thus of a new world coming, I did not notice that Sir George Griffin's party was breaking up, for when I looked again and saw his lawns empty except for the chairs scattered about on the grass and one lace parasol which a guest had left behind, I felt as if the thronged scene had been magically dissolved with a Prospero's wand of my own fancy.

The following afternoon when I visited Mr Joliffe to grapple with the Syracusan expedition and a particularly difficult speech of Nicias which I had ill prepared I took the opportunity of my tutor's preoccupation with some alternative reading of Thucydides to replace the green volume of *Intentions* upon his shelf.

'Did you enjoy that book?' he asked, without looking up.

I was taken aback for a moment and stammered some would-be jaunty but in effect imbecile reply.

'Well, I hardly think you are old enough to appreciate it,' my tutor observed, 'and I'd rather that in future you didn't borrow my books without consulting me first.'

The chance to escape from the Athenian camp and that long speech of Nicias by involving Mr Joliffe in an argument about my ability to appreciate the glittering Vivian and the plausible Cyril was too valuable not to be seized, and in the end I had the gratification of making my tutor shake that head of his, which was by this date almost denuded of those bright little golden curls.

'Well,' he said, 'I suppose each generation is just a little more knowing than its predecessor.'

Knowing was hardly the epithet I should have used myself for the profound worldly wisdom I felt I already possessed; but I let it pass, and happy over what I considered an intellectual victory I did not grudge Mr Joliffe the opportunity of demonstrating to me that, however thorough my appreciation of the paradoxes fired at one another by Vivian and Cyril, the very first sentence of the speech of Nicias could tie me up into knots. But though at the time I was feeling I was much too brilliant a young creature to be cooped up any longer in the restricted sphere of our street, I feel now that in recapturing that phase of my life there it is a most unwelcome intrusion of self-conscious modernity, and I am wrath with myself for not having managed to avoid it. But this shall be the end of such vapourings. Aubrey Beardsley and Oscar Wilde and the immature ambitions of approaching adolescence shall all be forgotten in the completely Victorian atmosphere of Number 23.

WHEN recalling the past the tendency is always to make it static in retrospect. My tutoring by Mr Joliffe must have been spread over six or seven years; but I always see him as I saw him first standing on the doorstep of Number 9 in that light Newmarket overcoat and then a moment afterwards as I saw him for the last time, leaning over his desk in a cloud of tobacco smoke to check some reference in Thucydides, the top of his head already bald except for two or three isolated curls. My intercourse with the Gurneys must have extended over several years, but I always see them when Gladys was about fourteen, Muriel about twelve, Dorothy about ten, and Bob about thirteen. They were living in our street when I first went to stay with my aunts, and they were still living in it when, very soon after that state of mind induced in myself by reading *Intentions*, my aunts ceased to live there and my own frequent visits to our street became past history. Yet I can only think of the Gurneys as they would have remained for no more than a single year. This subjugation of time by memory adds much to the pleasure of looking back especially to childish friendships, for these wax and wane, and so what stays in the mind is always a friendship in the zenith of its intimacy.

I once read in an American magazine for the young, which may or may not have been *St Nicholas* a story about an extremely naughty family called the Scaramouches who were under the sway of a fantastically severe governess. No incident from the story remains with me except this governess's punishment for leaving fat upon their plates, which was to be made to eat the equivalent quantity in yellow soap. I regret to say that I do not remember the name of this remarkable woman, who, however, had a rival in real life called Miss Bearsted.

To look at Miss Bearsted one would never have suspected her of being a martinet. She was a little woman always dressed in the depths of dark dowdiness. Her figure simply did not exist. It looked just like something which had been pushed hastily into a bag, so hastily that it had made a hole in the bottom and allowed a pair of elastic-sided boots to slip through. Miss Bearsted wore, winter and summer, a black straw hat fastened to her head by a piece of elastic under a bun of skimpy hair, and, winter and summer, whenever she went out of doors she wore a respirator of black gauze over her mouth, the elastic fastener of which was pinned by a black safety pin to the elastic band of her straw hat. I never see people wearing respirators nowadays; but they were not uncommon at that date, and they gave to the faces of those who wore them an expression of open-mouthed astonishment, until one was close enough to see what it really was that made them appear to be gaping perpetually. In spite of her severity Miss Bearsted was apparently capable of rousing affection in the hearts of her pupils, and seldom was she seen walking along the pavement of our street without two of them hanging on her arms and looking likely to drag the poor little woman prone on the pavement.

Mr Gurney was a magistrate or official of some kind in one of our tropical colonies, so he was only seen at long intervals in our street. He was a big jovial man with a complexion like mahogany and a voice of brass; but, though when he was home on leave, Number 23 radiated hospitality and entertainment, even he dared not plan a visit to the Zoo or the Earl's Court Exhibition without obtaining leave from Miss Bearsted first for her pupils to enjoy the treat. As for Mrs Gurney, she deferred entirely to the little governess in all matters connected with her daughters. She was a tall handsome woman of the statuesque type; but beyond shaking hands with her at the end of a party and thanking her for the jolly evening we had passed we saw little of her, and she did not make much impression on the young people of the neighbourhood. For us Miss Bearsted and her Draconian rule represented the personality of Number 23. Even Bob Gurney when he was home from school for the holidays had to bend before Miss Bearsted's frigid disapproval, and it was rumoured that she illustrated with a hairbrush her views on the conduct of schoolboys.

Yet in spite of Miss Bearsted's discipline the Gurneys were the naughtiest children of our acquaintance. The Spinks without any kind of discipline at home except an occasional outburst of rage from their father were not really naughty. It was empiricism, not naughtiness, which led Almeric Spink to give Polly a bottle of ink to drink. He was not trying to mesmerize her out of mischief but in an access of scientific curiosity. The Gurneys, on the other hand, once they did escape from the range of Miss Bearsted's stern and somewhat ichthyoidal eye, made up in a few minutes for hours of chastened behaviour under her supervision.

Tea on Saturday afternoon at the Gurneys' was a solemn affair, with Miss Bearsted sitting at the head of the table. Even guests did not like to expose themselves to her biting sarcasm.

'Let me see. Did you open the door for me?' she once said to me when tea was over and I happened to be nearest the door of the morning room at the moment when Miss Bearsted led the way upstairs to preside over the intellectual games set out for our diversion. I had not opened the door for Miss Bearsted. I had been gazing out of the window just then to watch the progress through the November dusk of a Guy Fawkes procession. Blushing with confusion, I hastened to display the courtesy she expected, for which I received an icy 'Thank you.'

Should one of the guests at Number 23 find himself leaning upon the table with his elbows, he would presently become aware that from the other end of it a pair of coldly critical eyes under a pair of arched eyebrows were fixed upon his slovenly posture, while the Gurney girls sat with downcast looks and chewed with most ladylike mastication the large and thick slice of bread and butter which had to precede, thrice repeated, the small piece of madeira or seed cake allowed us a reward for the successful dispatch of the bread and butter. When that basilisk glance of Miss Bearsted was cast upon the lounging guest, she might have been in the act of raising her own cup of tea to her lips. In that case the cup of tea would remain poised in mid-air until the guest removed his elbow from the table, which done, Miss Bearsted would utter a deep sigh, shake her head, and allow the interrupted cup to reach her lips at last. My friend Olive used at first to be able to hold out longest against Miss Bearsted's blasting stare; but in the end even Olive surrendered. Perhaps she dreaded being ordered out of the room by Miss Bearsted and her own inability to refuse to obey the humiliating command. But what definitely broke Olive's nerve was when one afternoon she whispered such a funny story to Muriel Gurney that Muriel, despite Miss Bearsted's quelling presence, exploded, unfortunately at a moment when her mouth was full of the faintly coloured liquid that Miss Bearsted called tea. She always drank her own from a specially brewed pot.

'Muriel,' said Miss Bearsted, in a tone of frigid disgust, 'retire to your room. I will see you there in due course.'

Muriel was an exceptionally pretty girl with wavy chestnut hair kept like everybody and everything else at Number 23 in severe restraint by Miss Bearsted, a large semicircular comb dragging it back from her high forehead and two black ribbons preventing the plaits behind from breaking over her shoulder in a foam of curls. Her complexion was always high; but when she heard Miss Bearsted's sentence her cheeks crimsoned in a deep blush as she murmured her penitence and begged the governess to overlook the accident.

'Are you venturing to argue with me, Muriel?' Miss Bearsted inquired in a tone of shocked incredulity. 'Surely you know by now that argument always involves you in still further unpleasant consequences.'

'But I say, Miss Bearsted,' Olive broke in, as Muriel rose to obey her sentence, 'you can't punish Muriel for what was my fault. She only laughed because I told her something.'

'No doubt your mother, Lady Marjorie, has often reminded you, Olive,' said Miss Bearsted, 'that when a little girl is invited out to a friend's house it is not her business to comment upon what takes place there. And even if you suppose the tea table to be a suitable place at which to whisper stories, Muriel does not. Muriel will take her punishment, fully aware that she deserves it, for an unpardonable breach of table manners, and if, as I hope she will, she takes her punishment with a proper sense of how much she had deserved it, Muriel may be allowed to rejoin us in the schoolroom after tea and take her part in the games.'

'But, Miss Bearsted – ' Olive tried again.

'Silence, Olive, if you please, or I shall have to ask you to put on your hat and coat and return to your own home.'

'And that's what I jolly well ought to have done, Olive said to me afterwards.

'But you didn't,' I observed a little sarcastically, for Olive had laughed a good deal at my snub from Miss Bearsted over the door at the last tea party, and I wished her to recognise that she was no better able than the rest of us to stand up to Miss Bearsted.

'No, dash it, I didn't,' Olive candidly admitted, and I noticed that she never again whispered funny stories at the Gurney tea parties.

The thought of Muriel waiting up in her room for Miss Bearstead kept us all silent for the rest of the meal, and it comes back to me that we tried to propitiate the fierce little governess by listening with extra attention to her tale of how Cleopatra's Needle was brought all the way from Egypt as a present to Queen Victoria.

Miss Bearsted left us in the schoolroom to prepare for the games while she 'saw' Muriel in her room, and those of us that were guests sat ill at ease, wondering at the callousness of Muriel's two sisters, who took advantage of the absence of their governess to show us with what skill they could turn cartwheels.

The suspense became intolerable. I think we were expecting to hear at any moment the house rent by Muriel's shrieks.

'What will she do to her?' somebody asked at last in an uncomfortable whisper.

'She'll probably use a slipper,' said Dorothy Gurney, 'because that's what Muriel hates most.'

As she spoke she turned another cartwheel and with her whirling legs knocked the wind out of a very fat boy called Hungerford.

'Goo!' Hungerford gasped. 'Goo-gah! Goo! Goo! Gah! Goo-goo-goo!'

I am glad to be able to record that Hungerford was still bent double when Miss Bearsted returned with Muriel, and still making those strange noises, because it enabled us all to concentrate upon Hungerford's efforts to recapture his breath, and so to avoid the embarrassment of pretending not to notice that Muriel had been crying.

'What is the matter with you, Claude?' Miss Bearsted inquired, with a frown at his contortions.

'Goo!' the fat boy answered ambiguously.

'Have you hurt yourself?' she pressed.

'Ooo! I'm all ri – ah now,' Hungerford averred.

Miss Bearsted looked round the room for enlightenment, and I, fearing for Dorothy to whom about the time of the tea party I was inclined to fancy myself sentimentally attached, explained hastily that I had pushed Hungerford against the table by mistake and knocked his wind out. In taking upon myself the blame for Hungerford's odd sounds I felt a bit of a knight-errant, and I was a little hurt to perceive no trace of a grateful smile upon Dorothy's pretty face. She was not living up to the romantic conception of her I had formed, and turning to look at Muriel I decided that she was more attractive than her younger sister. At the moment with her tear-stained cheeks she appeared to me the perfect damsel in distress, and I longed to rescue her from Miss Bearsted and by my devotion make up for all that she had suffered.

'Strange behaviour indeed,' Miss Bearsted observed. 'I hope we shall have no more of this horseplay. We are not used to horseplay in our schoolroom. And now, I think, we had better sit down to the Counties of England, Northern Section.'

This was not an invitation to lessons but to a game.

Counties of England was played on the same principle as Happy Families; but instead of collecting the family of Mr Potts the Painter or Mr Chip the Carpenter one collected the chief towns of an English county. Now, in Happy Families when one has a member of the Dip family one may ask another player if Miss Dip, the Dyer's daughter, is at home. If Miss Dip does happen to be at home she is surrendered without a murmur by the player who holds her picture. Not so in Counties of England. Suppose the aim was to complete the County Palatine, of which one might hold Manchester and Bolton. After racking the brain to remember another town in Lancashire, one might ask for Oldham. Was Oldham immediately surrendered by the player who held it? By no means. Before parting with Oldham he had a right to ask his opponent the population of Oldham, the chief industry of Oldham, and its geographical situation. If the petitioner failed to answer, the player who held Oldham might refuse to part with it and might extract from his late petitioner the city of Manchester, provided of course that he knew more about Manchester than his late petitioner had known about Oldham. This game, designed for instructive amusement, was in practice severely trying to the nerves of the contestants, and it invariably caused heated arguments over some of the replies.

Miss Bearsted's methods of dealing with any arguments

among her own pupils was to say in a sharp voice, 'Cease arguing!' and rap the offender on the head with a forefinger encased in a thimble. If the guest argued, she ruled the county involved out of the game. Perhaps this was the only way the game would ever have come to an end, for I never remember any of the players managing to collect all the towns of a county and thus complete even one set. When this game had come to and end because Miss Bearsted had withdrawn all the cards from circulation, we played another game the name of which I forget, but I know that counters were gradually amassed by answering questions like, 'What is ink made of?' or, 'Which is the world's highest volcano?'

After this, Miss Bearsted was wont to relax for a few minutes and join us in a game of Snap.

The conclusion of that game was foregone. The victor was always Miss Bearsted. The little governess loved Snap, and she was a demon player. Normally she had a frigid but somewhat shaky voice. Her devastating rebukes and threats of punishment were drawled out. They communicated to the listener a feeling that Miss Bearsted was staggering like Bunyan under a pack of sins – the sins of her pupils, of course, not her own. The way she walked gave an impression of utter weariness, as if her frail and crooked body could not much longer support the burden of her moral responsibility. Her eyes usually lacked lustre. Her hands were cold as frogs. But the instant the cards were dealt for a game of Snap and we all sat round the table waiting for her to give the signal for the first player to turn his card, Miss Bearsted's personality changed. Her shoulders which normally drooped like a bottle squared themselves. Her fishy grey-blue eyes glinted. Her voice lost that fatigued drawl and took on the timbre of a rattle.

'Be careful now, everybody, to turn the cards towards the table. The first player who turns a card away from the table and towards himself will forfeit all his cards to the pool and will not be allowed to snap in again. Are you all ready? Begin, Gladys.'

It was almost frightening to see the way Miss Bearsted's eyes would dart round the table as bright as a hawk's. She made us so nervous that we stammered and hesitated every time we thought we saw two similar cards lying face upwards. Not so Miss Bearsted. Snap! Her voice cracked like a whip, and she would sweep an arm across the table to scoop up the two heaps she had captured. Snap! Snap! It was always the voice of Miss Bearsted which was first. We none of us stood a chance against her passionate will to win. I recall few spectacles in the course of my life which have inspired such awe as the sight of Miss Bearsted when only one opponent was left and she held before her nearly all the rest of the pack. A rabbit fascinated by a large and sinister snake; a mouse in the claws of a cat; even an English heavyweight boxer stepping into the ring to meet an American defender of the title – none of these provides a sufficiently vivid contrast between weakness and strength to be used as an effective comparison for one of us, with a few cards left, turning the top card under the eyes of Miss Bearsted, leaning forward hungrily over the rest of the pack.

Snap! The rabbit is swallowed. The mouse has been crunched up. The English heavyweight boxer is on his back. Miss Bearsted has won the game.

One day after Miss Bearsted had won two games of Snap and one of Cork Grab at which she was no less of an adept, her hand coming down for the cork with the ferocity of a falcon's talons striking a pigeon, Olive suggested a game of Old Maid.

I do not believe Olive intended to score off Miss Bearsted. It was a game we often played among ourselves. But the little governess took it personally.

'We do not play such vulgar and stupid games in this house,' she said. 'Were Gladys or Muriel or Dorothy to suggest such a game, she would be severely punished.'

And Miss Bearsted glared at Olive with an expression of such malevolence that Olive stirred uneasily upon her chair as if she were half afraid that Miss Bearsted would in another moment deal with her as rigorously as she was accustomed to deal with her own pupils.

Yet, as I have said, remove the young Gurneys from the immediate overlooking of their governess, and they were the worst-behaved children in the neighbourhood. Such an episode as that when Olive and I drank the mould of unset lemon sponge was exceptional. But let Dorothy Gurney find herself in another house, and she was inside the store cupboard within ten minutes. Currants and sultanas were her particular fondness, and she could turn a pound of currants into an ounce like magic. Candied peel attracted her. So for that matter did ordinary lump sugar. I suppose it was Miss Bearsted's belief in bread and butter which aroused this protestantism in Dorothy's inside. Our cook Hetty once declared she would as soon turn a giraffe loose in the kitchen of Number 9 as that long-necked young Turk from Number 23.

'Believe it or not, Janet, but if she didn't turn the bread pan upside down and stand on it to reach up and start in picking at my mincemeat, and which I'd carefully pushed away to the back of the very top shelf. "Well," I said, "well, if that don't beat the band." And what do you think she had the blaring impudence and sauce to give me as a back answer?'

'I wouldn't like to say what she mightn't give you,' observed Janet dourly.

' "Oh," says her highness as calm as a cucumber, and really I could have boxed her ears, "Oh," she says, "your mincemeat isn't half so nice as what the Clyburns' mincemeat is. There's too much suet in it." '

' "Suet?" I said, speaking very sharp for me, for I was really a bit aggravated by now, "suet," I said, "I'll suet you, you naughty girl, if you don't get down off of that bread pan and take your messy fingers out of my mincemeat. Let me just tell Miss Bearsted what you've been up to, and you know what you'd get." And what do you think she up and flung back at me as daring as a savage? "Yes, Hetty," she says, "I know what I'd get and where I'd get it," and with that she grabbed a handful of coffee beans with one hand and a tomato with the other and took her hook out of my kitchen before I could say Jack Robinson.'

If Dorothy Gurney's *forte* away from Miss Bearsted was robbing larders, her sister Muriel's was climbing ladders. Muriel could not see a ladder without climbing up to the top of it and then sliding down with her legs and arms round the uprights.

Claude Hungerford, the fat boy of the neighbourhood, was once standing at the foot of a ladder up which Muriel had climbed.

'Watch me slide down, Claude,' her light laughing voice called.

And before Claude's slow gaze had focused itself upon Muriel's dainty form, he was lying prostrate on the ground with Muriel on top of him.

'You've hurt my nose, Muriel,' he blubbed.

'Pooh, you cry-baby,' she scoffed, 'it wouldn't hurt *your* nose if a ton of bricks fell on it.'

'It would,' Hungerford moaned.

'No, it wouldn't, because it isn't a nose at all.'

'It is a nose,' the injured boy contradicted.

'It isn't. It's a greasy lump of putty.'

'It isn't putty,' Hungerford insisted.

'No, putty's too good for a nose like yours,' Muriel agreed. 'It's just mud. Mud I've wiped off my boots on the scraper.'

And before Hungerford, goaded to unchivalrous violence by her taunts, could attack her, Muriel was up at the top of the ladder again and beaming at the painter, who had by now come to the window to see what was happening to his ladder.

If there were no outside ladders for Muriel to climb, she climbed stepladders indoors, and since the mere ascent of a stepladder is not in itself immensely exciting, Muriel had to invent trimmings for this pastime, such as rehanging the pictures in a friend's house, or giving imitations of famous statues on the top. Once at the Clyburns' she put the twins' rocking horse on the stepladder, mounted it, and proclaimed herself to be Lord Napier of Magdala or some distinguished general whose equestrian monument had recently been erected.

No sooner had she announced who she was than step-ladder, rocking horse, and Muriel crashed.

She was only bruised herself, but her blue sash was torn, and buttons kept falling from her for the remainder of the afternoon.

'Look here,' Muriel warned her sisters, 'I'm going to tell Miss Bearsted I fell downstairs trying not to tread on the twins' kitten. Don't you forget, if she asks you what happened.'

'She won't believe you,' said Gladys emphatically. 'She'll probably use that slipper of Father's she said she'd use next time if she couldn't teach you to behave yourself better.'

'Bother it,' said Muriel pensively. 'And I've got rather a big bruise. I shouldn't think she'd be so caddish as that.'

'Won't she?' Gladys exclaimed. 'You wait and see.'

'Oh, well,' Muriel retorted. 'I shan't get it as you did last Friday for blowing a kiss to the butcher's boy. You nearly yelled the house down.'

The classic features of Gladys were obscured by a scowl. The ivory of her skin was darkened by an angry flush. It was not that she minded the revelation about the butcher's boy. Indeed, she was inclined to flaunt her gallantries at us. We had even discussed in whispers among ourselves whether Gladys Gurney might not deserve the damning epithet 'fast.' But that her sister should publish to the world the sequel of her coquetry with the butcher's boy wounded her pride.

'You beastly little sneak,' she cried, with which she seized Muriel by one of her plaits and slapped her face.

Muriel was two years younger than Gladys, and not nearly so robustly built, but she had *élan*, and without waiting to console her smarting cheek she made use of that *élan*, by lowering her head and butting Gladys in the midriff. Then she sprang up and bore her sister to the ground with more *élan* than ever. The Clyburn twins stood hand in hand in a corner of the schoolroom, looking in their long brown velveteen frocks more perfectly Kate Greenaway than ever. The rest of us withdrew to the other corner of the schoolroom, to leave space on the floor for the contending sisters, who were rolling over and over in a whirligig of white frocks and black stockings, the blue sash of Muriel and the amber sash of Gladys like standards in the murk of battle.

Presently, kind Mrs Clyburn appeared upon the scene, her hands held up in dismay, her widow's weeds lending a touch of extra solemnity to her shocked feelings.

'Children, children, do not quarrel like this. I thought there had been an accident.'

Gladys and Muriel ceased to roll over and picked themselves up.

'We often fight like that at home,' Muriel explained to the distressed hostess.

We who knew the state of affairs within Number 23 found this difficult to believe.

'You won't fight any more, will you, my dears?' begged Mrs Clyburn, preparing to withdraw, for she thought that children's tea parties were better enjoyed without the discouraging presence of grown-ups.

'No, Mrs Clyburn, we won't really,' the two young Amazons promised, and that kind and gentle creature in her widow's weeds left us to ourselves again.

'Well,' said Muriel to her elder sister with a weight of satisfaction in her tone, 'if I get into a row for tearing my sash, so will you.'

Gladys and Muriel dallied at the Clyburns' as long as they could in order to postpone the reckoning with Miss Bearsted; but at last in decency they had to go. Both of them took a preoccupied leave of the twins. Only Dorothy was able to express with any enthusiasm their gratitude for a ripping time, which was in the circumstances a felicitous epithet. as a matter of fact we heard afterwards that Dorothy miscalculated the capacity of her handkerchief as a receptacle for currants and that an unpleasant-looking stain on her frock where they had oozed through involved her in Miss Bearsted's vengeance as painfully as her elder sister's. Miss Bearsted must have had a magnificently energetic evening.

Bob Gurney's naughtiness was not less marked than his sisters', and though like them he dared not display it within sound and sight of Miss Bearsted, his holidays always provided us with some signal display of mischief. Bob was very like Muriel to look at. There was a year between them, but they might easily have passed for twins. He was a slim boy with an engaging persuasiveness of speech, and when in the still decorum of his own home he conceived a 'lark' he seldom had much difficulty in tempting us into playing our parts in it.

Bob had a passion for secret societies; but his secret societies, unlike so many of the secret societies of childhood, seldom evaporated in a cloud of rules, signs, countersigns, and gatherings. Bob's secret societies were formed to attain some definite object, and when that object had been attained the secret society was dissolved and another was formed. He had a secret society for ringing other people's bells and running away, and when this palled he founded a still more esoteric society to ring the bell of a strange house and ask if somebody or other who did not live there was at home. This ended in a grim joke played upon the unfortunate Hungerford, who was bidden by the chief of the secret society to ring the bell of some house and ask for Mrs Carmichael-Smith. Now it happened that a Mrs Carmichael-Smith actually did live in this particular house. I can still vividly remember the exquisite rapture which seized the secret society when, standing in a group at the corner of Burton Road, it watched the wretched Hungerford invited in by the maidservant. I can still hear the excited murmur of, 'Will he scoot?'

But Hungerford did not scoot. He evidently lost his head when the maidservant asked him to come in, and he went in. The secret society shouted aloud in ecstasy. The secret society indulged in a kind of Bacchic dance of triumph. The secret society bent over and held its sides in Olympian mirth.

'What will he say to her?'

'What will he do?'

'He must be feeling a most frightful ass!'

'He must be almost catting with funk!'

'Perhaps she'll send for a bobby.'

'Here he comes!'

The door of Mrs Carmichael-Smith's house opened, and the wretched Hungerford, crimson-cheeked, staggered down the steps without his cap and started to run towards the safety of his own home, there to lay his confusion and mortification upon the wide bosom of his mother.

The secret society, every member of which could run twice as fast as poor fat Hungerford, rushed whooping in pursuit.

'What happened?'

'What did she say?'

'What did she do?'

Hungerford turned on the secret society and resigned from it with bitter words.

'You cads! You swizellers!' he moaned savagely. 'I won't ever belong to any secret society any of you beasts belong to.'

'Where's your cap, Hungerford?' asked one of the members.

'Fish and find out, you cheat,' Hungerford snarled, and then spurning his late comrades he resumed his lumbering trot in the direction of home.

The tragedy was that we were never able to find out from Hungerford what did happen when he found himself inside Mrs Carmichael-Smith's house. We could not even extract from him if he waited long enough to see Mrs Carmichael-Smith herself. We tried insults. We tried flattery. We tried tuck. Nothing would induce Hungerford to reveal what had happened.

The next secret society Bob Gurney founded was one for breaking the windows of empty houses. As Bob outlined the objectives of this society they sounded fascinating; but when it came to actually flinging the first stone the other members drew back. Ringing other people's bells was one thing; but breaking other people's windows – for we realised the emptiest house in London was not an orphan – was another. We did not feel clear what the penalty would be if we were caught. It might mean prison. We were not prepared to face the treadmill, even under the sway of Bob Gurney's seductive tongue.

'Well, what's the good of having a secret society to break the windows if you're all too funky to do it?' Bob demanded with what was indubitably logic.

One of the members, stung by the scorn in Bob Gurney's accents, asked why he did not invite the secret society to climb over the garden from Number 23 and break the windows in Number 25, the empty house next door.

'Well, we can't very well do that,' Bob demurred.

'No, because you're afraid of your governess,' the disaffected member pointed out caustically.

Bob flung down his cap.

'I'll fight you for that,' he challenged.

But the other members of the secret society intervened and pleaded for harmony.

'Well, if you think I'm afraid of Miss Bearsted,' said Bob, 'I'll jolly well show you funks that anyway I'm not afraid to break windows by myself.'

'Not the windows of 25,' the disaffected member sneered.

Bob Gurney disdained to reply.

Later on, I tried to turn him from his resolve, for I knew Bob, and I knew that except Miss Bearsted there was not a human being of whom he stood in awe.

'Look here, Bob. You'd better not go and break any windows. You might get caught. And I think you could get put in prison.'

Bob swept aside my prudence with a lofty gesture.

'I started this secret society for breaking windows, and I'm going to break some windows, even if all the rest of you *are* afraid of your nurses.'

It was exaggeration to accuse us of having nurses. We had outlived them. But I bore him no ill will, for I knew how deeply the gibe about Miss Bearsted had rankled. In an access of devotion I volunteered to come and break windows with him.

He looked at me critically. I did not flinch under his eagle glance.

'Right-o! We'll show these funks that we're not funks even if they're funks,' Bob proclaimed, and there was in the gesture which accompanied this decision resolution in the grand style. Robert the Bruce might have made a similar gesture when the spider persuaded him to try again.

'I've thought where we'll break the windows,' Bob told me a day or two later. 'There's an empty house looking over the Rec.'

The 'Rec' was our affectionate abbreviation for the Recreation Ground, a stretch of about six acres of waste land near the playing fields of St James's School, for which the owners were awaiting their price before handing it over to the builder of new streets. Various families in West Kensington had agreed to subscribe ten-and-sixpence a year for the key, and with the income thus derived, the Recretion Ground Committee paid a gardener to keep the grass down in the middle of it and repaired the fence which ran round two sides of it. The other two sides were bounded by the backs of houses and their gardens. A few old elms, hawthorns, and elders still dotted this relic of open country, and the variety of the landscape was pleasantly enhanced by a large gravel pit. A road with houses on either side now runs straight through it, indistinguishable from the other roads all around; but in wandering about the scenes of my childhood recently I noticed that one small corner of the Recreation Ground had survived the builder and was the headquarters of a local lawn-tennis club. There was no lawn-tennis club in our time. Our principal forms of exercise were rounders and excavation of dugouts in the side of the gravel pit in which we might smoke without fear of detection from any of the numerous windows that overlooked the Recreation Ground. It was a set of such windows in an empty house that Bob Gurney had decided to break.

'But everybody will see us,' I objected.

'Not in the middle of the night, you fathead.'

'In the middle of the night?' I gasped.

'Well, you don't suppose we can do it any other time?'

'But how are we going to get out in the middle of the night?' I asked.

'I'm going to slide down the drain pipe outside my room,' he answered.

'But that's at the back. You won't be any nearer to getting

out into our street.'

'Yes, I will,' Bob proclaimed. 'Because I'm going to break into the empty house next door and get into our street that way.'

My heart almost stopped beating in awe of such a reckless enterprise. I looked at Bob in dazzled admiration. Here indeed was the stuff of which the heroes of long ago were made. Evidently the imputation upon his courage levelled by that disaffected member of the secret society had festered.

'But, Bob, I don't think I can slide down a drain pipe. I'm not so good at it as you and Muriel.'

It was painful to be admitting such lack of agility; but discretion in this case completely smothered valour.

'Well, you can get out of your front door,' said Bob. 'And I'll meet you at the corner at twelve o'clock.'

'But my aunt might hear the bolts being drawn, and if I get out I can't get back.'

'I'm going to leave the area door of Number 25 open. Then you can climb back over the garden walls in between to your garden and climb back into your room by the drain pipe.'

'But I can't climb up a drain pipe.'

'Can't climb up a drain pipe?' Bob echoed in contemptuous astonishment. 'If you can't slide down and if you can't climb up, what can you do?'

Put thus, my qualifications to lead a life of adventure did sound inadequate.

However, not even for a smile from Bob Gurney's crystal-clear blue eyes could I muster up enough confidence to join his nocturnal sally, and in the end I funked it.

Perhaps Bob in his heart was rather glad that he was to do the deed alone, for I remember with gratitude that he was not unsympathetic over the failure of my nerve.

'All right,' he said with the condescension of a Coeur de Lion for some camp follower, 'perhaps you *are* rather a kid.'

'I say, Bob, you won't let yourself be caught by a bobby, will you?'

'Rather not,' he promised. 'The only thing I'm a bit funky over is whether Miss Bearsted hears me. But I don't think she will, because I've got some laudanum to put in her gruel.'

'Laudanum? But that's poison, isn't it?'

'It's marked "poison" on the bottle,' said Bob simply. 'But I looked up in a book about it and it only says deadly if some-body swallows an awful lot.'

'I say, where did you get this laudanum?'

'I found an old bottle in a cupboard. The cork was out. But it stinks. So I expect it'll still work all right.'

'But suppose Miss Bearsted tastes it in her gruel?'

'She won't know what it is, you ass. And anyway she won't taste it. I put some Gregory Powder in her gruel yesterday, and if she didn't taste that, which she didn't, she won't taste laudanum.'

I implored Bob not to run the risk of killing Miss Bearsted with laudanum. I had recently been reading *Oliver Twist,* and I could not bear the thought of my gallant friend going through what Bill Sykes went through in the condemned cell. I recog-nised that for the hero to be caught by his governess would be a humiliating climax to his adventure, if as rumour said such a capture would mean the application of the flat side of a hairbrush. Still, a whacking was less drastic than a hanging, and it was better Miss Bearsted should wake up and catch him than that she should never wake up again.

In the end I flatter myself Bob was convinced by my plead-ing. Anyway, he told me he should use the laudanum for kill-ing butterflies instead.

The story of Bob's escape from Number 23 unheard and unseen by Miss Bearsted and of his return equally inaudible and invisible thrilled us for weeks. Casanova's escape from the prison in Venice, Monte Cristo's escape from the Château d'If, Lord Nithsdale's escape from the Tower, Jack Sheppard's escape from Newgate – none of these was able to compete for some time with Bob Gurney's escape from Miss Bearsted. We could sit and listen by the hour to his narrative, fascinated not merely by the authenticity of it, but also by the narrator's ges-tures and clear bright eyes and strangely attractive voice, to which the very faintest suspicion of a stammer added a delicious piquancy. The story was told so often that we knew every detail of it, and when Bob was relating his adventure to one who had never heard it before, we would always prompt him if he for-got one of the incidents over which we were wont to gloat.

Briefly, the story was that Bob, when the two hands of his Waterbury watch merged at midnight, rose from his bed, dressed himself with fearful caution, and left behind him under the bedclothes the bolster garbed in his nightshirt, with the ostrich egg from the Gurney museum to represent his head upon the pillow, covered, however, with the top of the sheet. The next risky business had been to get the window open wide enough, without creaking, for him to reach the drain pipe. One of Miss Bearsted's strictest rules was that no bedroom window must be opened more than two inches, and that at the top. She had more horror of a draught than of a blackbeetle, as we who knew her respirator could easily imagine. Fortunately he had been allowed some oil in which to soak chestnuts for the game of conquerors (now corrupted by the verdigris of time to 'conkers,' a hideous example of the vulgarity of the most vulgar age in history), and with this he had coaxed the window into silence. Then he had slid down the drain pipe to the balcony and climbed over on to the balcony of the empty house next door, whence he had descended into the area at the back and with his Norwegian knife (we all had Norwegian knives in those days, but I never see them now produced from schoolboys' pockets) He pulled back the hasp of the kitchen window.

The notion of entering that empty house alone at midnight made the hair of our heads stand on end, and when Bob told us how he had walked through the dark and empty kitchen and forgotten that the inside of Number 25 was the other way round from the inside of Number 23, so that he had miscalculated the direction of the open coal-cellar door and had been precipitated down the steps into the coal cellar, we used to feel quite faint with the shock of it. But there was worse to come. Let me take up the narrative for a while in Bob's own words.

'I got rather a biff on my forehead, and when I had groped about for a bit and got back into the passage I felt a big giddy, and by mistake, instead of opening the area door, I went into the room which is our morning room.'

'And ours,' we used to echo sympathetically at this point for by this time Bob was such a hero that we could not bear him to feel that we would venture to criticise even his sense of direction.

'Well, I was just turning round to go out when I saw a body lying on the floor close to the window. I couldn't see its face, but I could see it was a body because there was just a little light coming into the room from the lamp-post at the corner of our street. I felt in a most frightful funk.'

How Bob endeared himself to his listeners by this candid admission! He was, we felt, a mortal like ourselves.

'And then I started to walk backwards on tiptoe. And the body groaned.'

At this point, the first time Bob told his story, one of the Clyburn twins let out a piercing scream, rushed from the room, and was sick halfway up the stairs before she had time to reach a less inconvenient spot. And I remember that because Gwendolen did not follow her twin sister and do the same thing we were for ever afterwards skeptical about that intense sympathy which was supposed to exist between twins. To be sure, Gwendolen was very pale; but she neither screamed nor moved from her chair.

'Well, when the body groaned I nearly rushed out of the room like billy-oh. But I didn't.'

Marvellous sang-froid! How we worshipped it!

'I kept on walking backwards on tiptoe, and the body groaned again. And just as I got to the door it said, "What's that?"'

Even at the twentieth repetition our handkerchiefs used to come out at this point in order to mop the nervous perspiration from our foreheads.

'I didn't hardly dare to breathe,' Bob used to continue, for emotion recollected in tranquillity never failed to make him ungrammatical at this crisis in the tale. 'I just kept absolutely still for five secs, and then I started to go on going out backwards on tiptoe. And when I got into the passage and was creeping along to the area door I heard a footstep in the hall up above. But I didn't make a row, though I was in a frightful funk they'd hear the way I was breathing. And then I opened the area door and crept up the steps very quietly because I thought there might be a bobby coming along our street. And there was! There wasn't a dustbin or anything to hide behind in the area, and I felt almost dead with funk when the bobby walked past. But he didn't shine his bull's eye down into the area. He shoved it up to shine on the front door and walked on. I think if I hadn't heard that footstep up above I'd have bunked back at once and gone out to the back and over our wall again. But I couldn't do it then. I was shaking all over.'

We always betted he was at this point in the narrative.

'I bet you were' took on the character of a liturgical response, and we should have felt quite irreverent if we had omitted it.

After his hair-raising transit through the basement of the empty house, Bob had actually had the nerve to walk for ten minutes of empty gaslit roads to the gate of the Recreation Ground, had climbed over the paling, had bunged two stones through two windows, had crawled on his belly through the long grass to the gravel pit, had remained for over an hour inside the dugout of the secret society, had smoked a suitably named Pick-me-Up cigarette, had climbed out of the Recreation Ground on the other side, and had reached our street just before two o'clock.

'And then I got in rather a funk again,' Bob used to relate, 'because I suddenly thought that they might see me from inside and murder me when I opened the area door. So I looked to see if there was a bobby coming, and then I crawled along the pavement on my belly and crawled down the area steps on my back and crouched under the window and pushed at the door to see if it was still open. And it was.'

We never failed to utter a deep sigh of relief here.

'I pushed the door open very quietly and listened, but I couldn't hear anything; and then I crawled along the passage to the kitchen on my hands and knees, because I thought if anybody came out suddenly I could easily trip them up.'

I do not like the idea of skepticism nearly forty years later; but I fancy that at this stage of his narrative the triumphant escapade must have gone to Bob's head. I believe that, even at the time when he told us about his plan to trip up possible assailants, we did not really believe that this was the inspiration of his going down on all fours. But we never expressed our doubts. We felt he had a right by now to say that he had fought three burglars single-handed and knocked out the lot.

Anyway, Bob undoubtedly did make that second perilous transit through the basement of the empty house; he undoubtedly did climb back over the garden wall to the balcony of Number 23; he undoubtedly did manage to climb up the drain pipe to his own room; and he undoubtedly did succeed in hiding from Miss Bearsted the whole business.

It was a remarkable triumph for Bob when next day he was able to show us the broken windows in the house over the

167

Recreation Ground, a triumph even more exquisite than he had anticipated because by mistake he had broken two windows not of the empty house, but of the house next door, which was inhabited.

The epilogue, however, was the greatest triumph of all. Two days later Bob came to us, dancing with elation and justifiable self-esteem, to inform us that there was a reward offered for him.

'Rot!' we cried.

'I swear there is.'

And then he invited us to accompany him to the Terrace.

'Look,' he exclaimed proudly, pointing to a printed notice stuck on the window of Eardeley's Dairy.

We looked and read enviously:

TEN SHILLINGS REWARD

Whereas on the night of September 17th some person or persons maliciously broke with stones the windows of . . . (the number of the house and the name of the road followed here) . . . *the above reward will be paid to anybody who can give information which will lead to the detection of the person or persons responsible for this wilful damage.*

It was indeed worth while belonging to a secret society when there was a price upon the head of its leader.

Yet when some of us suggested to Bob that we should explore the empty house next door by daylight he shook his head.

'Miss Bearsted is sure to spot us getting over the wall,' he objected.

This tribute to Miss Bearsted's quelling eye was surely noteworthy from a boy who had carried through the escapade just narrated. It may be urged by critics of mid-Victorian methods of education that the little governess did not succeed in really curbing her charges. They might even suggest that her methods brought out all that was worst in them. Perhaps the sentimental and lazy methods of today are more genuinely effective. Perhaps our earnest educationalists have really sharpened the youthful sense of what the jargon of the moment calls 'values.' An age which is so optimistic of the future of democracy must in mental self-defence believe in the moral advance of its own children. Miss Bearsted is already as remote in the great backward and abysm of time as Mrs Crabtree of *Holiday House*.

NUMBER 25 *To Be Let or Sold*

BOB GURNEY'S tale of the empty house next door played upon the imagination of all the children in the neighbourhood throughout that autumn after Bob himself went back to school. I was in the country with my father, because Aunt Adelaide and Aunt Emily were travelling in Italy; but when I arrived to stay with them as usual at Christmas, the empty house had acquired the status of an enchanted castle. We would stand outside to gaze up at the begrimed windows and fancy we could see shadowy faces watching us from within. We would peer down into the area over the railings, and try to shape that huddle of something in the farthest corner of the bare morning room into the sleeping body which had muttered 'What's that?' to the venturesome Bob. Time after time somebody would vow he had distinctly seen it move, whereat we would scatter in terror. As for the young braggart who swore he had gone down the area steps, stared into the room, and discovered that the body was nothing but a heap of old sacking, we scorned him. He did not live in our street, I am glad to remember. He did not even live in Burton Road, or Carlington Road, or Cronmore Road, or any of our allied roads. He was indeed nothing but a refugee from Notting Hill, who was spending his Christmas holidays with a grandmother owing to the presence of mumps in his own home.

I fancy it must have been about now that the legend of the little old woman was born. She was said to accost children in the street and, after inquiring of them the road to somewhere or other, to stab them in the eye with a long hatpin. That a little old woman with this unpleasant whim did exist in Kensington had long been known and had long been shivered over as a potential adventure. There were several children in the neighbourhood who declared they had seen her. She was reported to have a very red face and to wear a crape bonnet always askew. But until she took up her abode in the empty house her headquarters had been a mystery. We thought of informing one of the bobbies who passed at intervals with majestic tread along our street. We felt that the police ought to know about this little old woman. In the end, however, we were always deterred by a suspected lack of sympathy in the bobbies, large men with stolid faces, the incranation of blind justice in their remoteness from the frailties of ordinary human nature. I once did get as far as saying to one of these ponderous embodiments of the law's slow but sure and ruthless course, 'Do you know – ' but when he stopped and gazed down at my upturned face my courage failed.

'Do you know the time, please?' I asked instead.

It was about this date that a popular song began:

> *If you want to know the time,*
> *Ask a policeman.*

So perhaps the Metropolitan Police were unduly sensitive about this question. Anyway, this particular bobby replied gruffly:

'Time you stopped playing about in the road and went off home to your ma.'

In the end we decided to consult the postman, who was the friend of every child on his round. He was a good-looking young man with such conspicuously curly hair that we always called him Curly, and so fond were we of him that we always came down extra early on the morning of Boxing Day so as to make certain of seeing Curly presented with his Christmas Box of half a crown.

I can see him now turning the corner by Doctor Arden's house about eleven o'clock, always in a hurry because he would always have been delayed with the second delivery by the conversations he would have had with children's nursemaids and nurses on the way.

'Curly put down his bag this morning and caught a ball I threw to him.'

What a triumph for a child who could boast of such a special mark of Curly's favour.

His very rat-tats all along our street had a peculiarly inspiring sound. The postman who went round with the last post at night used to give rather an ominous rat-tat, and as there were always much fewer letters at night those rat-tats lacked the cheerful continuity of Curly's morning delivery at door after door right along our street. At night there used to be irregular silences when a couple of houses were passed over before the next rat-tat. Curly had been married about a year, and when he and Mrs Curly had their firstborn son some of us were actually invited to go and have tea with the young couple and admire the baby. We thought it a tremendous adventure to visit a postman at home, and we were particularly impressed by the way Curly wore an ordinary coat with the red-striped trousers of his postman's uniform. We wondered if the policemen kept on their blue trousers with an ordinary jacket when they were at home; but somehow we could not conjure up the picture of a bobby in his domestic surroundings. Even without their helmets bobbies looked pretty rum. There had once been a bobby on our beat who had been exceptionally popular with the cooks along our street, and several of us had seen him at supper in our kitchens, his helmet resting on the kitchen dresser. Not that I ever saw him in Hetty's kitchen. She used to say she had no patience with the way some girls carried on. So cheap, she called it.

We asked Curly about the little old woman with the hatpin, and he declared that she had certainly made the empty house her home.

'How do you know, Curly? Have you seen her?'

'No, I wouldn't actually say I'd seen her.'

'Well, how do you know she's there?'

'Why, I left a letter for her only yesterday morning.'

'You didn't!'

'Oh, I didn't, didn't I? Well, if you all know more about the inside of my post bag than what I know myself, what's the good of asking me questions?'

'What was her name, Curly?'

'Her name? Let me see now. What *was* her name? Why blowed if I haven't forgotten *what* it was.'

However, Curly's habits of playing jokes on us made us hope that he was not serious now. He had once told Clara Lockett that her brother had sent her a skeleton from the hospital where he was working and that this skeleton had come to life and gnawed its way out of the parcel and goodness knows where it had got to. Clara, however, was too stolid a girl to be frightened by such a tale.

'Skeletons can't walk, you stupid,' she told Curly in that heavy voice of hers.

'Skeletons can't walk?' Curly had echoed. 'All right, when you see it popping its head out of the cupboard and grinning at you, don't say I never warned you.'

And there had been the same twinkle in Curly's eyes when he had told Clara that story about the skeletons as now when he was assuring us that he had left a letter for the little old woman with the crape bonnet and the long hatpin. All the same, we began to avoid passing the empty house after dark, and if we came back from a late message to one of the shops in the Terrace we used to keep on the other side of our street until we had passed Number 25. The silence and gloom of it in the twilight cast a chill.

And then one morning during these Christmas holidays Bob Gurney suddenly announced that he was prepared to take a personally conducted tour round the empty house.

'But what about Miss Bearsted? Won't she mind?' we asked, for now that entrance to the empty house was apparently to be made easy for us we were not quite so sure if we wanted to go in, and we were inclined to use the bogy of Miss Bearsted as a counterpoise to any bogies in Number 25.

'She's got to go away today to see her mother who's ill in the country. She'll probably be away at least a week. Isn't it spiffing?' said Bob.

We pondered awhile the thought of Miss Bearsted's mother. She must be a pretty grim figure, we decided.

'Miss Bearsted's going away by the 3.30 train this afternoon from Euston. The cab's ordered at a quarter-past two,' Bob announced the next day.

Nobody who had seen Gladys, Muriel, and Dorothy clinging to Miss Bearsted and hanging upon her last farewell and even standing on the front-door steps to blow kisses after the lumbering cab, until it had turned the corner of our street by Doctor Arden's and taken the handkerchief fluttering from the window out of sight, could have supposed anything except the liveliest affection between pupils and governess. Was it hypocrisy? Or was it the propitaiation that is used by savages toward the tribal god? Or was it really the affection of creatures for a being of superior strength?

There was a great gathering at Number 23 that afternoon when Miss Bearsted was gone. At first a certain amount of order was preserved, because someone put a damper on too much exuberance of spirit by suggesting that she might miss her train through a block in the traffic. Traffic in London was already a problem even forty years ago, and I daresay it will be just as much of a problem forty years hence, by which time it is unlikely there will be anyone in our street, except perhaps the Bond baby, to know whether it is or not.

By five o'clock a large party of us sat down to tea and all danger of Miss Bearsted's return seemed to have vanished. We could now feel confident she was well on her way toward the Staffordshire vicarage where her sick mother was expecting her.

The sense of freedom was eloquently expressed by Bob Gurney when Mabel, the parlourmaid of Number 23, brought in the usual plates piled up with thick slices of bread and butter, for he commanded her to take away that beastly bread and butter and bring in the jam.

'No such thing, Master Robert,' said Mabel, attempting to understudy the austere manner of the absent governess. 'You know perfectly well that you're only allowed jam on Sundays.'

'Pelt her! Pelt her!' shouted Bob. 'Pelt her with bread and butter.'

'Pelt her!' screamed Dorothy.

Muriel did not wait to urge action. She had flung three slices as hard as she could without a word.

'You wicked girl,' exclaimed the angry maid. 'You see if you don't get a good whipping for that when Miss Bearsted comes back.'

'Sneak! Sneak!' cried Dorothy, turning to the ammunition and carrying on the assault begun by Muriel.

'We'll give you a jolly good whacking yourself if you sneak,' Bob declared.

We guests, I am glad to remember, neither joined in such threats to the prim Mabel's dignity nor in the pelting of her with bread and butter.

'I'll go and fetch your mother down to you, Master Robert, if you don't desist from your boldness and wickedness.'

'Ha-ha! Sucks for you, she's out,' Bob shouted gleefully.

'So bring the jam.'

'The jam! The jam!' his sisters echoed in high-voiced excitement.

'Not a blessed spoonful of jam will you have, you daring children,' Mabel declared.

'Then we'll get it for ourselves,' Gladys announced, and with a rush the four young Gurneys swept past Mabel to pillage the store cupboard. Groans of astonishment from their portly cook were heard. Cries of alarm from Edith the housemaid shrilled. Cupboard doors banged. A dish crashed.

We guests kept our places and looked at one another. Could this in very truth be the severe morning room of Number 23 where we had so often sat demurely round the tea table? It was an incredible transformation.

Presently our unruly hosts returned with their plunder. We saw no reason to refuse to share in it. Whatever happened we could not suffer at Miss Bearsted's hands as accessories. Our only expiation would be from within. So we tucked in with the plunderers, and cordially agreed with Dorothy that currants eaten *ad libitum* with madeira cake added much to its flavour. We assured Bob that anchovy paste when spread three times as thickly as usual was indubitably three times as good. We congratulated Muriel on the happy inspiration which had led her to combine sardines and bananas as her contribution to the feast. We had never found bananas so delicious as when eaten thus immediately on top of sardines. But it was Gladys who won the loudest applause for her contribution, for it was Gladys who produced the bottle of orange wine which we poured into our tea cups and drank with a gusto that made us ask ourselves why fortune did not allow us orange wine instead of watery tea every afternoon. The only guest who did not enjoy the orange wine was Clara Lockett, and that because it was the medium at Number 3 to disguise the cod-liver oil she had been ordered by Doctor Arden. She sat looking at her cup with a sickly expression on her stolid countenance until we asked her if she did not like orange wine, and when she shuddered at the memories of cod-liver oil which surged over her we gallantly drank the contents of Clara's cup.

When this boisterous tea was finished it was voted by Bob Gurney too late to explore the empty house that afternoon, and looking at the drear January evening without we agreed with him. The broadest daylight was essential for such an adventure.

I believe most of us fancied we should hear no more of the Gurneys after that tea for some time. I think we expected to be told they had been locked up in their rooms on a diet of stale bread until Miss Bearsted returned from Saffordshire to complete the expiation. However, we were wrong; Bob Gurney was early abroad the very next morning and whistling for me to come down and join him for the exploration of Number 25.

'We're not going to have any girls with us,' he said severely. 'They'll only scream all the time.'

I agreed with Bob that an empty house was no place for girls, and when presently he suggested that there was no point in making a squash of the business by asking anybody else at all, I was too sensible of the compliment he paid me to show the least sign of disappointment that we were not going to invade the empty house with all the boys we could collect.

'You remember when they offered that reward for me last hols?' Bob asked as coolly as if he had been a mere puppy dog lost, stolen, or strayed.

'Rather.'

'Well, a chap at my school said it would be rather a lark to denounce somebody, and I read a rather ripping book about Russian anarchists, so I know the right way to denounce anybody.'

'How do you, Bob?'

'Well, if you think a chap in a secret society is going to betray you, you write him a warning in blood. You write "Beware. You have trifled with us too long. The vengeance of your comrades will overtake you in a way you know not of."'

'Wouldn't it take an awful lot of blood to write all that?' I demurred.

. 'Oh, well, I know where my mater has some red ink. So we can use that instead.'

I thought this a good opportunity to try to find out what Mrs Gurney's reaction had been to that riotous tea party of yesterday.

'Mabel didn't tell her. She's going to wait and sneak to Miss Bearsted when she comes back. At least she says so now; but I told her if she did I'd put hundreds of blackbeetles in her room, and so perhaps she won't. Anyway, I shall start collecting them in case. But don't let's jaw about Mabel. I want to send this warning to Hungerford.'

'Why?'

'Well, because you always warn a traitor.'

'Is Hungerford a traitor?'

'He resigned from our secret society, didn't he?'

'Oh, rather.'

'Well, then, of course he's a traitor. I shall warn him to leave the country,' Bob went on.

'You can write him quite a long warning,' I suggested, 'now you're going to use red ink instead of blood. But he can't leave the country. He's got to go to school next term.'

'No, I don't suppose he will leave the country,' Bob agreed. 'But if he doesn't, he must pay the penalty for being a traitor.'

'What's that?'

'He'll be denounced.'

'Who to?'

'The police, of course, you fathead.'

'What for?'

'I tell you. For being a traitor. Is your head made of wood?'

'I meant what are you going to denounce him for doing?'

'For breaking those windows, of course.'

'But he didn't break them.'

'I know that. But I can't denounce him for blowing up the Czar or anything, because the police would know it was all rot, and nothing would happen. But if I denounce him for something they really know did happen, they'll search his mother's house, and arrest Hungerford, and –'

'Yes,' I interrupted, 'but suppose he denounces you. He jolly well might, and if he did, the police might find out it was you, and Hungerford would get the ten shillings reward.'

'Oh, well denouncing is rather rot,' said Bob. 'Come and let's climb over the wall now and get into the empty house.'

Bob could drop a project of which he was tired as casually as a kitten can cease chasing a paper ball.

When we stood in the sunken yard outside the window of the kitchen and our footsteps were muffled by the sodden leaves of the Virginia creeper, I began to wish again for company and told Bob that I thought Almeric and Aylmer Spink (they were still living in our street at this date) would enjoy exploring the empty house with us. It was then that Bob revealed to me for the first time his purpose in choosing only a single companion.

'You know, if burglars have been living here,' he murmured in a low voice, 'they may have left some jewels and gold in the house, and if they have we don't want to divide it with thousands of other people. It would be rather ripping to be rich. I'd buy a skit of things. And now wait a jiffy. If the window is fastened, that means there *are* people living in the house, because I left it open.'

I decided inwardly that if the hasp was fastened I would do all I could to dissuade Bob from venturing inside; but the window was open and presumably had been ever since Bob had opened it with his Norwegian knife last September.

We explored the basement thoroughly without finding any signs of human habitation, and what we fancied might be a body in the morning room proved after all to be sacking as the Notting Hill youth had said.

'Well, it wasn't sacking when I saw it under the window that night,' Bob said.

The front hall, when we reached it through the door with panels of ground glass which led down into the basement, chilled our spirits. Perhaps it was the effect of the circulars which had been pushed through the flap of the letter box and which finding no letter box on the other side, had fallen upon the floor, to be blown hither and thither by the draught coming under the matless front door.

There is nothing so eloquent of abandonment as an unread circular about coals, and the whole of the hall of Number 25 was littered with the prices of Derby Brights and Wallsend and Silkstone.

We explored the drawing room and the dining room; but we found nothing of interest, though we enjoyed the view of our street from the dining-room window, because to look at it thus from an empty house gave us a feeling of ownership.

'If we find the burglars' treasure I vote we buy this house for ourselves,' said Bob.

I agreed that this suggestion was an attractive one.

'Only if we do,' he continued, 'bags I the drawing room, because I want a place where I can have a really decent model railway.'

We went on upstairs to explore the first floor, and in that desolate square with peeling strips of wall paper hanging down from the walls which in Number 9 was my Aunt Adelaide's sitting room I began to play with the idea of expressing myself through the medium of a room. It should be draped with curtains of violet velvet with a golden ceiling, and I would have a lattice window inside the ordinary window like Mr Mellor. . . .

But Bob did not give me long to indulge in these dreams of decoration, for he was already leading the way up to the floor above. I was finding the silence and emptiness of the house more eerie the farther we went up, and the prospect of the top floor with the inevitable noises in the cistern cupboard was not tempting. I could not help wondering what we should do if we looked over the balusters and saw far down in the hall below a moving shadow on the tiles. By this time Bob was opening the door of the back room, and a second later he exclaimed:

'Somebody *has* been in here, by gum!'

My first instinct was to rush helter-skelter back down the stairs and out of the front door into the safety of our street; but my legs turned to cotton-wool and feeling as if I were in the middle of a nightmare, I stumbled after Bob to see in one corner of the room a mattress with a couple of frowsy blankets tossed up in a heap on top of it. There were no chairs; but there were some battered pots and pans lying about by the fireplace, which was full of dead ashes; and in another corner there was a pile of rags with a pair of boots beside them, and hanging from a nail on the wall a crooked bowler hat with a collar balanced upon it.

'Look out,' I gasped, 'he may come back and catch us. Let's scoot.'

But Bob declined to scoot. He was now firmly convinced that a little search would reveal a robbers' hoard. In vain did I argue with him that nothing in the appearance of that decayed mattress or those dirty blankets indicated the existence of a successful burglar. He was bent on making us rich for life.

At last in desperation I suggested that here was a genuine opportunity to denounce somebody to the police, and to my relief Bob was taken with the notion.

'Well, come on and let's get out of the house before he comes back,' I urged.

'But we must warn him,' said Bob. 'We must give him a chance of escape.'

'Why?'

'Because you always do warn anybody before you denounce them. Except the familiars of the Inquisition. They didn't.'

Until then I had always been prejudiced against the methods of the Grand Inquisitor, but now I began to see the point of them.

'I know, we'll denounce him here,' Bob exclaimed.

'But you've got no red ink,' I objected.

'No, but I've got some blue chalk. And Morgiana in the *Forty Thieves* used chalk. I wonder if she used blue chalk though?'

'Use any chalk you've got,' I urged him fretfully. 'Only do be quick.'

So Bob chalked on the wall above the mantelpiece of this squalid hermit's abode:

BEWARE!

Your hiding-place has been discovered by the slueths of the police. Fly from the country unless you wish to rest for ever in a fellon's cell.
                                    Signed
                        A WELL-WISHER.

'But you're not a well-wisher,' I pointed out. 'If he doesn't fly, you're going to denounce him to the police.'

'No, *you're* going to denounce him,' Bob contradicted. 'And then I'm going to help him to escape.'

A long argument ensued about this. I pointed out to Bob that I never wanted to denounce anybody and that I didn't see why I should.

'Suppose he finds out that I denounced him?' I asked. 'He may come and murder me when he gets out of prison.'

'But you'll send the police what's called an anominous letter – '

'It isn't anominous. It's anonymous.'

'I bet you it isn't,' Bob challenged.

'What will you bet?' I asked.

'I'll bet you – '

But with what Bob was willing to back his spelling was never to be known, for at that instant we were interrupted by the sound of a cough somewhere down below in the empty house.

How I cursed myself for stopping to argue with Bob the ethics of denunciation and the orthography of anonymous! There seemed now not the slightest chance of avoiding being murdered. A contingency which had kept me in a stew on many a night when I had been lying awake in the long hours of darkness was about to happen in the full light of day. Escape was impossible .The hollow cough was already nearer, and we could hear by now the laboured breathing of somebody toiling up the stairs. I looked at Bob bitterly. This was where his recklessness had landed us; at the top of an empty house with a murderer coming upstairs, slowly indeed, but all too surely. And for us no more chance of escape than a couple of minnows in a jam jar. Even Bob's debonair confidence was shaken. Even the serene roses of his complexion were mottled with apprehension at last.

'We'd better hide upstairs in the cistern cupboard,' he whispered. 'And when he goes into his room, we'll try to creep past and get downstairs. Or perhaps, when he sees the warning,' he added hopefully, 'he'll be in such a funk that he'll run away himself.'

So treading the bare boards as tenderly as we could we reached the topmost story of the empty house, and crouched among the cobwebs at the back of the cistern.

To our horror the footsteps instead of turning aside into the room we had just left continued up the top staircase.

'He's heard us,' Bob gasped.

In my agitation I managed to get a strip of unusually substantial cobweb into my mouth, and owing to the way Bob was packing me still deeper into the corner I could not raise my arm to pull it out again. I knew it was only a matter of moments before I must cough and betray our presence. But just as I did cough, by great good fortune the mysterious unknown coughed himself, so that my lapse was unnoticed. At least it would have been if Bob in turning round to urge silence with a warning grimace had not caught the cistern a bang with his elbow. The hollow receptacle rang like a gong.

To our amazement and relief instead of hearing the savage growl which we associated with the elocution of murderers, we heard a voice quavering in obvious alarm:

181

'I didn't mean no harm by coming here. Don't go and treat a poor old man harsh. I'll go away quiet. So help me bob, I will.'

Naturally Bob himself did not suppose that the old man was appealing to him; but perhaps the use of his name as a variant for the Almighty's added a touch of dignity to his emergence from the cistern cupboard, which might otherwise have been endangered by the large smudge on his face. As for me, I was heartily thankful not to be murdered and so much relieved by being able at last to extract that disgusting cobweb from my mouth that I could have hugged the decrepit figure we found quavering on the landing.

He was indeed as old as he had announced he was. He had a long white beard, much matted, and ragged white hair. He was dressed in what may once have been the frock coat of somebody as tall as General Brackenbury. On him it looked like a mouldering green dressing gown. He was wearing on one foot a boot through the cap of which four toes were twitching nervously, on the other foot a carpet slipper. Through holes in his trousers we could see a pair of emaciated knees, and round his middle to serve as shirt and waistcoat combined he had rolled a piece of green baize which was kept in place by strings of various thicknesses. He had a collar; but nothing to which he could fasten it; so he had pinned it together with a decayed boat-race favour, a pale blue Cambridge swallow made of plush. Even in those days, when figures of utter destitution like this were more often to be seen than now, this old man presented an extreme example of human misery.

Bob and I recognised him at once as a poor old rag-picker, and indeed, beside him on the landing, was a sack full of the fruits of his assiduous and melancholy contemplation of the gutters. We had seen him sometimes venturing timidly down into the areas of our street and taking a nervous surreptitious peep into the dustbins when twilight was falling.

'I didn't mean no harm,' he quavered to us. 'I been out for two nights and I slep' yesterday in Waterloo Arches. I didn't think as it 'ud hurt anybody if I slep' here of a day sometimes. I can get a morsel of fire here with bits of coal sometimes.'

We assured him that we sympathised with his desire for shelter, and we earnestly promised that we would never reveal his refuge to the police.

'Good boys! Good boys!' the old man muttered. 'You

wouldn't go for to do anything as 'ud hurt a poor old man what never did no harm, on'y just picked a living as best he could.'

'And I say,' Bob put in, 'when you read what's chalked up over the mantelpiece in your room, you needn't be frightened. We only wrote it for a lark.'

'Thank'ee,' said the old man, 'thank'ee, young genelmen. But I can't read a word, printed or wrote, so that'll be quite all right, that'll be. But I can make my mark,' he added proudly. 'And I made 'un once years ago when there were a big set out about a right of way as the new squire had closed agin the public. "Can you sweer, William Cobb, as you can mind your grandfeyther saying as how he'd used this here path by Tangley Copse, man and boy, without obstructionation by anybody?" "I can sweer it," I up and told them, "if I was to lie down and die this blessed minute." And wi' that they wrote William Cobb his mark, and I put a cross, and Lawyer said he couldn't have put a better cross himself, and nex' day he give me a new half-crown. But I were wild in those days, and I hadn't a fourpenny piece left nex' morning.'

While the old man was telling this story of a remote triumph, there had crept back into his speech the burr of some distant countryside, and we might have been listening to an aged labourer in a smock frock and tall beaver hat maundering on across a stile. In those days there were still plenty of old men like that in Gloucestershire where my father lived among his orchards.

But the present intervened, and it was in husky cockney again that William Cobb suddenly and suspiciously asked:

'You didn't go and hurt my cat, did you?'

'Your cat?' we echoed. 'We never saw a cat.'

The old man chuckled faintly his relief.

'No, he'd lie low, would Mouser. That blooming cat's made of brains. Artful? Well, I reckon he's the artfullest cat in London. But he don't like strangers. Can't take to them at all, and for which, Mouser ain't to blame. He'd been treated bad, Mouser had, when I found him lying in a dustbin one pouring wet winter's night. Yes, ye'd been treated bad. And if I hadn't have lifted the lid off that dustbin, I reckon as he'd have been dead by morning, Mouser would. But I took him back home along of me, and him being a black cat he must have brought me luck, for I found a sov'rin lying on the edge of a drain just where the white buses stop at the corner of Redcliffe Gardings. So I was able to buy a bit of meat and make some soup for Mouser. Drunk it like a infant in arms, he did.'

'Do you often find sovereigns?' Bob asked.

'On'y found that one all the time I been picking. Coins is scarce. I found a two-shilling bit. Standing up on edge, that was, right against the curb. And I found a bob once among the greenstuff in Berwick Market after the barrers had gone off. Two tanners both on the pavement, and a thruppeny bit in the gutter just outside of a church. And nine coppers – two pennies, four browns, and three joes. That's all the coin I ever found. I found a wedding ring once, but it was only nine carat. And I found a tooth with some gold in it, but I couldn't get nothing on it. So I kep' it for luck; but it didn't bring me no luck, because a cab wheel run over one of my feet, and which is why I can't wear a boot on it.'

We looked at the four toes of the uninjured foot protruding through the boot, by which it really seemed less hampered than the injured foot by the carpet slipper.

'But I've had blooming little luck since I dossed in this house,' the old man went on. 'Here, come on in and I'll show you.'

He opened the door of the attic at the back, and as he led the way in, a big black cat ran forward to greet him, then caught sight of Bob and myself and retreated into a corner, growling.

'All right, Mouser, them's is friends of mine. They won't hurt you, my old boon companion.'

However, the boon companion, who had lost the whole of one ear and half the other, and who had a scar which apparently doubled the size of his nose so that he resembled a battered hobgoblin, continued to growl in the corner occasionally arching his back and spitting at us.

'He'll quieten down presently,' the old man assured us. 'But he never did like strangers and he never will. Yet you can't blame the cat, for he was treated bad by somebody. Very bad.'

We bothered no more about Mouser's hostility in looking at the queer sight the attic presented, one side of it a foot deep in rags, pieces of coloured paper, bits of iron, bottles, and bones, the other side bestrewn with what the old man evidently considered objects of comparative rarity. Among these were rusty curtain rings, broken keys, the seamed yellow handles of table knives, cracked saucers and cups, cigarette tins, bits of rubber tires from bicycles and perambulators, a couple of balls of silver paper, several balls of variously coloured tape and string, the rims and crowns of straw hats, and most conspicuous of all in the very centre of this museum of rubbish the nosebag of a horse.

So Bob had been right in suspecting the existence of a hoard, albeit we should have been nothing the richer by our discovery of it.

'Yes, that's my little bit since I dossed in this here house,' William Cobb informed us. 'And it's not what it would have been years ago. Picking gets worse every year. I don't know whether it's my eyes ain't what they used to be or whether as these here munciple cleaners spoils the ground or whether people's getting more careful what they throw away; but picking ain't what it was. It's the same with eatables. You'll find a crust now where once you could find half a blooming loaf. Then there's cigars. You'd be surprised, too, how far I've got to tramp before I'll find enough cigar ends to fetch a tanner. Well, I suppose I haven't got much longer. I reckon I'm over eighty years now, and I won't be sorry to doss down for good and all under the ground. Except for Mouser. Mouser 'ud miss me. Well, you can talk about human beings; but that blooming cat's got twice the sense of a human being. Come on, Mouser, these young genelmen won't hurt you.'

And sure enough the black cat seemed to understand what the old man was saying to him, for he came out from his corner and allowed us to stroke him.

'There you are, you see. He knows what a young genelman is. That cat? Why, he's a walking book. He caught a mouse the other night and kep' it till I come back in the morning and then went and lay it on my chest when I was dossed down. Wanted to share it with me. So to please him I got up and cooked this here blooming mouse the same as I might a bit of sausage or any other bit of relish I might find, and Mouser he sat and watched me cook this mouse with a grin on his dile like a happy kid. And arter I'd pretended to have a bite he eat that mouse of his like it was roast beef. Yes, that's the on'y thing as'll worry me when I doss down for the last time – what's to become of Mouser?'

Bob asked the old man if he had been sleeping in the empty house last September; but it transpired he had only taken up his quarters here since the beginning of October after an empty house where he had been living in Hammersmith had found a tenant.

'I reckon what you saw was a tramp,' he told Bob. 'They'll often leave a door open and set a chalk mark on it to let another know where there's good dossing. But I don't want no blooming tramps in here. So I always bolts the door when I comes back early in the morning from my rounds.'

'But what do you do when you go out at night? Have you got a key?'

The old man looked at us intently for a moment. Then, as if he had reassured himself of our good will, he said mysteriously:

'I got a skelington key. Open any ornary door. A feller left it behind him in a doss house at Whitechapel. But I never use it except on an empty house like what this is. I've lived rough, I have, very rough; but I was always brought up honest, and I've been honest ever since. It gets a regular habit after a bit. I never done a day in quod all my life. But come to think of it now, how did *you* get in?' the old man suddenly asked.

We told him about the kitchen window and the way over the garden wall.

'Then you both live in this here street. Fancy that now! Mouser, do you hear that? Neighbours, that's what these young genelmen are.'

Mouser twitched his tail in acknowledgement.

'There you are, you see. He's got you all according now.'

'I live in the house next door,' Bob announced, a note of pride in his voice. He evidently felt that propinquity to the habitation of this aged ragpicker added something to the distinction of living at Number 23.

'Fancy that now,' exclaimed Mr William Cobb, wagging his unkempt white beard at us. 'Well, we *is* neighbours and no mistake.'

'If I tapped on the wall of my room, you'd hear me tapping in your room downstairs where you sleep,' Bob told him.'

'I reckon I would,' the old man agreed.

'I *will* tap sometimes if you like,' Bob offered.

'Well, it'ud be a bit of company in a manner of speaking,' the old man allowed.

'Well, I will,' Bob promised. 'And I say, do you mind if we bring some other chaps to see you?'

'Not coppers?'

'No, no, of course not. Well, as a matter of fact,' Bob continued as nonchalantly as his blushing honours would allow, 'there's a reward offered for me. So I couldn't very well bring any bobbies here. No, these chaps are friends of ours.'

'Friends of yours is friends of mine,' the old rag-picker declared. 'That's right, ain't it, Mouser?'

Once again the battered black cat twitched his tail in assent.

So long as Miss Bearsted was in attendance on her sick mother old William Cobb led what was probably a more social existence than at any period of his life, for Bob Gurney introduced through the kitchen window of the empty house every boy and girl of his acquaintance. It goes without saying they all had to join a secret society first and swear the most bloodcurdling oaths never to divulge to anybody outside the secret society the presence of the ragpicker at Number 25. The old man became as much of a children's pet as Jumbo the Zoo elephant. Instead of raiding store cupboards on our own account we now raided them in his interest. Even when Miss Bearsted did come back and the kitchen-window entrance was no longer feasible, by posting sentinels we managed to visit him from the front of the house. In return for our presents of food the old man entertained us with stories of his past, which we found of absorbing interest. He also taught us many of the signs which tramps chalk up outside houses to give useful information to their fellows of the craft, and we had a splendid time chalking up hospitable hieroglyphics on the houses of people we did not like. There must have been far more tramps in those days about London, for I well remember what a pest they became to some of our neighbours on whose gateposts we had chalked up cordial recommendations of the good cheer to be expected by begging at their area doors.

Bob went back to school at the end of January, and I went back to the country soon afterwards; but friends of ours maintained William Cobb with supplies, and when Bob and I saw him again at Easter we thought the old ragpicker was looking less emaciated. As for Mouser, he was positively sleek. Yet the black cat, though he would let any of us stroke him now

187

without growling or spitting, would never accept food from our hands. We had to give it all to the old man before he would touch a morsel.

Bob went back to school again after the holidays; but this time I stayed on with my aunts.

One morning at the end of May, when Olive and I went to pay the old man a visit, we found him lying on his decayed mattress, a strange look in his eyes.

'I was out again picking last night,' he told us. I have forgotten to mention that, since Bob had arranged for him to be supported by the secret society expressly incorporated for such a purpose, the old man had seldom gone out. 'Out again picking I was,' he repeated in a kind of puzzled voice. 'And when I came back this morning I felt all of a shiver, and which is why I'm dossed down like this here. But it was a lovely fine night, and when I looked out of the window it come over me all of a sudden as I'd like to make the round again. It come over me sudden and peculiar like as perhaps if I went out picking I might find a sparkler. Ever since I took to picking I've thought I might find a sparkler; but I never did. And I didn't find one last night. Well, no one can have everything in this world, they say. And if I hadn't have found that sov'ring I told you about, I might have found a sparkler. It don't do to be *too* greedy. Yes, I went out picking again last night.'

He lay back, staring up at the ceiling for a while in silence.

'Did you find anything?' Olive asked presently.

The old man pointed a withered finger at a disreputable dog collar on the floor beside his bed.

'On'y that, and the usual bits and pieces. And it come over me lying here just now as that dog collar wasn't much to leave behind for Mouser.'

'Leave behind you?' we echoed.

'I wouldn't say nothing as 'ud frighten any of you kiddies. Not for nothing I wouldn't,' the old man declared apologetically. 'But it come over me sudden when I come through the door this morning as I wouldn't go out again except feet first. And I stood listening for a minute to some sparrows as was cheep-cheeping round the chimbley pots, and then it come over me as they sounded like what they used to sound when I was half as big as what you are now. Yet coming back from my picking of a morning early. I've heard thousands of sparrows, as you might say; but I never thought nothing of the way they used to sound years afore even I come up to London. Not till this morning I didn't. And when I come on up here and laid down it come over me as I wasn't feeling so strong as I used to feel, and I've been laying here thinking what poor old Mouser's going to do?'

We looked across at the battered black cat who was lying curled up asleep where the May sunlight was shining on the floor. He did not seem anxious about his future.

'You wouldn't let them treat Mouser bad, missy?' the old man asked anxiously of Olive.

'Of course I wouldn't,' she declared.

'He'd been treated bad when I found him. Very bad. And if ever an animile was grateful, that cat of mine was grateful. Well, you see for yourselves what he thinks of me. You might have thought with all you young ladies and genelmen coming here and bringing him tit-bits and making a lot of him, he'd have thought me a bit beneath him. But you see for yourselves he never turned against me, not a hair. Thanks to all you kind young ladies and genelmen he's a cat now as could go anywhere, barring of course him having only half one ear and the other one gone for good. But he's going to miss me. I know that. So if you found him alone one morning, I don't think he'd disgrace a genelman's house, barring of course his poor old ears.'

Neither Olive nor I grasped what the old ragpicker was trying to warn us of. We thought he meant to go away literally and leave his cat behind.

'But why do you want to go away and leave Mouser?' we asked.

The old man stared at us.

'It ain't as I particularly wants to go,' he muttered.

'Then don't go,' we urged.

'You won't let anybody treat Mouser bad?' he asked again anxiously.

'No, no. We won't really,' we promised.

'The sun falls nice and warm where he's laying now,' the old man observed with an approving nod.

Soon after this we left him.

It was two days before Olive and I went again to see William Cobb. And when we opened the door of his room we saw that

189

Mouser was lying on his chest. We thought the old man was asleep, and then suddenly the black cat uttered a kind of wail, a most eerie sound, and standing up began to claw at the green baize which the old man wore for shirt and waistcoat. We could not make out why Mouser's behaviour did not waken him. Olive suddenly turned white.

'I believe he's dead,' she whispered.

My heart gave a great jump, and I am sure I turned as white as Olive.

'What shall we do?' I asked, horrified.

'We must get Mouser to come with us,' she said. 'And then I suppose we'd better tell a policeman.'

I was about eleven at this date, and Olive was about a year older. It was a tremendous experience for two children, and looking back at it now I feel rather proud of our behaviour in not rushing out of that empty house at once. We could not bring ourselves, however, to go very close to the body of the old ragpicker, and Mouser refused to leave it. He had given up clawing at the baize, and he now sat with his back to us, gazing, I suppose, with those big yellow eyes at his old friend's lifeless face. We were afraid after we had told a policeman what had happened we should not be allowed inside the house again, and knowing Mouser's feelings about strangers we dreaded what they might do to him if he would not leave the body.

'Mouser,' said Olive at last in a solemn tone of voice. 'Mouser, do listen. Your master is dead. You can't wake him up with your claws. He asked us to look after you. Please, Mouser, do come with us.'

I suppose that those who claim for the dog a greater power of personal devotion than the cat will say that Mouser left the body of his dead master to follow Olive because he was thinking about his own comfort. But I am sure the old ragpicker would have said it was a sign of his wonderful intelligence, and I agree with William Cobb.

Anyway, Mouser went to live with Olive at Number 7, where he lived happily until his death ten years later. Lady Marjorie was anxious at first for the safety of her bullfinch; but Mouser's sagacity was too great for him to repay kindness by trying to kill something his protectress loved. I never heard that he was even caught looking at the bullfinch. Gradually, too, he grew less hostile to strangers, and really except for that

190

disreputable lack of ears and hobgoblin's nose he might have been a drawing-room cat all his life.

After the death of the old ragpicker in the empty house the owners took care to keep it more carefully closed. It remained empty for another three years, and it must have been empty for quite ten years when one day we saw a cheerful party of workmen arrive and take down the board on which was painted TO BE LET OR SOLD.

I REALISE now that the Linwoods were pioneers of a new order in our street, and that with their coming Mr Lockett might as well have abandoned finally his ambition for that select and exclusive neighbourhood of which he had dreamed when he had moved a little farther west from Old Kensington and bought Number 23. What particularly annoyed him was that the Linwoods had secured Number 25 at a lower rent owing to the anxiety of the owners to be rid of a house which had been unprofitably empty for so many years.

'I always said it was fatal to allow that house to stand empty all that time,' Mr Lockett declared. To hear him one could have supposed the landlords had kept it from being occupied for the express purpose of defeating his own plans. 'From what I can gather these people at Number 25 have turned it into what is nothing better than a common lodging house.'

This was rather an exaggeration; for although three young men were permanently established under Mrs Linwood's roof, there was no evidence that she was prepared to let any of her rooms to casual lodgers.

'I knew when those confounded Spinks took Number 13 that we should pay for it sooner or later.'

The Spinks had faded out of our ken for quite two years, and the Rosenthals had been installed in their old house for a long time before the Linwoods arrived, so it was hardly fair of Mr Lockett to blame the Spinks for the newcomers.

'We don't want these wild bohemians,' he grumbled. 'Excellent at a smoking concert, but altogether out of place in our street. The way those two young women spend their time lolling out of the window is revolting. And I have a strong impression that their faces are covered with powder.'

The two young women in question were Bella and Madge Linwood, then both in their early twenties, with buxom figures and full lips and that dressing-room air which the more or less emancipated young women of Queen Victoria's last years so often conveyed without ever having passed through a stage door.

It was difficult to guess why Mrs Linwood should have produced such a bouncing pair of daughters. She was herself a shrivelled little woman whose clothes were put on anyhow and whose vagueness was so extreme that she might easily have lost her husband as one loses a pocketbook. Anyway, she had no husband, and I fancy there was a general belief in our street that she never had had a husband. Although Mrs Linwood was outwardly so unlike Bella and Madge, it was easy to see from whom they inherited their bohemianism. It would never have struck Mrs Linwood to suggest that they should not lean out of windows and stare down at the people in our street. And Mrs Linwood would have been as much surprised by people's criticising her daughters as by their suggesting that she herself smoked too many cigarettes. Mrs Linwood's notion was that people should do what they felt like doing at the very moment when they felt like doing it. This theory of ethics produced a certain amount of irregularity in the household meals. If nobody at Number 25 felt like cooking nobody did cook, and if nobody felt like eating nobody did eat. Then again if nobody felt like getting up in the morning nobody did get up, and usually nobody did feel like getting up, because usually nobody at Number 25 went to bed until very late indeed. If the young men living with Mrs Linwood had been business men they might have objected to such complete indifference to time. But they were not businessmen. Arthur Lloyd was intending to be a composer. Geoffrey Moore was intending to be a singer. Dick Fanning was intending to be an author.

The chief evidence our street possessed of their artistic aspirations was the way they used to play the piano and sing songs at all hours of the night. Besides being heard they were seen, for the gas was always full on and the blinds never drawn. Owing to the very high choker collars that Geoffrey Moore used to wear he always had to take his collar off when he was singing, and this gave him the appearance of a music-hall comedian, so that he never looked as if he were singing one of those drawing-roof ballads which at this date were inevitable in every house.

Geoffrey Moore had a charming tenor voice and used to sing with much emotion ballads about old gardens and maidens walking within them with hair of sunny brown, and about bringing violets to his lady love every morning and roses every evening; ballads that expressed the most respectful feelings towards womanhood. But singing them like that without his collar created a wrong impression, and we often used to hear Mr Lockett and General Brackenbury grumble to one another about the way those people at Number 25 kept bawling out vulgar music-hall ditties, regardless of their neighbours' peace. There was some excuse for General Brackenbury, because he was not musical; but after all Mr Lockett was a singing master himself, and I am sure he could not really have thought that Geoffrey Moore was singing music-hall ditties. He was just as severe, too, on Arthur Lloyd, chiefly, I fancy, because Arthur Lloyd had such a passion for Wagner. Mr Lockett hated Wagner's music. He said it was ugly, perverted, unhealthy stuff. I remember that he nearly resigned from his post at St Jude's when the vicar asked him to play some of the *Parsifal* music as a voluntary. I happened to be up in the organ loft with Mr Lockett that Sunday and was a witness of the scene.

'Ah, Mr Lockett,' said the vicar, 'it has been suggested to me that membahs of our congregation would greatly appreciate an opportunity to hear some of the music of *Parsifal* by the German composah Wagner and I wondahed if next Sunday evening you might indulge them. Or possibly you might even contrive to arrange it for this evening?'

'Who suggested such a thing?' demanded Mr Lockett, his grizzled carroty locks bristling like the back of a pugnacious old Irish terrier.

'It was in point of fact our esteemed friend and helpah, Miss Girdlestone.'

'Miss Girdlestone ought to know better,' Mr Lockett snapped.

The vicar gasped. Miss Girdlestone subscribed more heavily than any member of his congregation to parish charities, and I think the vicar was convinced that Miss Girdlestone knew the best.

'Miss Girdlestone assures me that Wagner has written a great deal of music which though more often performed in the

194

theatah may be performed with the greatest propriety in a sacred edifice.'

'Wagner wrote for a mob of perverted degenerates, Vicar,' Mr Lockett affirmed. 'And I won't defile my fingers by playing a note of his so-called music.'

'Defile, Mr Lockett? Defile is a very strong word to use.'

'It's not strong enough to express what I feel about playing Wagner's pernicious stuff on my organ.'

'Dear me, this is all very unexpected,' the vicar sighed. 'I'm sure our kind Miss Girdlestone had no ideah that you would feel like this about her little suggestion. It's most painful, most painful. Yes, Hutchinson? What is it, Hutchinson?'

This question was addressed to a choir boy who with glazed pink cheeks was trying to gulp out some message from the vestry.

'Please, sir, Mr Oliphant sent me up to say did you know it had gone eleven o'clock.'

'Dear me, I am coming at once. Perhaps after Matins, Mr Lockett . . . '

The vicar hurried away to join his two curates and the waiting choir, while Mr Lockett sat down to crash out upon the organ an unusually martial introit which seemed to be playing the clergy and choir into their seats like a regiment on to the review ground.

So when Arthur Lloyd banged out transcriptions of *Tanhäuser* and *Lohengrin*, with the windows of his room so wide open that the perveted music could be heard all along our street, no wonder Mr Lockett, who had refused to oblige even Miss Girdlestone, spoke bitterly of those noisy mountebanks at Number 25.

It was rumoured that Dick Fanning, the other member of the trio, was destined one day to become a great novelist; but his literary output at present seemed to consist chiefly of lyrics which Arthur Lloyd set to music and Geoffrey Moore sang.

It was some time before I contrived to get to know the inmates of Number 25. In the end the introduction came about through Gladys Gurney, who by this date must have been close on seventeen and had developed into a handsome and dashing young woman. Miss Bearsted had retired from the control of the young Gurneys about a year before the Linwoods took Number 25. Muriel had gone to school in France,

Dorothy had gone to school in Germany, and Bob was now at Clifton. So Gladys, finding home life uneventful, made friends over the garden wall with Bella and Madge Linwood, and being invited by them to join in their evenings flirted ardently with the three young men in turn until she ended by imagining herself deep in love with Dick Fanning.

I fancy that some faint lingering influence of Miss Bearsted's education may have led Gladys to take me with her to Number 25 as a kind of chaperon first of all. Or it may have been that she just thought I was often at a loose end for companionship at this time and, being a generous warm-hearted girl, wanted to give me a chance of amusement. My great friend Olive Doyle had gone away to a school in France like Muriel, and my father was talking now of sending me to spend a year with some family in Hanover, a prospect I did not view with the least pleasure. However, my Aunt Adelaide advised me not to argue about it and guaranteed that after a year in Germany I should have a year in France and, if she could persuade my father, a year in Italy before I went to the university.

Probably it was my aunt's knowledge that the stretches of boyhood I had spent so happily in our street would soon belong to the past which led her not to object to my frequenting Number 25. I know one or two of her friends were hinting Number 25 was no place for the boy of fifteen; but she paid no attention and, provided I did not overstay the time allowed me, my visits were not interfered with.

These gatherings at the Linwoods' made me feel tremendously grown up, which I could never manage to feel at any of the other houses in our street, the people in them having most of them known me from such very early years. Of course, Mr Mellor had always treated me as his equal in age ever since I met him first on that drizzling evening outside Elson's bookshop; but he lived a life entirely outside the ordinary intercourse of our street, and when I was with him it was more like taking a walk in the Elysian fields and holding converse with the mighty dead than having tea with an elderly bachelor. To visit him was to feel the agelessness of the remote past. To be at one of Mrs Linwood's gatherings was to step forward and take one's place in that immediate future which dances so alluringly before a boy of fifteen and from which he usually sees himself debarred by those difficult years of later adolescence through which he has yet to live. If this were autobiography I should be tempted to enlarge upon my impressions of and reactions to that happy-go-lucky society I found at the Linwoods'; but conventions have been discarded so fast that I could not hope to entertain the modern reader with what at the close of Queen Victoria's reign seemed the license of such a house as Number 25. It is too remote for profitable or entertaining psychologising. Why, already it is the mode to refer even to the Edwardian decade as we in youth referred to the Regency or even to the Restoration.

I have spoken of Arthur Lloyd's playing of Wagner to the disgust of Mr Lockett, but it was really Tchaikovsky who was thrilling us at this date. The Pathetic Symphony seemed the ultimate expression music could offer to the modern world. I never hear the Pathetic Symphony but there comes back to me the first time I heard those heart-rending melodies. It was upon a Sunday afternoon in late autumn when fog had turned to a thin rain before the shutting in of dusk. The sitting room at the Linwoods', which bore no kind of resemblance to the drawing rooms along the rest of our street, had gradually filled up since dinner with a crowd of people who had taken refuge here from the gloom of a London Sabbath. Geoffrey Moore had sung for us, and a young woman in a floppy green dress with a fuzz of bright red hair had recited for us from one of the slim volumes of minor verse that drifted steadily down throughout the 'nineties like autumn leaves. Another young woman in a floppy brown and orange dress had read us a short story about some man who had committed suicide so beautifully that we felt at the end of it we all ought to commit suicide ourselves just as beautifully. There had been a long discussion about the object of life, in which it looked as if the supporters of hedonism would completely annihilate, the other side, until somebody on the other side asked, 'But what is pleasure?' This turned the conversation into a series of confessions which might have been interesting if only everybody had not been so anxious to confess that nobody had time to listen.

And then, chiefly I think to persuade Bella and Madge Linwood to abandon the discussion and go and make tea, because it was the 'girl's' Sunday off, Mrs Linwood asked Arthur Lloyd if he wouldn't play that thing he liked so much by that man with a name like a sneeze, which he couldn't expect her to say or anybody else either, such names as these Russian – he was Russian, wasn't he? – these Russian musicians managed to think of, but he had played them some of it the other night and it had made her feel so shivery that she knew it must be good.

'So do play it to us, Arthur, there's a dear,' Mrs Linwood wound up, and lighting a cigarette from the stump of the one she had just been smoking, a continuity she had been achieving with cigarette after cigarette all the afternoon, Mrs Linwood flung herself back on the divan and prepared to shiver.

'I suppose you mean Tchaikovsky's Pathetic Symphony?' Arthur Lloyd asked.

'Yes, that's it. I don't know how you remember the names, Arthur, leave alone the tunes. I think you're marvellous. Bella! Madge! Do go and see about tea.'

Bella and Madge would probably have argued for a while about the necessity of getting tea at that particular moment if there had not been two young men in the party whom they rather liked and who themselves were delighted to escape from Tchaikovsky in order to indulge in badinage with Bella and Madge down in the kitchen.

So the usual argument between themselves and their mother was avoided, and Arthur Lloyd sat down to play a large part of the Pathetic Symphony upon the cottage piano of which Mrs Linwood never failed to say that it was a jolly good piano once. Arthur Lloyd had a really good piano in his own room on the first floor upon which he was wont to play the transciptions of Wagner that so much irritated Mr Lockett; but he did not regard his performance of the Pathetic Symphony by ear as serious piano playing, and so he did not mind sitting down to that cottage piano of Mrs Linwood which once upon a time had been such a good one.

It may have been that people were tired of talking and were content to lean back and smoke quietly, or like Gladys Gurney and Dick Fanning hold hands until the gas was lighted and the blinds were drawn; but I prefer to think that there was some magic about Arthur Lloyd's playing which cast a spell upon his listeners, whatever their mood. I remember that I was sitting on a cushion leaning against the wall of the room and that through the French windows I could see at the end of the garden the poplars already bare of all except a few withered leaves, and beyond the poplars the backs of houses melting into the on-coming dark, as the fog was displaced by that thin melancholy rain, and here and there in the dim line of houses a lighted room with shadows moving about it. While Arthur Lloyd played those yearning melodies I felt that the whole of human nature's misery was being expressed in this room. I had lately been reading the poem of Arthur O'Shaughnessy's which begins:

> *We are the music makers,*
>   *And we are the dreamers of dreams;*

and looking round that darkening room I thought how splendid it was that the Linwoods and Arthur Lloyd had come to live in our street and touch it with the breath of that immense *au delà* of which these yearning notes sounded the appeal. I felt a great pity for people like the Locketts and the Rosenthals and Doctor Arden and the Bonds and General Brackenbury who were content to lead a circumscribed existence of stuffy con-ventionality, entirely unaware of that *au delà.*

Ah, exquisite melancholy of adolescence, would that I could feel again your clutch at my heart! Ah, luxury of youthful sorrow which is but a lover's quarrel with life!

Now when years later I find myself trying to recapture the emotion of listening to the Pathetic Symphony in that untidy smoke-haunted room on that mournful London dusk of a Sun-day at the end of October, a generation of years ago, I can only feel a faint resentment against the Linwoods and Arthur Lloyd and his friends and against Tchaikovsky himself for spoiling the symmetry of our street. They intrude upon my picture. They have no business to be in our street at all. I wish Mrs Linwood had never taken Number 25 and that it might have stood empty for evermore.

NUMBER 5

THE earliest recollections I have of my Aunt Adelaide and our street are linked with the Jubilee of Queen Victoria in 1887, and thanks to the cooperation of the historical background my last recollections of her and of our street are linked with the Diamond Jubilee of 1897. The decade stretches from one azure June to another. When I sat between Aunt Adelaide and Aunt Emily in a stand not far from Hyde Park Corner, I do not suppose that any of us in that stand or any of those serried crowds upon the pavements or any of the scarlet troops that lined the route of the procession felt even the slightest touch of mortality's chill hand. It was a day of fanfares and gold lace and brazen marches and glittering uniforms. It was a day of imperial splendour and imperial power unsurpassed in the history of our planet. It was the peak of the British Empire's greatness, the ultimate expression of its grandeur. It was a long cloudless June day of Queen's weather, the culmination of daylight's waxing.

Two evenings later, the trumpets still resounding in my brain, the drums still beating, the illuminations still sparkling, I wandered along to Elson's bookshop to search the shelves for some volume that would gratify the thirst for barbaric colour which had been raised by the Jubilee procession. My interest in pastel shades, in the 'New Art' of Munich, in neo-hedonism and Verlaine's poetry and Aubrey Beardsley's drawings and Tchaikovsky's music, was in abeyance. I was in the mood again for that coloured plate of the cavalry regiments of the British army in the *Boy's Own Paper*.

However, I found nothing within reach of my purse, and was just turning homeward when I saw Mr Mellor's beard sweeping the dust from the pages of some folio. I asked him if he had seen the Jubilee procession on Saturday.

'Great Scott, no!' he gasped. 'You don't mean to say you went out gaping with the mob? Astonishing vigour of body and strength of mind!'

One of Mr Mellor's charms, as I already indicated, was his implication that I was the same age as himself. The average elderly bachelor would have reminded me of the forty or fifty years' difference in our ages by adding that he was too old for that sort of thing. Mr Mellor merely conveyed his astonishment that another elderly bachelor should have preserved enough pristine energy to put up with the fatigue of sitting in a stand from six o'clock in the morning just to see a procession go past.

'You must be worn out,' he continued.

I assured him that I was quite all right.

'Then come to supper with me. Mrs Jutsom felt regrettably impelled to goo gallivanting off on Saturday to what she calls the Joobly, and she may or may not have provided the wherewithal to fill our bellies. But the wine is red and abundant. There is a Camembert cheese which tomorrow will require a spoon and therefore must be eaten this very night. I have lettuces and cherries, new bread and fresh butter. What the devil more do we want? Let Mrs Jutsom's larder be a vacuum, we shall survive. Ah, yes, and ginger. I had forgotten the ginger. There is a jar of it unexcavated as yet.'

Mr Mellor's invitation occurred conveniently, for when I reached Number 9 I found my Aunt Adelaide had retired to bed early with a headache brought on by the long outing in Saturday's sun, which she had been fighting against all yesterday in order not to miss church, and that Aunt Emily had met some friends up in town for the Jubilee and was going out to a theatre. Hetty and Janet had both been to the Jubilee, too, and to let them go to bed early I was for the first time in my life entrusted with a latchkey, the time of my return being fixed as a special favour for as late as half-past ten o'clock. These details will be sounding extremely trivial; but this evening of June, 1897, became a date of much importance in my life in our street, and consequently the attendant circumstances possess for my imagination the portentous attributes of fatality.

When I rang the bell of Number 5 the door was opened by Mr Mellor himself. He held in one hand a basket.

'Eggs!' he shouted. 'Some of Mrs Jutsom's rustic connections have been in London for the Joobly and the house is full of new-laid eggs. Mrs Jutsom is sitting in her kitchen surrounded by perspiring brothers and sisters and brothers-in-law and sisters-in-law, every one of whom has presented her with eggs. He that would have eggs, saith the old adage, must bear with cackling. And Mrs Jutsom bears with it nobly. As for me I will e'en make an omelette *aux fines,* choosing that as the noblest of the six hundred and eighty-five ways of cooking an egg.'

The dining-room table was laid with the very supper Mr Mellor had promised, and to this, with the aid of a chafing dish, he set about adding an omelette of a lightness and aromatic flavour such as even I had never tasted, though my Aunt Adelaide had trained Hetty to make a really good omelette, trained her austerely to be as light with her hands as ballet dancers are trained to be light upon their feet. But Hetty's best omelette would have seemed earthbound if eaten after this sylph conjured from the chafing dish by such a Prospero of a cook. He made it in the dining room, and in that medieval chamber he looked like a genial alchemist brewing a potion that should confer invisibility on him who partook of it.

After supper we retired upstairs to Mr Mellor's den, carrying with us bottles of red wine. It was always pretended when I took supper with Mr Mellor that I should be drinking glass for glass with him for the rest of the evening. So I always used to be told to bring upstairs my wine, and this evening, as I had been sipping slowly one glass, while Mr Mellor gulped down a dozen, he said:

'Look here, young fellow my lad, if you're going to boggle at Château Yquem like a Harrogate dowager at her morning dose of water, pass your bottle over to me. Good wine is a familiar creature if it be well used, but, as Dr Johnson once observed to Sir Joshua, no good and worthy man will insist upon another man's drinking wine.'

By putting it thus, Mr Mellor prevented my feeling the least embarrassment over my own comparatively timid performance. He would usually become meditative for a while after finishing his second bottle, and so it was tonight. He leaned back in a long silence, while I contemplated upon the mantelpiece a shell on which was painted a little naked girl standing on golden sands beside a blue sea. It was painted so cunningly that the texture of the shell had apparently given life to the colours. The sea glittered in the sun; the body of the child glowed with pulsing blood; the sands were sheened veritably as the tide had left them.

'Bah!' Mr Mellor burst out suddenly. 'Horace was right. Lettuce after wine does float about upon an acid stomach. I can't remember the exact Latin, but Horace was right. And you were wiser than I in sipping your wine discreetly. How shall I anchor this wine-logged lettuce? By the holy poker, there shall be no harbour for this derelict lettuce, for I will sink the sodden brute. It shall no longer float upon a few beggarly wineglassfuls. It shall be soused with a beaker full of Falernian.'

With this Mr Mellor heaved himself up out of his chair and went across to a cupboard hanging in a corner. When he opened it, I saw that the shelves were crowded with glasses of every shape and colour. My host plunged his hand into the middle of them and drew out a goblet of green cut glass, which he filled to the brim and swallowed at a breath.

'I will sink thee, lettuce, with a craft of thine own colour,' he proclaimed. '*Vinum vincit viridem. Submersa est lactuca.* But to make perfectly sure that wine-logged lettuce is finally sunk, I will repeat the dose.'

After settling the lettuce Mr Mellor became expansive, and started to tell me those stories I could listen to by the hour of Rossetti and William Morris and Swinburne and all the rest of them. I remember, too, he had a lot of good tales this evening about Whistler, whose *Gentle Art of Making Enemies* I had just discovered on Mr Joliffe's shelves and had read in an ecstasy of wonder that such wit could be.

The one-handed clock which I had by now learnt to read was marking ten when we heard the voice of Mrs Jutsom from the hall. No message was considered of sufficient importance to warrant Mrs Jutsom's invading Mr Mellor's den with it. If the master of the house felt in the mood to answer her, he came out from his den and shouted down across the balusters of the landing to know what the devil she wanted that she was making such a shindy about it in the hall. Mrs Justom always humoured his eccentricity, but she did once say to me that to look after Mr Mellor was more like being a keeper at the Zoo than anything else.

'Fancy him thinking as I don't ever take the chance of him being out to go up and flick the worst of the dust off everything. Well, really it's childish. But don't you let on to him, my dear, what I told you, because I really believe he thinks I've never set foot on one stair above the dining-room floor.'

I do not know what the upper rooms at Number 5 would have been like if Mrs Jutsom had not disobeyed the rules of the house at every opportunity. They were thick enough with dust as it was.

'I hear the voice of Mrs Jutsom, do I not?' Mr Mellor now asked this evening. 'What do you suppose she wants?'

I said had no idea.

'And I have no idea,' he added, wagging his beard.

'Mr Mellor, sir,' we heard again, 'Will you come out, please, and speak to me a minute?'

'There is an unwonted urgency in her tone,' Mr Mellor decided gravely. 'I cannot imagine why she should come up and bellow at me at such an hour. What *can* she be wanting, do you suppose?'

I offered to go and find out for him, if he felt disinclined to drag himself out of his comfortable chair.

'Yes,' he agreed, 'yes, your suggestion is a practical one. It would, if carried out, probably go far towards solving the problem of why Mrs Jutsom should at this tranquil hour of ten o'clock be yelling for me like this. But wait a moment. Do not forget my rule that, if I do not answer her summons by word of mouth, she may, if she feels that the message is of sufficient importance, blow a blast upon the horn. So let us wait a little. Why should we disturb ourselves unless we are completely convinced that Mrs Jutsom has a genuinely important communication to make to us, as for instance that the lower part of the house is on fire?'

He had hardly finished speaking when we heard the noise of the Swiss cow horn, which hung in the hall for an emergency like this.

'Mrs Jutsom does not blow with the compulsion of a Roland. I have heard her blow her own nose with a richer sonority than she seems able to evoke from that horn. However, blown it she has, and so spare me the labour of extracting myself from this chair by finding out for me what that pertinacious woman wants.'

I hurried outside and leaned over the balusters to see Mrs Jutsom standing at the foot of the stairs and shaking her head reproachfully.

'Will you tell Mr Mellor that there's a gentleman wants to

see him? I've shown him into the dining room, and lit the candles. Here's his card.'

I ran downstairs and looked at the name:

Oliver Darrell

'Somebody to see me?' exclaimed Mr Mellor. 'But nobody ever calls to see me. Occasionally people write. It must be the Joobly. Even I am visited by someone who has come to London for the Joobly. Confound the Joobly, I say, and confound Mrs Justom for letting her hospitality exceed her discretion. Mrs Jutsom, you are, since Eve, the silliest woman that ever afflicted a man.'

But Mrs Jutsom, having delivered the visitor's card, had retired to the basement, where not even Mr Mellor's voice could reach her.

'What is the name of this pestilent intruder?' the owner of the house asked.

I put the card in his hand.

'Oliver Darrell! Now why the deuce didn't that idiotic woman tell me it was Oliver Darrell?'

Mr Mellor went galumphing down the stairs in the way he did when he was excited, which always reminded me of a big sea lion galumphing down a chute into his pool.

'Darrell, my dear fellow, how are you? How are you?' he was roaring as he burst into the dining room, whence in a moment he came galumphing out again with his arm in the arm of a tall man in rough brown tweed who impressed me at once as the most distinguished-looking man I had ever seen.

When they reached Mr Mellor's den, I at once said that I ought to be going, because I supposed that these two friends would not want the company of a boy at what was evidently a meeting after a lapse of years.

'I thought you told me you hadn't to be home before half-past ten?' Mr Mellor asked.

'Well, I havent.'

'Then what's the use of going twenty minutes before you need? Sit down again.'

With this he gave me a push that sent me backwards deep into one of those old armchairs covered with blue and red tambour work.

'This is Mr Oliver Darrell, the painter,' he told me.

The tall man nodded with a sort of indifferent cordiality; but when Mr Mellor told him my name he glanced at me a sudden searching look and seemed on the point of asking me something before he evidently thought the better of it in the same instant, and turned away to tell Mr Mellor that he did not look a day older than when he saw him last in Paris in '83, fourteen years ago.

'More than I can say for you, my boy,' said Mr Mellor.'

'I'm forty-two now. There's a difference between twenty-eight and forty-two,' the younger man answered quickly.

'And I'm seventy-two,' Mr Mellor roared triumphantly.

I myself was at the age when thirty seemed like an extreme antiquity; but even I was astonished to hear that Mr Mellor was over seventy.

While he and Oliver Darrell were talking about people and places I knew nothing of, I watched the newcomer with an ever-increasing and fascinated interest. He was clean-shaven, with a profile as clear-cut as one of Flaxman's heroes, his likeness to whom was accentuated by the terra-cotta to which the sun had burnt his complexion. I thought how splendid he would look as Hector or Diomed. Not that he did not to my eye look splendid enough in that suit of rough brown tweed with tie of faded amber silk.

'I was glad to see La Belle Dame again,' he was saying to Mr Mellor. 'It's a great picture.'

'It's the only good picture I ever painted,' Mr Mellor agreed. 'So I would never sell it.'

'A good picture,' the visitor repeated, 'and a good subject,' he added half to himself.

Then he caught sight of the little naked girl painted upon that shell which was leaning against the wall above the mantelpiece, and he asked Mr Mellor if it was his work.

'Yes, I painted it on a shell I picked up on the beach at Rapallo. Do not think, my dear Oliver, that you are the only great painter who has visited Rapallo. That was one of your favourite haunts, wasn't it? Yes, as Johnson once said to Bozzy, the man who has not visited Italy is conscious of an inferiority, and so I hasten to remind you that I *have* visited Italy.'

'On the beach at Rapallo,' Oliver Darrell murmured.

Then looking full at me he said:

'You have the same name as an old friend of mine,' at the

very instant that I said:

'My Aunt Adelaide has a picture of the beach at Rapallo.'

'Your Aunt Adelaide?' Darrell repeated, and those veiled blue eyes of his suddenly flamed.

'Yes, I'm staying with her. She lives next door but one to Mr Mellor. She lives with a friend called Miss Emily Culham.'

'And your aunt is not married?' Darrell asked.

I shook my head.

'And she lives next door but one to this house?'

'At Number 9, yes. And I think I must be going now, Mr Mellor, because I said I would be home by half-past ten and,' I added in as nonchalant a voice as I could manage, 'I've got the latchkey.'

'You'll be seeing your aunt in a minute or two?' Darrell asked, staring at me.

I told him I should not disturb her unless she called to me when I passed the door of her room, because she had gone to bed early with a bad headache after the long outing for the Jubilee on Saturday.

'Does she often have bad headaches?' he asked.

'Pretty often,' I told him.

I do not believe as a matter of fact that my Aunt Adelaide's headaches really were so very frequent; but young people always suppose that the ills of their seniors are chronic, because their incidence so often interferes with a youthful pleasure.

The visitor seemed anxious to say something more and kept knitting his eyebrows as if puzzled how to express himself; but I with the responsibility of that latchkey to justify was fidgeting to be off, and finally I thrust out an awkward hand to bid him farewell.

'I'll see you safely off the premises,' said Mr Mellor, shutting the door upon his visitor and leading the way downstairs. 'Come in here a moment,' he told me by the dining-room door.

The wax candles lighted by Mrs Jutsom for the visitor's reception were still burning on either side the picture of the knight in sea-green armour. Between them stood the hourglass in which the sands were half run out. Darrell must have turned it over idly while he was waiting for the housekeeper to rouse the master of the house. Mr Mellor snatched up one of the great pewter candlesticks and held the golden flame so that it lit up the knight's face, the while he half chanted:

> *'I saw pale kings, and princes too,*
> *Pale warriors, death-pale were they all:*
> *They cried – 'La belle dame sans merci*
> *Hath thee in thrall!'*

Then he looked hard at me.

'Do you recognise that face?' he asked.

And I saw that the face of the knight-at-arms was the face of Oliver Darrell, but death-pale like all those victims of unhappy love.

'I painted that in 1883 when I was working for a time in France. Oliver came haggard and woebegone one day to my studio in no mood for the companionship of his contemporaries, and I asked him to sit for that head. It was and it is and it will remain the only good picture I shall ever paint. I was fortunate in my model. *Alone and palely loitering.* I can see him now in the studio. He was going to be married to a charming girl, and there was some quarrel – I say quarrel, but I never heard the story – there may have been no quarrel at all. Anyway, the engagement was broken off. And now of course her name comes back to me. It was your aunt. When you first spoke to me about her, the name was vaguely familiar; but you know my horror of female intrusion, except by gay young rosebuds like Olive who, by the way and alas, is growing up much too fast. I always put a woman's name out of my head as quick as I can. But look here, now that Oliver's come back like this, oughtn't you and I to do something about it? The sands are running out,' he went on, pointing a grubby stubby forefinger at the hourglass.

I did not like to tell Mr Mellor about that Browning of my Aunt Adelaide's in which she had pencilled those records in her fine hand beside the text. I could not speak of that O. whose name I knew at last, and of that wild happiness he had brought to my aunt upon that morn of Rome and May. Besides, some years had passed since that anniversary afternoon when I had found my aunt's bookcase unlocked and when in the tempered sunlight of her study to the sound of that blind filling and flapping in the May breeze I had trespassed upon her secret.

'I might tell Aunt Emily,' I suggested. 'And then she could

say if Aunt Adelaide would like to know that Mr Darrell was in London.'

'No, that's no good. The only way is for your Aunt Emily to see him. And I suppose that means I shall have to invite Aunt Emily to my house. Well, he gave me the only good picture I shall ever paint. Ask Aunt Emily if she'll come to tea with me tomorrow and meet Oliver. I hope I'm not being an interfering busybody . . . but the sands are running out very fast . . . very fast.'

I agreed earnestly, for I was thinking by now it must be nearly a quarter of an hour later than I had promised to be home.

'All right, cut along,' said Mr Mellor.

It was hardly fifteen yards from the door of Number 5 to the door of Number 9 but either because of Oliver Darrell's appearance and all that it might mean to my Aunt Adelaide – or as I fear may be more likely – because for the first time in my life I was about to let myself in with a latchkey, the picture of our street on that June night is still with me. The three lamp-posts still burn as brightly, though were we to see them today they would not seem to be burning at all brightly after the electric light we now enjoy. The midsummer sky is still as deep and glimmering a blue above the high wall of Sir George Griffin's garden. I can still hear the bolts being pushed in and the chain on the door being fastened at Number 7 as I pass. I can still hear the low murmur of conversation from the Bonds' front balcony, and from the open windows of Number 25 a feminine voice is still singing, *I wish I could remember the first day, first hour, first moment of your meeting me.* To this day, whenever I hear those words of Christina Rossetti and that so poignantly perfect melody of Maude Valérie White I see a faded photograph of my Aunt Adelaide in a tight flounced skirt of the earliest 'eighties, standing by that latticed window which was one of the favourite scenic properties of the Baker Street photographer of that period and looking down into some imaginary studio garden. I can still fancy that I smell the sweet pungency of Lady Marjorie's geraniums watered at twilight an hour since, and the pots of yellow musk along the sill of the dining-room window in our house.

I WISHED as I opened the front door with the latchkey that somebody I knew could pass and see my first gesture of manhood; but not a footstep was heard along the pavement of our street as I closed the door gently behind me.

I walked upstairs and listened outside the door of my Aunt Adelaide's room. I even turned the handle of her dressing-room door to hear if she would call to me. When I first came to stay at Number 9 ten years ago·I had always slept in this dressing room, and it had always been my ambition to wake up when Aunt Adelaide came to bed and to call her drowsily that I might hear that reassuring voice murmur gently:

'Go to sleep. It's Aunt Adelaide.'

And sometimes, though very seldom, I would beg for a glass of water in order to have the joy of seeing her wavy chestnut hair falling in a cascade over her shoulders.

But tonight when I whispered, 'It's me, Aunt Adelaide. I've come in,' there was no answer.

This decided me to do what I had wanted to do and sit up for Aunt Emily so that I could tell her at once about Oliver Darrell and about Mr Mellor's invitation to tea. I felt that if I were to wait until tomorrow morning the effect of my announcement would be killed by the critical light of day. It seemed to me that Aunt Adelaide's not answering me was a sign that I was meant to speak to Aunt Emily this very night. I would have given a great deal to have the courage to go into Aunt Adelaide's sitting room and see if by chance that volume of Browning's poems was attainable. But I so much dreaded causing some fresh catastrophe in my aunt's life by what would appear nothing except inquisitiveness that I did not dare.

Down in the drawing room where I had made up my mind to sit and wait for Aunt Emily's return, the faint pop of the gas when I lighted one of the burners sounded like an explosion in the silence of the house, and the luminous globe of porcelain through which the gas jet glowed opalescent seemed to be flaming like naphtha. There was a framed Arundel print of Botticelli's picture of Venus Rising from the Sea hanging on the wall, and too much agitated by now to read, I sat down and stared at it, thinking of that picture of the little naked girl painted by Mr Mellor on the shell he had picked up on the beach at Rapallo. I wished the water-colour of that beach in my aunt's bedroom were down here, for I was sure that it was linked with some moment of her engagement to Oliver Darrell. I should have been none the wiser if that water-colour had been before me; but I think I should have conjured beside those silvery blue ripples the figures of two lovers parting fourteen years ago. It was strange that this very evening Mr Mellor should have put that painted shell on his mantelpiece, strange that I should have had an extra half-hour's leave, and strangest of all that Oliver Darrell should have called upon this night of all nights. Everything had conspired to bring those parted lovers together, and nothing must now happen to separate them again.

The elfin chimes in my Aunt Emily's travelling clock struck eleven. I wondered if that same clock had struck the hours away for those two lovers in Italy. If I were writing a story of a boy of fifteen made aware of what I was made aware of then, I do not believe I should venture to attribute to him that fancy about the clock. I should probably imagine that he would have been perhaps a little shocked by the notion that an aunt of his, drawing near to forty, could ever have been in love at all without marriage as the conventional ending. But as I look back now to what I was thinking as I sat there waiting for Aunt Emily in the empty drawing room of Number 9 on that June night so many years ago, I cannot recall that for a single instant did I regard my Aunt Adelaide as other than the heroine of a romance, ageless and fair and worthy to be loved. It is true my mind was crammed with ideas of romantic love nigh as thick as was Don Quixote's. In spite of my adventures with modern writers I was the child of an earlier age and, for all my fascination by the glittering paradoxes of Vivian and Cyril in Oscar Wilde's *Intentions,* I was entirely without a touch of the precocious cynicism by which it is so difficult for the poor child of the moment to escape being touched.

It must have been a quarter of an hour from midnight when

211

at last I heard the noise of the latchkey and the jingle of a departing hansom cab.

'My dear boy,' Aunt Emily exclaimed, 'what in the name of goodness are you doing, up at this hour?'

I wish I had the technique to describe Aunt Emily's dress that evening; but all I know is that she was a shimmer of pink satin and that she let her train fall in astonishment at sight of me emerging from the drawing room.

'I waited up, Aunt Emily, to tell you something. Something important. Aunt Adelaide's asleep. It's something about her that I want to tell you.'

'But, dear boy, it's nearly midnight.'

'Yes, but really it's something frightfully important. Do come into the drawing room and let me talk to you.'

Aunt Emily hesitated for a moment at the foot of the stairs and looked in the direction of Aunt Adelaide's room.

'No, no, we must go to bed. You can tell me tomorrow.'

'It's about a Mr Darrell.'

Aunt Emily, white as her own hands, stared at me. Then she went quickly into the drawing room, and the swish of her silk petticoats comes back across the years like the sound of violins playing incidental music to this scene.

There was hanging on the wall of the drawing room at Number 9 a painting of Aunt Emily as a child of about four. It was a circular canvas, and she was seated in tall grasses among blowballs and poppies and ox-eyed daisies. She was holding a blowball herself and, a grave expression on her face, look of wonder in her speedwell eyes, she was blowing the plumed seeds into the air. Now, while she sat listening to my tale of the evening's encounter, the same look was in her eyes, and the child on the wall behind her seemed somehow to be a third in the conversation.

'And Mr Mellor wants me to go to tea with him tomorrow afternoon and meet Mr Darrell?' she murmured at the end of my narration. Then in a lowered voice so low as hardly to be audible she whispered to herself: 'The heart that has truly loved never forgets.'

I did not know whether she referred to him or to my Aunt Adelaide by this line, and I hoped that I might be told something more about this old love affair, about how it began and how it ended.

But Aunt Emily said no more, and I heard not another word from her except a sudden sharp command to take myself off to bed.

As was leaving the drawing room Aunt Emily told me to be sure not to say a word to Janet of my having met Mr Darrell.

'And of course you'll not say anything to your aunt?'

'Of course not,' I said indignantly.

For the first time it evidently occurred to Aunt Emily that she was treating me a little unfairly.

'Of course I never really thought you would,' she said. 'Indeed, nobody could have been more tactful than you have been. And so you'll understand, I know, that it isn't my secret. Aunt Adelaide wouldn't like to think that we had been discussing her most private affairs, would she?'

I believe if Aunt Emily had not added that question at the end as if she were trying to explain something to a very young child I should have gone off to bed quite content. But we are sensitive at the age of fifteen to the imputation of extreme youth, and I could not resist paying Aunt Emily back for having imputed youth to me.

'It was you who said that the heart which has truly loved never forgets,' I reminded her.

'Did I say that?' she asked in surprise. 'It was a line from a song I used to sing once. Come back into the drawing room for a moment. I think that as you have been the means of perhaps bringing together two who loved each other very truly you are entitled to know a little more than you do.'

I seated myself on a footstool at Aunt Emily's feet.

'Once upon a time,' she began, as if it were a fairy tale she was telling me, 'once upon a time long ago . . . well, not so very long ago really, though it was before you were born . . . Aunt Adelaide and I were travelling in Italy. I was engaged to be married and had been studying singing in Milan and Rome, and Adelaide had come out to spend the summer. We met Mr Darrell who was a painter, and he proposed to her.'

'On the beach at Rapallo?' I put in.

'No, no, it was on the Campagna near Rome on a morning in May. I had gone off to scramble about the arches of the old aqueduct for flowers, and when I came back I heard the news. I had been wondering if he would propose to her, and I had sat foolishly blowing the seeds from a cuckoo-clock to find if he loved her.'

'Like you're blowing them in that picture?' I commented.

Aunt Emily turned round and looked at the picture of herself as a child.

'Yes, like that,' she said. 'How observant of you. All the years that picture has been hanging there it has never once reminded me of that day on the Campagna. Well, they could not get married, because Oliver thought he had not enough money. And then the man to whom I was engaged was killed in Egypt, and Adelaide was very kind to me and . . . well, her engagement with Oliver Darrell was broken off because . . . oh, well, it began with an argument over religion . . . and of course it ought never to have ended as it did . . . but both were proud . . . and, well, two people who loved one another were foolish enough to suppose that they would be happier apart from one another. I've often reproached myself since. I've often wondered if I did all I might have done to help. I'm afraid I was selfish. The sad thing is that suffering is apt to make people selfish, and I had suffered a great deal.'

I longed to be able to tell Aunt Emily how little she had ever seemed selfish to me during so many happy visits to our street; but youth finds it hard to make statements of fact about its emotions until that fatal hour when it finds it much too easy.

So to escape from feeling this desire to say something I could not muster up enough self-confidence to say, I asked if the engagement had been broken off at Rapallo.

'Yes, it was at Rapallo.'

Then my vision of lovers parting beside that silvery blue sea had been justified.

'My dear boy, look at the time!' Aunt Emily suddenly exclaimed. 'Out with the gas and away to bed.'

'You will go to tea with Mr Mellor tomorrow?' I pressed.

'Why, of course I shall.'

I wished next day that I could be hearing what she said to Oliver Darrell, and what he said to her. It was a strain to be having tea with my Aunt Adelaide while next door but one that momentous interview was in mid-course.

'Why do you keep looking at me so curiously?' Aunt Adelaide asked. 'I did not think that a headache would have

214

altered my appearance to that extent.'

I assured her with a blush that I was not thinking at all about her personal appearance. At which she laughed; and then what must she think of to talk about but my supper with Mr Mellor last night.

'I'm bound to say this friend of yours is a most ungallant old gentleman. I think he might have invited your two middle-aged aunts to tea with him at any rate once. I fear you have given him a most discouraging account of us in order to have a safe refuge. I overtook him in our street one day last week, and he made for his front door like an alarmed bear.'

'I think he is a misogynist,' I volunteered.

My aunt's eyebrows slanted more than ever, as they always did when she was amused, and her grey eyes danced deliciously.

'Well, isn't that what you call anybody who doesn't like women?' I asked.

'Indeed yes. You use a most impeccably correct word, and you must forgive my smile. I was just thinking what a grand word it was for you to be using. I can't quite get used to your growing up in this rapid fashion. You're still such a very little boy to me.'

And as last night I had longed to express to Aunt Emily some of my affectionate gratitude for a thousand kindnesses, so now I would have sacrificed all my grand words like misogynist to be able too give Aunt Adelaide even the smallest hint of how dearly I loved her. But all I could do was kick the leg of the table in embarrassment and fill my mouth with cake.

However, after tea I asked her if she would read some poetry to me. In making that request I was trying to tell her that I was as much dependent on her as ever in spite of having been allowed last night a latchkey for the first time. Owing to my newly awakened interest in modern poetry it had been quite a long time since I had asked her to read the poems she loved, like Coleridge's *Christabel,* or *Goblin Market,* Or Keats's *Eve of St Agnes.* Thrilled though I was by Arthur Symons and Ernest Dowson, I did not feel that I wanted Aunt Adelaide to be reading that she had flung roses, roses riotously.

She asked me what I should like her to read, and on an impulse I asked her to read some Browning.

It was only when my aunt moved across to her desk and un-locked the bookcase above, apparently to take out that volume of Browning's poems bound in soft leather, that my heart began to beat. Suppose she should offer to read that poem, *Two in the Campagna*? And suppose that in the middle of it Aunt Emily should come back with Oliver Darrell, would not my aunt fancy I had had some knowledge of those dates and places recorded on the pages of that book in her fine hand? In a spasm of apprehension I begged her not to read Browning after all.

'Have you ever read *The Statue and the Bust*?' she asked.

I had to confess that I had not, and I could hardly dissuade her from reading a poem of which I had had to confess ignorance. But what a relief it was when she did not take out of the bookcase that little volume, but chose instead another and larger volume into which I had never looked. Yet even so I wished for any poet except Browning, and I asked her if she was sure that her headache really was completely gone, explaining that when I had asked her to read to me I had forgotten about the headache.

'Yes, yes, it's quite gone.' And sitting by the window she began the poem.

I tried to pay proper attention; but my mind was wandering next door but one, and I was speculating in which room at Number 5 Aunt Emily and Oliver Darrell were meeting. But perhaps Oliver Darrell had not allowed Mr Mellor to arrange the meeting. Perhaps he had gone off last night as suddenly as he had come and was already across the Channel again by now.

> Still I suppose they sit and ponder
> What a gift life was, ages ago.

Aunt Adelaide was reading these words when Aunt Emily came abruptly into the room. A speck of crimson was burning on each of her rose-leaf cheeks, and both cheeks were smudged with tears. And through the open door came up the song of her canaries, all of them singing together.

'Adelaide, my darling, there is somebody –'

'Somebody?' my aunt cut in sharply.

I was nearly on the point of jumping out of the window to escape from the pallor of her face, for I felt frightened by what seemed the noise of our three hearts beating in this quiet room.

'You'll see him, Adelaide?' her friend was leading.

'Will I?' my aunt asked in a dazed voice, as if she were incapable of making the decision for herself but must leave it to Aunt Emily's decision.

Aunt Emily signed to me to come out of the room with her, and we went downstairs to the dining room where Oliver Darrell was waiting.

'Go up to her,' she told him.

And I remember feeling so sorry for that tall distinguished man in his rough brown tweed suit when he said helplessly, 'But I don't know which room,' that I leapt forward and offered to show him which room. The tone of his voice in which he said, 'Thanks very much' when I pointed to the door of my aunt's sitting room is with me yet. It was as if he were thanking me for some casual courtesy. Yet he was in such a state of nervous agitation that instead of going into my aunt's room he went to the wrong door and walked into the housemaid's cupboard. I shook my head and pointed to the right door.

'Oh, yes, I see, thanks very much,' he said once more in that absurdly nonchalant tone of voice.

As for me, I went back to the drawing room, where I found Aunt Emily arranging some carnations in a bowl.

'These were a present from Mr Mellor,' she said. 'Wasn't it kind of him?'

But I was not going to be treated like this by one of my fellow conspirators, and I asked bluntly if Mr Darrell and Aunt Adelaide would be married now.

'That will depend on Aunt Adelaide,' said her friend.

'I think I'll go round and see Mr Mellor,' I was inspired to say, for to sit here in suspense and watch Aunt Emily arranging carnations with so little idea of how she seemed to want them to look was likely to become unendurable presently, should the suspense be prolonged.

Mr Mellor opened the door for me himself. He was in his shirtsleeves and was smoking one of those long Italian cigars.

'For goodness' sake come and eat some of this tea,' he bellowed, and he dragged me into the dining room, where I found the table spread with cakes of every size and sort.

'That aunt of yours is a stunner,' he told me. 'but she hasn't the appetite of a goldfinch. Why didn't you bring her round to see me before?'

'You said you didn't want to meet any of my female relations.'

'Did I? Well, you should have insisted. That kind of dusty corn-coloured hair is very unusual. Well, are the star-crossed lovers united?'

I said I did not know yet.

'You cold-blooded little eft!' he shouted. 'Do you mean to say you came gorging in here after your aunt's tea without waiting to be sure?'

'Well, I couldn't go up to my aunt's sitting room and ask her. You can't ask things like that.'

'Look here, stuff your mouth full of cake and stop talking nonsense.'

Half an hour later I went back to Number 9 and entering by the area door inquired cautiously of Janet if Mr Darrell was still upstairs with my Aunt Adelaide.

'Mr – who?' Janet snapped, her eyes popping.

'Mr Darrell.'

'When did he come here?' she asked indignantly.

'He came this afternoon with Aunt Emily.'

'I never saw him.'

'Ah,' I said maliciously, 'but you don't see everything always.'

'I wish for no rudeness from you,' said Janet.

I did not wait to argue with the disconcerted Janet, but went upstairs. There were voices in the drawing room. Happy voices. And the canaries were singing louder than ever.

'I'll be back in a minute,' I said, putting my head round the door; and glad to postpone the embarrassment of being told by Aunt Adelaide that she was going to be married to Oliver Darrell, I hurried back to Number 5.

'It's all right,' I told Mr Mellor. 'they *are* going to be married'

'The world is full of stupid people,' Mr Mellor observed. 'Still, I should have thought a good deal less of them if the pair of them had been clever.'

NUMBER 9 *To Be Let or Sold*

THERE is danger of sentimentality in writing so many years later of a love affair turned in a moment from unhappiness to happiness like this of my Aunt Adelaide's, and I would rather say brusquely that she and Oliver Darrell were married a month later and went south before the swallows. That lament of Christina Rosetti's for exile from the sweet south was a favourite poem of my aunt's and she always read it with a poignancy in her voice that used to embarrass me slightly when I was listening. It was easy now to understand why Christina Rosetti's poetry had meant so much to her, for she must have been thinking how much her own love story resembled that broken romance in the life of the poetess. But now she was going back to the sweet south, and our street would soon be no more to her than a northern memory.

Indeed I was actually to see the boards up in front of Number 9 before my turn came to leave our street, not for the sweet south, alas, but for Hanover, which to me was by no means so pleasant a prospect. However, my father was determined I should spend the next year in Germany, and there was no more to be said.

The knowledge that my aunts were leaving our street made my impending banishment from it less bitter, and Aunt Emily's promise that she would make a point of spending with me all my holidays in Germany, so that she could take me round all the quaint old cities with richer legends and history than Hanover, if not such impeccable German, was a great solace to my regretful frame of mind.

I wish I could say that Aunt Emily had a love affair as fragrant as the delicate first roses of autumn; but she remained true to that dead lover of hers in Egypt, and she gave the rest of her heart to her friends.

NUMBER 9 *Sold*

I HAVE one more satisfactory event to report. In spite of the lower rent which the Linwoods were paying for Number 25 my aunts' house was sold early in September for fifty pounds more than they paid for it, and Mr Lockett must have walked along our street as jauntily as if he had had a happy love affair himself.

THE END

THE SYLVIA SCARLETT TRILOGY

by Compton Mackenzie

D. H. Lawrence considered the Sylvia Scarlett saga to be
Sir Compton Mackenzie's masterpiece. Covering the same
colourful period and including many of the same
characters as the classic SINISTER STREET, this story
breaks brave new ground in its exploration of a heroine
acclaimed as 'one of the few really great women in
fiction'.

Sylvia is a beautiful girl with a bitingly sharp tongue.
She is married at the tender age of nineteen to the dashing
Philip Iredale, and their three-month whirlwind of passion
drives their relationship to cataclysmic destruction in
SYLVIA SCARLETT. Shattered by a brutal divorce, she
throws herself into a hedonistic life in Europe, which
prepares her for the second great passion in her life –
SYLVIA AND ARTHUR. Finally, in SYLVIA AND
MICHAEL, she fights down despair only to be confronted
by the horror of the First World War, and her last and
greatest love.

'In the great tradition of English picaresque novels – in
many ways it is a twentieth century *Moll Flanders*.'
—*Antony Sampson*

SYLVIA SCARLETT   30p
SYLVIA AND ARTHUR   30p
SYLVIA AND MICHAEL   35p

NEW ENGLISH LIBRARY

NEL BESTSELLERS

Crime

T013 332	CLOUDS OF WITNESS	*Dorothy L. Sayers*	40p
W002 871	THE UNPLEASANTNESS AT THE BELLONA CLUB	*Dorothy L. Sayers*	30p
W003 011	GAUDY NIGHT	*Dorothy L. Sayers*	50p
T010 457	THE NINE TAILORS	*Dorothy L. Sayers*	35p
T012 484	FIVE RED HERRINGS	*Dorothy L. Sayers*	40p
T012 492	UNNATURAL DEATH	*Dorothy L. Sayers*	40p

Fiction

W002 775	HATTER'S CASTLE	*A. J. Cronin*	60p
W002 777	THE STARS LOOK DOWN	*A. J. Cronin*	60p
T010 414	THE CITADEL	*A. J. Cronin*	60p
T010 422	THE KEYS OF THE KINGDOM	*A. J. Cronin*	50p
T001 288	THE TROUBLE WITH LAZY ETHEL	*Ernest K. Gann*	30p
T003 922	IN THE COMPANY OF EAGLES	*Ernest K. Gann*	30p
W002 145	THE NINTH DIRECTIVE	*Adam Hall*	25p
T012 271	THE WARSAW DOCUMENT	*Adam Hall*	40p
T011 305	THE STRIKER PORTFOLIO	*Adam Hall*	30p
T007 243	SYLVIA SCARLETT	*Compton Mackenzie*	30p
T007 669	SYLVIA AND ARTHUR	*Compton Mackenzie*	30p
T007 677	SYLVIA AND MICHAEL	*Compton Mackenzie*	35p
W002 772	TO THE CORAL STRAND	*John Masters*	40p
W002 788	TRIAL AT MONOMOY	*John Masters*	40p
T009 084	SIR, YOU BASTARD	*G. F. Newman*	30p
T012 522	THURSDAY MY LOVE	*Robert H. Rimmer*	40p
T009 769	THE HARRAD EXPERIMENT	*Robert H. Rimmer*	40p
T010 252	THE REBELLION OF YALE MARRATT	*Robert H. Rimmer*	50p
T010 716	THE ZOLOTOV AFFAIR	*Robert H. Rimmer*	30p
T013 820	THE DREAM MERCHANTS	*Harold Robbins*	75p
W002 783	79 PARK AVENUE	*Harold Robbins*	50p
T012 255	THE CARPETBAGGERS	*Harold Robbins*	80p
T011 801	WHERE LOVE HAS GONE	*Harold Robbins*	70p
T013 707	THE ADVENTURERS	*Harold Robbins*	80p
T006 743	THE INHERITORS	*Harold Robbins*	60p
T009 467	STILETTO	*Harold Robbins*	30p
T010 406	NEVER LEAVE ME	*Harold Robbins*	30p
T011 771	NEVER LOVE A STRANGER	*Harold Robbins*	70p
T011 798	A STONE FOR DANNY FISHER	*Harold Robbins*	60p
T011 461	THE BETSY	*Harold Robbins*	80p
T010 201	RICH MAN, POOR MAN	*Irwin Shaw*	80p
W002 186	THE PLOT	*Irving Wallace*	75p
W002 761	THE SEVEN MINUTES	*Irving Wallace*	75p
T009 718	THE THREE SIRENS	*Irving Wallace*	75p
T010 341	THE PRIZE	*Irving Wallace*	80p

Historical

T009 750	THE WARWICK HEIRESS	*Margaret Abbey*	30p
T011 607	THE SON OF YORK	*Margaret Abbey*	30p
T011 585	THE ROSE IN SPRING	*Eleanor Fairburn*	30p
T009 734	RICHMOND AND ELIZABETH	*Brenda Honeyman*	30p
T011 593	HARRY THE KING	*Brenda Honeyman*	35p
T009 742	THE ROSE BOTH RED AND WHITE	*Betty King*	30p
W002 479	AN ODOUR OF SANCTITY	*Frank Yerby*	50p
W002 824	THE FOXES OF HARROW	*Frank Yerby*	50p
W002 916	BENTON'S ROW	*Frank Yerby*	40p
W003 010	THE VIXENS	*Frank Yerby*	40p
T006 921	JARRETT'S JADE	*Frank Yerby*	40p
T010 988	BRIDE OF LIBERTY	*Frank Yerby*	30p

Science Fiction

T007 081	THE CANOPY OF TIME	*Brian Aldiss*	30p
W003 003	CARSON OF VENUS	*Edgar Rice Burroughs*	30p
W002 449	THE MOON IS A HARSH MISTRESS	*Robert Heinlein*	40p
W002 697	THE WORLDS OF ROBERT HEINLEIN	*Robert Heinlein*	25p
W002 839	SPACE FAMILY STONE	*Robert Heinlein*	30p
W002 844	STRANGER IN A STRANGE LAND	*Robert Heinlein*	60p

T006 778	ASSIGNMENT IN ETERNITY	Robert Heinlein 25p
T007 294	HAVE SPACESUIT – WILL TRAVEL	Robert Heinlein 30p
T009 696	GLORY ROAD	Robert Heinlein 40p
T011 844	DUNE	Frank Herbert 75p
T012 298	DUNE MESSIAH	Frank Herbert 40p
W002 814	THE WORLDS OF FRANK HERBERT	Frank Herbert 30p
W002 911	SANTAROGA BARRIER	Frank Herbert 30p
W003 001	DRAGON IN THE SEA	Frank Herbert 30p

War

W002 921	WOLF PACK	William Hardy 30p
W002 484	THE FLEET THAT HAD TO DIE	Richard Hough 25p
W002 805	HUNTING OF FORCE Z	Richard Hough 30p
W002 632	THE BASTARD BRIGADE	Peter Leslie 25p
T006 999	KILLER CORPS	Peter Leslie 25p
T011 755	TRAWLERS GO TO WAR	Lund and Ludlam 40p
W005 051	GOERING	Manvell & Freankel 52½p
W005 065	HIMMLER	Manvell & Freankel 52½p
W002 423	STRIKE FROM THE SKY	Alexander McKee 30p
W002 831	NIGHT	Francis Pollini 40p
T010 074	THE GREEN BERET	Hilary St. George Saunders 40p
T010 066	THE RED BERET	Hilary St. George Saunders 40p

Western

T010 619	EDGE – THE LONER	George Gilman 25p
T010 600	EDGE – TEN THOUSAND DOLLARS AMERICAN	George Gilman 25p
T010 929	EDGE – APACHE DEATH	George Gilman 25p

General

T011 763	SEX MANNERS FOR MEN	Robert Chartham 30p
W002 531	SEX MANNERS FOR ADVANCED LOVERS	Robert Chartham 25p
W002 835	SEX AND THE OVER FORTIES	Robert Chartham 30p
T010 732	THE SENSUOUS COUPLE	Dr. C. 25p
P002 367	AN ABZ OF LOVE	Inge and Sten Hegeler 60p
P011 402	A HAPPIER SEX LIFE	Dr. Sha Kokken 70p
W002 584	SEX MANNERS FOR SINGLE GIRLS	Georges Valensin 25p
W002 592	THE FRENCH ART OF SEX MANNERS	Georges Valensin 25p
W002 726	THE POWER TO LOVE	E. W. Hirsch M. D. 47½p

Mad

S003 491	LIKE MAD	30p
S003 494	MAD IN ORBIT	30p
S003 520	THE BEDSIDE MAD	30p
S003 521	THE VOODOO MAD	30p
S003 657	MAD FOR BETTER OR VERSE	30p
S003 716	THE SELF MADE MAD	30p

NEL P.O. BOX 11, FALMOUTH, CORNWALL

Please send cheque or postal order. Allow 6p per book to cover postage and packing.

Name...

Address ....

....

Title ....
(SEPTEMBER)